LEGACY

LEGACY

JIM CHAMBERS

Copyright © 2025 Jim Chambers

The moral right of the author has been asserted.

Apart from any fair dealing for the purposes of research or private study, or criticism or review, as permitted under the Copyright, Designs and Patents Act 1988, this publication may only be reproduced, stored or transmitted, in any form or by any means, with the prior permission in writing of the publishers, or in the case of reprographic reproduction in accordance with the terms of licences issued by the Copyright Licensing Agency. Enquiries concerning reproduction outside those terms should be sent to the publishers.

The manufacturer's authorised representative in the EU for product safety is Authorised Rep Compliance Ltd, 71 Lower Baggot Street, Dublin D02 P593 Ireland
(www.arccompliance.com)

This is a work of fiction. Names, characters, businesses, places, events and incidents are either the products of the author's imagination or used in a fictitious manner. Any resemblance to actual persons, living or dead, or actual events is purely coincidental.

Troubador Publishing Ltd
Unit E2 Airfield Business Park,
Harrison Road, Market Harborough,
Leicestershire. LE16 7UL
Tel: 0116 2792299
Email: books@troubador.co.uk
Web: www.troubador.co.uk

ISBN 978 1836282 167

British Library Cataloguing in Publication Data.
A catalogue record for this book is available from the British Library.

Typeset in 10.5pt Adobe Garamond Pro by Troubador Publishing Ltd, Leicester, UK

*This book is dedicated to Barbara,
whom I met at college over fifty years ago.*

ABOUT THE AUTHOR

Jim was born in Derby in the East Midlands, the eldest of three children born to Dick and Barbara. His working-class roots are a source of pride, his father an enduring point of reference. But the world of butchery was not for him. Instead, he opted for business, subsequently enjoying a career in education technology where he became a CEO in an education, training and services business before moving on to lead a vocational training business in the apprenticeship sector. In more recent years he has operated as a non-executive chair of various successful 'ed tech' companies, a role that continues as part of his semi-retirement. Now more time-rich, Jim follows his passions for hiking, golfing, and writing. The *Paradigm Shift* marked his first foray into fiction, self-published in 2013, and was prescient in foretelling the Brexit journey that was to follow. *The Hope Affair* was published in 2021 and *Urban Scarecrows* in 2022.

Jim is a long-standing Derby County season ticket holder and recalls the glory days of Clough and Taylor, and then of Dave Mackay in the 1970s.

Jim lives in the Peak District of Derbyshire with his wife of nearly fifty years, Barbara. They have four offspring, Nicola, Andrew, Christoper, and Elizabeth, and, at last count, five grandchildren.

ONE

10TH DECEMBER 2020

Julian was met by a young woman, warrant card at the ready: DS Ruth Dodds.

'May I have a word please, sir?'

'It's my dad's funeral today.'

'Just a few minutes.'

Julian showed her into his study and watched as she took in views to the moors beyond manicured gardens: frosted lawns, skeletal trees adorned with feathery hoar frost. An Aston Martin gleamed on the drive.

She turned towards Julian, scanned the twin computer set-up, high-end music system, decanters of whisky. 'About our misper, Scott Morrison. You said you were on the continent between 8th and 15th November 2017?'

'Yes.'

'You weren't. Twice now you've recollected incorrectly. *Twice.*'

'It was years ago.'

'The wheels of justice grind slowly, sir,' DS Dodds said with a tight smile.

'I'll check.'

'We need to know.'

'You previously asked about October,' said Julian.

'And now we need to know of your movements in October *and* November. As we explained on... let me see...' the DS rifled through her notebook, 'Friday 27th October at 15.10.'

'You'll have your reasons, I guess.' Julian was deadpan.

'Yes.'

He glanced at his watch. 'But not today. After all—'

'Of course, sir. And please accept my condolences. Oh, just one last thing – I'd appreciate you taking us through your confrontation with Scott back in 1996.'

Did the Covid rules allow the removal of face masks? No one took issue. Not today, not graveside. The pall-bearers lowered the casket into its final resting place: a slow, controlled descent. Everything about the day had been planned, controlled with businesslike efficiency. All very traditional: mourning of a death, rather than the celebration of a life. Mourners bedecked in black wearing dutiful, sombre expressions. The brief order of service had been chosen by Julian's dad. A musical prelude was deemed superfluous, entry in reverential silence preferred. 'Abide With Me' was the chosen hymn, the muffled rendition delivered by the small, masked congregation. Vicar Bates read the prepared eulogy, referenced his dad's notes, and the Bible reading was the classic John chapter 14, read by Luke, the elder son. Then the final goodbye uttered in time-honoured tradition: *Earth to earth, ashes to ashes, dust to dust.*[1]

Julian bowed his head (one had to go through the motions, show some respect), before his eyes slid over the family. Luke

---

[1] Copyright owned by Lawrence Weiner and Artists Rights Society (ARS), New York.

blew his nose noisily and brushed a tear from the corner of his eye. Emily wailed without restraint. Julian spurned the hand that reached for him. Was Lotte's intended faux motivation love? Sympathy?

Vicar Bates motioned towards Luke with an open hand extended and a gentle inclination of his head – Luke's cue to grab a fistful of dirt. Luke complied and watched it fall into the void. Emily did likewise, her actions accompanied by a mournful soundtrack as she flourished a wad of tissues. One fluttered from her grasp before coming to rest on the coffin. Vicar Bates then looked in Julian's direction. Julian declined with a gentle lateral movement of his head.

He was understood.

A final prayer was intoned.

Time to move on.

As the mourners walked away, Julian and Lotte brought up the rear until he paused, pulled away, assured her he was fine. He needed a moment alone. He walked back to the grave and peered down. They had not often seen eye to eye, had rarely agreed. But he was his dad: Terence Gerald Sinclair. Julian's whispered sentiments were unheard: *I'll sort it all out now. My way.* Turning on his heels, he marched briskly back as the family piled into cars. As he approached the limo, he felt his mobile vibrate and paused to read. His eyebrows arched before he tapped a response:

Will call later. Urgency understood.

At the wake Julian picked at a plate of room-temperature sausage rolls and tired-looking ham and egg mayonnaise sandwiches that looked as if they were past their best, and wondered what organisms might fester within. He sipped a glass of warm Chardonnay as the family settled into soft sofas and chairs around a roaring log fire. He distanced himself from Emily, whose sobbing and wailing had given way to an endless stream of mindless chatter as she and Luke rewrote history: wonderful dad, inspirational businessman, wonderful legacy…

'You're quiet,' said Luke in one lull. His lined face displayed his grief as starkly as bare trees display winter.

'Not much to say.'

'You could show some bloody emotion,' said Emily, who accepted another glass proffered by Lotte. Julian's wife had taken a bottle into her custody, the two of them well advanced in their assault on its contents.

'If you'll excuse me,' said Julian as he set aside the barely touched food and left the family group to their moroseness. They did not need him to assist in their recollections, would not appreciate what he might offer.

Julian removed his leather shoes, trod softly upstairs to the galleried landing, made his way to the nursery. Nanny Barlow had managed to get little Josh off to sleep, having bathed him and tended to his medication. Julian placed a gentle hand on Nanny's shoulder as she sat in the shadows; he nodded his gratitude, his appreciation of her efforts. She had minimal assistance. Julian was perplexed at the lack of maternal input but there seemed little he could do to persuade Lotte. He sighed inwardly, kissed two fingers, bent, and gently touched his son's forehead, receiving a soft murmur in response. He sat in a chair alongside his cot and just watched Josh in his slumbers, loving the occasional snuffle, his snoring; so peaceful, so perfect, so premature at just twenty-seven weeks. They had been warned of the side effects and had experienced the regular battle with at first pneumonia, then frequent stays in hospital necessitated by bronchiolitis. They hoped he had largely grown beyond this stage, was less susceptible. But they feared autism and certain telltale early signs were evident: few back-and-forth smiles, little responsiveness. They would monitor his development until a diagnosis was possible.

After half an hour or so Julian wandered into the kitchen and raided the fridge. He thinly sliced smoked salmon to drape over ripe avocado, served with a spoonful of Annie's homemade mayonnaise, a wedge of lemon, a twist of black pepper. He poured a glass of premier cru Puligny Montrachet as an upgrade on the wake's plonk and took his plunder to the study for respite and solitude.

Julian sank into his leather chair and sighed. It was a relief to escape the wake and his siblings' emotionally charged grief as he opted to listen to Brahms rather than Disturbed or Guns N Roses or Led Zeppelin – his usual fare. He closed his eyes and let the music wash over him, felt the tension seep away despite shards of guilt. He could not bring himself to mourn, and he worked hard to avoid the disapproving gaze of his dad from the portrait above the mantelpiece. It seemed to say, *I'm barely in the ground and here you are plotting to destroy everything your grandad and I built... you're lazy, useless, untrustworthy.* Julian shook his head, denied the accusation, but was soon distracted as his door was flung open. His heart sank when he saw a flushed Lotte on the threshold, glass in hand. With a contemptuous glare she slumped into an armchair, sloshed wine onto the carpet.

'What's wrong with you?' she said. Her green eyes flashed.

Julian glanced quizzically but said nothing; he did not seek an argument or a heart-to-heart. He preferred to keep the unwanted interruption to a minimum.

'You've said nothing, shed no tears. Just all... all... buttoned up. Nothing to say to Luke or Emily? You've just buried your dad, for God's sake, man. Why can't you let it go, let it all out?'

He said nothing; sipped his wine, self-contained and distant.

'Well?'

'Would it help? Would it change anything?' he said in barely a whisper.

'Oh, you're impossible. Don't suppose you've checked on your son either? Never home, always too busy even for little Josh.' She stood, threw back her drink, placed her glass in a puddle of wine on the mahogany table, and departed. The storm had blown, raged, moved on.

Julian sighed and picked up a photo of Lotte. The blonde-haired young woman had captured his heart with her rash of freckles over the bridge of a button nose and across high cheekbones; her outgoing, outspoken, outrageous character lived for the moment. She had brought such unbridled joy as she carried him to a distant place, but they now struggled to come close to rekindling such moments of extraordinary love. Their month-long honeymoon in the paradise of New Zealand and the Cook Islands was now nearly three years ago. And for a moment his dad spoke to him: *Are you sure you want to marry that girl?* His dad's words – so unwelcome, unnecessary, unheeded at the time. Now the observation seemed prescient. Julian resolved to try harder. Perhaps a holiday would be timely. Lotte enjoyed attention lavished upon her in exotic far-flung locations, blingy hotels and expensive restaurants. Perhaps the Caribbean, or maybe Indonesia.

TWO

2018

Lotte shook him awake and looked aghast. 'Julian... *Julian*. You're shouting and tossing and turning and... you're soaking wet.'

'Sorry,' he mumbled and reached for his glass of water. He pulled his hand through damp hair and took in the sweat-soaked sheets.

'The same old nightmare?' asked Lotte. She sighed. 'Yet again?'

'Sorry. I'll leave you to it. I'll be okay.'

She yawned and rolled over.

He grabbed a dressing gown and made his way downstairs. Julian glanced at the clock on the wall: just after four o'clock. The fragments of his nightmare assailed him: the steel-capped boot in his crutch, the vomit-spattered blue suede shoes. He shuddered. Always the same. Why could he not put it all behind him? And his dad spoke to him: *You need to grow up, son. Grow some balls.* Julian slurped coffee and took a couple of paracetamols. He crept into the spare bedroom. He needed rest before facing his dad's surprise call.

Julian breathed deeply in readiness. What could his dad possibly have to say? They had an unspoken pact to tolerate each other at family board meetings, to avoid one another socially. It was best for family harmony. It allowed the semblance of normality, the pretence of success, entrepreneurial brilliance. And given Julian's primary focus on his own business, that was just fine.

He pushed open the sitting-room door and surveyed the room as if with new eyes. It looked tired as he took in the threadbare arms of his dad's favourite armchair, the scorch marks on the fireside rug, and the heavy, old furniture that belonged in the '50s. It had been a while since the room had been cleaned and dusted, he assessed as he ran a finger along the sideboard surface. He glanced at one object after another: an old photo of Grandad, a framed commendation of an event held long ago in The Yorkshire Belle, an empty bottle of wine that might have provoked long-forgotten memories, dog-eared paperback thrillers, piles of magazines, a corkscrew, decanters, some with whisky or brandy within, others empty. Julian picked up an old photo of him and his siblings and swiftly replaced it as his dad joined him by the unlit fire.

'Dad.' Spoken guardedly.

'Julian.'

'How are you? You've not looked so well of late.'

'No.' Terence Sinclair's watery eyes could not hold Julian's, and instead focused on his arthritic hands, which fiddled with the newspaper in his lap.

Julian thought his dad looked unusually frail, diminished in the large armchair. He cut an altogether different image to the alpha male in the family home of Julian's childhood, to the one that dominated the family boardroom, that hectored staff in the Belle Hospitality pub chain business. 'Is it next month's AGM you wish to speak about?'

'No. No, not that.' His dad paused, took a sip of water.

Julian noticed the shaky hands. He said nothing, watched and waited.

Terence took a deep breath, sat forward. 'The family needs you, son,' he said before he sagged back in his chair. His pained expression revealed the effort to say as much.

'I offer my support at the board meetings. But we struggle to agree, don't we? And the business fails to honour our investment agreement—'

'Please. I didn't ask you for another argument. We'll no doubt cover that ground again... there's no easy way of saying this. I've not been well of late. Doctors, tests, scans... prodding, poking, pulling; treated like a pincushion. They all agree. I'm dying.' Terence lifted his eyes back to Julian's, and now it was his son who could not hold his dad's eyes.

'I'm sorry. Cancer?'

'Just so.'

'What's the treatment regime?'

'The quacks want me to have radiotherapy and chemotherapy, and God knows what else. But all it'll do is stave off the inevitable, make me ill, confine me to bed, ruin my taste buds and appetite, and generally screw up my life.'

'Sorry... I don't know what to say. How—'

'Two years if I'm lucky, three if I submit to their quackery.'

'What can I do?'

'Come and run the show as CEO: full operational responsibility of Belle Hospitality.'

'You want *me* to run it? Why me?' Julian was astonished. He had never expected such a request – far from it. Their antipathy toward one another was a constant cause of family angst, boardroom disharmony: his dad and siblings in one corner, the investors and Julian in the other. Snippets from the last board meeting assailed Julian as he tried to handle his incredulity.

The dismissal of his objections to the board reneging on their commitments to their external investor despite the powerful business logic, facts, figures was hard enough to bear. But the harsh words of his dad stung: *I run this business and take the broader view to control strategic direction. You need to learn to accept the wisdom of your betters.* 'We don't agree on the way forward. Why me?' he asked again.

'Luke's a solid enough accountant but he couldn't run a piss-up in a brewery,' said the old man.

'That's a bit harsh, isn't it? He has his own business.'

'A one-man accountancy operation. Not the same thing. And Emily… well, Emily's Emily. Love her to bits but best kept at arm's length from business. You're my only option.'

'You're really selling it to me,' said Julian. The sarcasm was lost on his dad. 'I have my business to run on the continent.'

'I thought you'd appointed someone to run it day-to-day?'

'True,' Julian conceded.

'And I wouldn't ask if…' Terence broke off, sipped more water, fell silent.

'I get to run it my way?'

'Subject to board approval.'

'I won't be a puppet for you to manipulate, Dad.'

'Always been your own man, Julian.'

'I need operational freedom, and I'm wedded to the wider strategy that you seem dead set against. If you want someone to do as you bid, to manage on blind faith… that's not me.'

'So, even in these circumstances you make conditions.'

'I need your agreement on this point. I won't be emasculated.'

'You've got it… subject to board approval.'

'And you're quite sure you want me to do this?'

'Who else?'

Julian looked at his dad sceptically, but how could he refuse him given the circumstances? 'When do you want me to take the reins?'

'Today. I've told Luke and Emily – about my prognosis.'

'How did they react?'

'As you'd expect,' said Terence.

Julian's brother, Luke, would always defer to his dad, his sister, Emily, too. Luke would be empathetic but practical, Emily a blubbing, emotional mess. But she would ultimately channel her inner Florence Nightingale.

Terence stood, drew himself upright, jutted his jaw out, attempted a smile – more of a grimace. Grasping the mantelpiece, he leant down to Julian and wagged a finger at his son. 'Got to keep the legacy going, haven't we? Your grandad's brilliance taken to new heights, and it'll soon be yours. You've got two hard acts to follow but I'll help you during this next period: an apprenticeship, if you like.'

That sounded more like his deluded dad, but at least it was good to see the return of spirit. Seeing his frailty was not easy, and him asking for help from Julian of all people was extraordinary. There was bitterness where love might otherwise have reigned, but he was still his dad. And he had swallowed his pride to ask. That would have hurt to contemplate, been painful to execute.

'That's really your assessment?' said Julian with a raised eyebrow, not willing to let the comment go without censure.

'Oh, I know we haven't always seen eye to eye, and you've made your mistakes, but we can let sleeping dogs lie. In the past. History. Gone and forgotten.'

Julian's hand reflexively reached up to his face. The scar had faded with time, but his limp persisted to this day. It was not forgotten; it never would be.

They assembled in an anteroom to enjoy a drink and lunch. Julian hoped this meeting would go better than the last one. Lotte was present by virtue of his gift of five per cent equity when they married. It had seemed a good idea at the time. It was interesting to note how the attendees gradually separated into their natural cliques: Lotte and Emily; the old man and Luke; Daisy and Elijah; and Julian, Thomas, and Zoe.

As they reluctantly moved into the boardroom and took their seats, Luke leant forwards and said, 'Congratulations, Lotte. A great cause.'

Julian's ears pricked up.

Lotte looked his way and smiled thinly before offering an explanation. 'I've volunteered to manage the fundraising of the local charity for the blind. Passed you by, no doubt.'

'Well done, you,' said the old man, his croaky voice weaker today. And Julian listened to the congratulations, saw Lotte revel in the spotlight.

'I know the hunk who runs the charity. Once knew him well. Very well. Jeremy Brash… well, I'll be blowed. You didn't say anything. Don't blame you, mind!' said Emily before she and Lotte giggled as they whisper-gossiped.

Julian looked on.

'How are you today, Daddy?' said Emily. Her laughing gave way to empathy as her eyes watered.

'I'm fine. Don't fuss.'

'Okay then, let's get down to business,' began Julian. 'First, some introductions. Some of you may not know Daisy, who runs the operational side of our business, having joined from a global contract catering company, and Elijah, who is our HR and talent director.'

'HR and what?'

Julian sighed inwardly. 'Talent, Dad. We agreed the appointment a couple of months ago. And of course, Zoe

Madden, the investment director of SI Investments. You're all welcome.'

When his dad had his off days – all too frequent now – he became especially irascible, but Julian hoped their guests would ensure he moderated his behaviour. His dad was the chairman and should conduct proceedings at shareholder meetings, but he interpreted his role as the guardian of The Yorkshire Belle and the ultimate decision-maker. So, it was left to Julian to lead.

'You will have received detailed papers prepared by Thomas with key inputs from Daisy and Elijah, who are here to answer questions. I'm sure you've all read the papers...' Luke fished out of his PC case a pristine information pack. Emily said she had misplaced hers, so was handed a set by Thomas, Julian's dependable FD.

'Our current trading position is weak,' said Thomas. 'Becoming critical. Room occupancy down, revenues down, margins down, and we will make both an operational and a PBT loss. Cash flow is weak, cash reserves have dipped.'

'The cash injected by investors,' added Julian pointedly.

'Contrary to the deal we had whereby you agreed to ring-fence investment funds,' said Zoe.

Thomas nodded his agreement, Julian remained impassive. His siblings and wife ignored Zoe.

'It's all a question of timing,' said Terence in an unusually emollient tone.

'So, the strategy remains intact?' asked Zoe.

'Of course.'

'Good. What are the proposed acquisition targets? And on the current business, all the analysis shows The Yorkshire Belle drags the rest of the group down. Why don't we dispose of it?'

'*Never!* Not the strategy – never was, never will be,' barked the old man.

'Strategically we need to consider all options,' said Julian. He wore his gravest expression, his tone serious, his eyes implored the directors to face reality. 'We'll run out of cash. We've already raided our investment funds, which will be further drained over the next six months – the minimum sale period.'

'Not for sale,' said his dad, who flushed and jabbed an assertive finger.

'Please bear with us,' said Julian.

'If you would just allow me to deliver a short presentation—' began Thomas.

'No. Let's reject this absurd proposal. Those in favour, please raise your hands.'

Luke's and Emily's shot up.

'Opposed?'

Thomas, Zoe, and Julian raised theirs.

'Neither Zoe nor Thomas are statutory directors, therefore you are *defeated*, Julian. The proposal is defeated, *my* motion is passed.' His dad's eyes mocked, revelled in the impotence of his son's position. This was not a board meeting, it was not a formal proposal either, but he was disinterested in such distinctions.

'I need to remind you of the investment agreement conditions, of changes to the articles of association. As investors we can—' said Zoe.

'Then write to me. Just one final thing it would be good for you to remember, Julian. I asked you back so you could learn, so you could run the business day-to-day. Strategy, policy, and ultimate decisions are mine as the primary shareholder and the one who built this business from scratch. Get used to the idea. Next meeting, please report what you're going to *do* to turn around the temporary downturn in The Yorkshire Belle's trading. The meeting is closed. Good day to you all.'

THREE

2019

The threatened storms failed to materialise as the clouds retreated to afford a glimpse of the beauty of the snow-covered Alps on the descent into Geneva. From there it was usually an hour to Hotel L'Angleterre, situated near Chamonix with excellent views of Mont Blanc. Today it took two hours with heavy traffic headed to the ski slopes in the busy post-Christmas period. Julian settled back and focused his mind on his hotel venture, placed on a back burner the family business, the idiosyncratic leadership style of his dad. It was satisfying to remind himself of his own business successes.

Having sold his first small hotel chain, JHS Hotels, Julian had soon started up again. He had a concept in mind. Many had their doubts, some were more forthright in their diagnosis, but he was not dissuaded. He had appointed a new general manager to run it day-to-day back in 2016: Lysander. Julian smiled as the dapper, charming GM flitted through his mind. Customers seemed to love him. A new head chef had been appointed and a coveted Michelin star secured. Occupancy was high and sales had boomed as Europeans flocked to experience this English hotel in the French Alps complete with its rose garden, English country-style bedrooms and lounges, English afternoon tea, and now haute cuisine of some repute.

'Mr Julian,' said a flustered doorman. 'I didn't know…'

'No reason you should have.' Julian shook his hand and allowed the doorman to take his bags.

'The usual suite?'

'Thank you.'

He sauntered into the lobby, where the portly, besuited Lysander was holding court to a small group of elderly ladies hanging on to his every word.

'Ladies, how nice to see you. I so hope our little abode will cope with such influx of glamour. But sexy ladies are always good for business.'

Cue gales of laughter…

Julian meandered through the hotel, then spent time with Lysander for an overview of progress, and met with the executive head chef. He pored over the accounts with the finance manager, and then decided to see for himself the hotel when in full swing, look at the refurbishment project and the new extension, which had increased the number of bedrooms from twenty to fifty; a multimillion-euro project overseen by a contracts manager. Julian inspected the recently finished bedrooms and the refurbished rooms, and generally felt the pulse. No, he did not need to be chaperoned. Yes, he would rather go solo. Lysander seemed to take this as some sort of personal slight. *Get over it.*

Reaching the expansive new lounge, he surveyed the busy traditional afternoon tea service. As he turned the corner, he paused to take in the spectacular scenery. The glass wall afforded unimpeded views of the Massif du Mont-Blanc. And yet the room's decor and furnishings and fabrics transported him to a Cotswolds country house hotel. The walls were adorned with pictures of English scenes interspersed with Alpine mountains and rivers, and snowfield paintings and photographs taken in the different seasons. The room was large, with different zones delineated by colour schemes, sofas, planters, and low tables. A grand centre table was adorned with colourful bone china tea sets in different patterns: wild strawberries, roses, peonies, birds, butterflies. Speciality teas were available: Earl Grey, Darjeeling, China, jasmine white tea, lapsang souchong... and the service of Yorkshire tea brought a smile to his face. The table was constantly replenished with a variety of finely cut sandwiches (including the inevitable cucumber sandwiches) and cakes; local patisserie offerings enhanced the English theme. And the customers were as eclectic as the teas as he took in a group of well-heeled elderly English couples, a gathering of Japanese tourists with cameras at the ready, and many French and Italian and German customers, all sipping their Yorkshire tea from delicate cups served mainly by local French waitresses adorned in traditional black-and-white uniforms with tiny, frilly aprons and wearing the small white paper hats as tradition dictated. He could almost have been in Bettys Tea Rooms in Harrogate, or in a trendy restaurant in Paris. But tea? It would never work, they said. Continentals don't drink tea, they said. In summer, the scenery changed to reveal Alpine fields awash with a riot of colourful wildflowers, a magical backdrop to the rose gardens as they spilled onto the manicured lawns through sections of the retracted glass wall. They had said roses would never survive the low temperatures, but they were wrong. Not if you procured from the right sources; they survive to minus twenty degrees centigrade and lower if cared for. Today they wore their insulated white blanket.

He emerged bleary-eyed after a poor night's sleep, which had followed an endless stream of staff eager to impress, and a raft of paperwork demanded his signature. Julian noted the huge Christmas tree in the lobby area, carols playing softly in the background. Groups awaited their transportation to the ski slopes and chattered excitedly in their colourful garb: rucksacks laden with additional layers, goggles, gloves. An elderly couple took in the hubbub while sipping coffees. Children created mayhem while staff attended to their guests. Lysander was very much the conductor of staff while lending an ear for customers who wanted to chat, always a tale to hand. Julian preferred to hover in the shadows before he moved through the lounge, took in the majesty of Mont Blanc, and made for the staff area where a coffee and a croissant could be enjoyed. A caffeine fix was needed to get him going for the day ahead.

'Mind if I join you?' Last time he had seen Cassandra she was off to get married to an English guy back home. It was good to see her again – a talented, bright, hard-working young woman of some potential. A bit of a plain Jane, but he found her thoughtful, interesting, and diligent – admirable qualities. 'Cassandra, isn't it?'

He detected irritation in her eyes as they lifted slowly, reluctant to admit an intruder. She nodded her affirmation.

'We worked together previously,' said Julian.

She squinted at him and seemed about to ask a question, but instead said, 'I was your employee.'

'Trainee manager, I recall.'

She delivered a half-smile of acknowledgement.

'May I sit down?'

She shrugged, then nodded.

'You were assistant manager last year,' Julian said. He had intended it as a question.

Cassandra closed her book, stifled a sigh. She glanced at Julian pointedly before her features relaxed. 'Sorry. I was engrossed, lost in the story... oh, yes please, a coffee would be nice,' she said to a waiter who had served Julian. 'I enjoyed my time as a trainee at JHS, met some interesting people. You and your team were hard taskmasters, mind. So, when the GM asked me to join as the assistant manager...'

She paused, and Julian sat back to finish his own coffee. He gave her space. The silence stretched as Cassandra turned back to her book.

'I'll leave you in peace...'

'No. Sorry. Didn't mean to be rude.'

'You weren't... how are you finding it?'

'The book?'

'The job.'

'It's okay.'

'But? I detect a but...'

'No buts.'

Julian looked at her quizzically.

'Well, your new GM brings an added dimension.'

'Lysander? Is there a problem?'

'Who knows?'

What could she mean? Julian had picked up on a few staff grumbles, yet all he had seen was positive: the business thrived as trade boomed, a GM who had lured a top chef to the hotel and who provided the centre-stage leadership successful hotels need, increased revenues and profits, and the refurbishment programme continued to roll. He had been impressed with the work itself. Perhaps he was a difficult taskmaster, but if it produced results...

Julian shook himself out of his reverie. Cassandra was untroubled, but he felt her eyes on him.

'Sorry. I was miles away... reflecting on your message...' Julian let the sentence hover, and Cassandra turned away, tight-lipped.

Cassandra had rejoined the hotel in a junior role in the accounts department. She was a quiet young woman. Perhaps a bit taciturn, but then, who was he to comment? Well, he did not care for frivolous young women anyway. *Except for Lotte?* He looked curiously at Cassandra as she sipped her coffee, and wondered what had brought her back so soon. What had happened to her marriage? Perhaps her husband worked for the hotel as well.

As he excused himself, he suddenly paused, turned, and said, 'I don't suppose you happen to know where I might find accommodation locally?'

Cassandra frowned, and he offered, by way of explanation, 'I'd like somewhere private, quiet – an escape from the hotel. Homely rather than glitzy.'

She stared at him and seemed to be toiling with her thoughts, and then he saw her eyes lighten and she said, 'I know just the place. I can take you, if you like.'

Cassandra thrust snowshoes at him, looked scornfully at his attire, and suggested he kit himself out more appropriately. She pointed to the snowfields to be crossed. It took them about forty minutes before coming to a hamlet, and then another ten minutes to reach their destination. Conversation had been impossible as they expended energy on the conditions, but he suspected it would have been meagre in any event. He enjoyed the physical exertion, and once he had mastered the technique he revelled in their awesome surroundings. At least the weather had relented, other than the occasional snow flurry. The small road connecting the hamlet with another village and from there to the hotel was inaccessible in the winter months, she explained. As they approached Cassandra's house, Julian noted faint graffiti on the side wall. That struck him as odd in this secluded spot.

'Is the owner in?' asked Julian, expecting to meet Cassandra's contact.

She raised a single eyebrow and smiled before saying, 'She soon will be.'

Cassandra opened the deadbolt locks on a seemingly new, sturdy wooden front door. As she lit the fire, he looked at the sparsely furnished room: two armchairs either side of the fireplace with a low-level coffee table, and a small dining table with two chairs also served as a sewing station. Simple bookshelves with hiking books and maps; mountain photographs and knick-knacks adorned the walls. No personal photographs anywhere of herself or loved ones.

She pointed to a door off the main room – the spare bedroom. 'It's very basic.'

He took in the double bed, wardrobe, and chest of drawers, opened a door into a toilet with a wash handbasin. Tiny, clean, and functional.

'There's a shower upstairs,' said Cassandra. 'We would have to come to some arrangement on timings. Not ideal. Hot chocolate before you head back?'

They took their drinks either side of the blazing fire now warming the bijou, chalet-style wooden house. He marvelled at the silence. No background Muzak, no excitable children, or alcohol-induced gregarious adults at play. Just silence bar the crackle of the fire.

'You did ask for homely. There's no Wi-Fi and mobile reception's dodgy.'

'It's perfect.'

They lapsed back into silence until Julian had finished his drink. He stared into the fire for a while, lost in thought but warmed physically and spiritually, savouring the serenity before Cassandra added, 'I'm no great conversationalist...'

'Nor me.'

'I like peace and quiet.'

'Me too.'

'But companionable silence can be…'

'Indeed,' Julian said. 'I'd love to take it.'

'Okay, but if it doesn't work for me—'

'No problem. I have my suite in the hotel.'

Back at the hotel, he worked on the accounts, but his mind was in reflective mode and strayed from his task. His marriage, rather than business for once, was uppermost as he viewed it from afar, like the eagle surveying its surroundings while soaring on thermals. So much had happened in just a few years; much still surprised him, a mystery. How he had been attracted to a gregarious, party-loving, live-for-the-moment girl he did not know, but she had transported him to places never dreamt of emotionally and experientially. It had been out of character for him to be drawn to someone like Lotte. It had caught him by surprise. It surprised him even now.

The spring wedding had been largely organised by Lotte; it was inevitably lavish, no expense spared. His dad's contacts and a family connection enabled them to marry in the York Minster with a special licence. They somehow managed to navigate around the requirement to attend services at the cathedral over the previous six months, although at Lotte's behest they had attended now and then. Julian's generous charitable donation may have oiled the wheels. The reception was held at the historic Merchant Taylors' Hall in the city: a fifteenth-century hall with medieval beams, it oozed atmosphere and privilege. Numbers being restricted to 120 people was a consolation. Julian left Lotte with the headache of whittling the numbers down while he focused on business. After all, she had left her head receptionist job in France months ago just to focus on the big day. It had gone like clockwork with no last-minute hitches, and the honeymoon had transported them to paradise. Even Julian had to admit it had been good to have a break, to indulge himself in water-based sports: kayaking, sub-aqua, waterskiing, snorkelling. Lotte generally preferred the palm-fringed white beaches with waiter service at their exclusive beachside hotels. And she steadfastly refused to join him on his hiking exploits; Tongariro Crossing with its emerald lakes, active craters, steam vents, and the Red Crater was a particular highlight for him. It had even inspired him to read Tolkien's *The Lord of the Rings*, the Middle-Earth location of the film.

Once back home he had been cajoled to hire a housekeeper; it seemed easier to concur. Quite why the two of them were in such need was beyond him, although their pile near Hutton-le-Hole, he conceded, was a substantial property. But his dad's housekeeper had had enough of the old man and quietly offered her services to Julian. Who could blame her? How she had suffered him for so long was another of life's mysteries. So, the redoubtable Annie was soon ensconced and quickly made her stamp on the house.

'Not sure we've made the right choice on the Annie front,' ventured Lotte one evening as they flicked through their wedding album.

'Mm,' grunted Julian, his mind elsewhere.

'She's blunt to the point of rudeness, seems to think she runs the house, and even commented on my outfit the other day. Told me my skirt was too short and my blouse too revealing. How dare she? And she tells me I drink too much.'

Julian arched an eyebrow before saying, 'She means well. You wanted someone to run the house. We're lucky to have her. Salt of the earth.'

'Certainly earthy! But if she can't learn to keep a civil tongue, she can sling her hook.'

Julian said nothing and poured himself a small Scotch, topped up Lotte's wine glass.

'And when the girls were round for lunch, you'll never guess what she did… *Julian?* Are you even listening?'

'To your every word.'

'Can you?'

'What?'

'I'll tell you, then. I can see you're not going to play. You can be a bit dull, you know, sweetheart.'

Silence.

'*Julian!*'

'Yes, my love.'

'I'd even planned the menu to save her the trouble. I couldn't be fairer, could I? You know the sort of things: canapés, langoustine and crab, salmon with a lemon mayo, Grand Marnier orange soufflé, all washed down with Chablis and bubbly and—'

'Sounds lovely.'

'And it would have been, but you'll never guess what she served. I was so embarrassed: bits of black pudding on sticks, small Yorkshire bloody puddings with slices of cold beef, and a jam roly-poly. I thought she was even on the point of offering poor Cynthia a bottle of brown ale. *Brown ale…* you're not smirking, are you? Oh, you're impossible. The bloody woman's impossible… and where are you off to now?'

'My study, love. Something I promised to do this evening.'

'Well, I'm off out, then. Find the girls and see if they're up for a bit of fun.'

Julian stared into the fire, watched the embers slowly die. Cassandra never demanded, was self-sufficient, and she seemed happy with her lot: her books, knitting, crocheting. They would occasionally listen to classical music played softly. It was a cocooning experience, with the warmth of her tiny chalet, the pursuit of simple interests, and snow falling around their abode. An island in a sea of white. She told him she enjoyed a little skiing; hillwalking in the summer – interests they had in common, although his skiing expertise was basic.

'Did you get married?' he ventured one evening.

She looked up sharply, opened and shut her mouth, but said nothing. Instead, she resumed her work: the early stages of a crocheted blanket. Julian reverted to his study of the hotel's accounts. They had an unwritten but well-understood rule not to intrude, to respect each other's privacy. She said nothing for a while, and busied herself in the kitchen before handing him a steaming mug of hot chocolate.

'The official version?' she asked, pointing to his papers.

'The accounts? Is there any other?' Julian answered with a puzzled expression.

'You don't think it's what Lysander wants you to believe?'

'Meaning what?'

'Figures tell the story you want them to.'

'And you have a different story to tell?'

She looked away and resumed a section of her work before reaching for her own PC. She opened a file and handed it to him. Julian looked at the figures; they were for the same period as the version he was studying. But the numbers were different.

'You're going to have to help me…'

'Capital costs coded to revenue expenditure as a direct cost. So, margins are depressed, capital costs artificially lowered. Although capital costs are still ahead of budget, the overshoot is understated.'

'Are you certain?'

'I'm chasing back every invoice over the last eighteen months to check the account codes they're posted to. I need a few more months…'

'Or additional resources,' Julian suggested.

'I'd rather not draw attention.'

'I'll get the contracts manager to check it out.'

'If I'm right, they'll just cover their tracks.'

'And you've taken it upon yourself to uncover… what?'

She shrugged.

'But, why?'

'I'm whacked.' She gathered her things. 'Goodnight.'

'Wait. Don't leave it there…'

Cassandra turned at the bottom of the stairs, and he saw anger flare in her eyes. In hushed tones she said, 'I have my reasons… oh, and it never happened. My wedding. What about you? Why did you never marry?'

Julian looked at her, the intrigue level notched higher, and he instinctively rubbed his naked wedding-ring finger. He removed the ring on landing in France. It just seemed a different world; his marital status a private matter of no relevance to anyone else. 'Goodnight,' he said.

The last few months had seen the trading position of Belle Hospitality worsen, and yet opposition to Julian's solution – the sale of the old pub – was intractable. Months were wasted as the crisis brewed. Being a hot summer's day in Yorkshire, they assembled in the garden for tea. As he wandered through the lounge towards the open French doors, he stopped short as he heard Emily talking excitedly, then Lotte's plaintive tones.

'Not found the right moment. He spends more time in France or in his study than he ever does with me. You wouldn't think we'd only been married five minutes. It's just so different to… oh, I don't know… he's as cold as… makes no effort to make me feel wanted or loved… we've not been out for ages, either.' Lotte sighed.

'Typical of Julian. You're a married couple now. He's got a

trophy wife to roll out for business functions, a big house, posh cars, sharp suits – all the accoutrements to transmit the image of success. He takes people for granted, uses them. Love him dearly but – what do you say, Luke?'

'Don't bring me into this.'

'Anyway, you've obviously found a bit of time to—'

'*Emily*. He'll be here soon. Change the topic, please. I'll tell him tonight if he's in the right mood.'

The exchange appalled Julian. He spoke into his mobile as he strolled through to the garden. 'Yes, yes, okay. Speak tomorrow. Thanks for the call.' Joining them, he shook Luke's hand briefly and kissed Emily on the cheek, his wife on the lips. Lotte looked at him in amazement. He helped himself to a glass of lemonade and a slice of Annie's fruit cake. 'How did you find Dad this morning?' he asked Lotte.

Apparently, he was in slightly better form, but his cancer had taken hold. The prognosis remained gloomy. They chatted about him for a while, steered clear of business.

'It's good to chat,' said Luke, 'but I only have twenty minutes or so. I'm sure you didn't suggest this meeting to talk about Dad. What is it, Julian?'

'No. And I've asked Thomas to join us as well. Ah, here he is. I just want to ensure we all have a clear understanding of the state of play.'

'I thought we did,' said Luke, his brow furrowing.

'The recent board meeting was emotionally charged. Let's take stock. This is business, though. We must leave the family emotions and politics to one side.'

'In a family business? How?' said Emily.

'She has a point, sweetheart,' Lotte offered, receiving a squeeze of the hand from her sister-in-law.

'We must try. Please. If only this once. Thomas has prepared an easily digestible analysis.'

'Don't be so bloody patronising,' said Emily, who immediately looked pleased with herself.

'These graphs show our actual results over the last three years for the whole business; these for just The Belle; these for the business without The Belle. The analysis is conclusive,' said Thomas.

Luke studied the graphs as Emily and Lotte looked at them quizzically. 'Are the results really as bad as you reported at the board meeting?' asked Luke.

'You're an accountant, Luke. You've seen the balance sheet, cash flow, P&L. What do you think? What's your professional opinion?' said Julian.

Luke pulled a face.

'And these graphs?' prompted Thomas.

'They're persuasive. Basically, without The Belle we have a business in need of attention, but just about profitable. With The Belle we are looking at—'

'*Luke!*' said Emily, her voice raised. 'We can't contemplate the business without The Belle,' she said, looking daggers at Julian.

'You do realise there can be no dividend this year, don't you?' said Julian.

Both siblings blanched, and, Luke protested, companies often paid dividends even in poor years.

'The investors will simply block any dividend proposal,' said Thomas.

'Can they?' asked Emily.

'Yes,' admitted Luke.

'Daddy will go berserk.'

'Which is why I want to discuss this informally,' said Julian.

'In my opinion we have little option but to sell The Yorkshire Belle,' said Thomas.

Luke was thoughtful, and slowly rose to his feet. He ambled over to stand in the shade of the beech tree, gazed over to the heather-clad moorlands in the distance. He stood with his back to them. He appeared to nod his head. Perhaps the inevitable conclusion had at last dawned. He turned back to the group, picked up his briefcase, and told them he must dash. As he strode away, he turned abruptly on his heels. 'We can't sell The Belle. The board gave their instructions to the executive at the last meeting. Find another solution and stop wasting time going over the same old ground. See you tomorrow, Em.'

Julian settled down to watch some television with Lotte. He would rather listen to music (preferably heavy rock, given his mood), but he had to make more of an effort, so went along with the soap opera she insisted upon. It was banal fare poorly acted, but his wife lapped it up. It was barely halfway through when she suddenly turned the TV off.

'Sorry about this morning again,' said Julian. Yet again he had been woken by Lotte in response to his shouted entreaties, his tortured nightmare.

'When are you going to tell me about these nightmares?'

'Hard to make any sense of them, hard to fathom,' Julian answered.

'Well, they're bloody disruptive. Anyway, we need to talk about something else. Come and sit with me. Why do you always opt for the armchair?'

Julian did as she asked, and she curled up on the sofa, pulled his arm around her.

'Sweetheart, there's something we need to discuss.'

'Oh, yes?' Julian frowned.

'How do you feel about becoming a dad?'

'*What?* A dad? Me? Why the question?'

'Answer it, please, darling.'

Sweetheart? Darling? 'I don't know. We've never discussed

it. Not sure it feels right just now. We've so much on our plate, and I just don't have time for—'

Lotte had pulled herself out from under his draped arm, and turned to look at him. Her emerald-green eyes sparkled with mischief above her rash of freckles. 'Well, you'll just have to make time,' she said firmly, a beaming smile lighting up the room. She looked as happy as he had seen her in months. 'You've got six months to get used to the idea.'

'What? You mean…'

'Yes: you're to become a dad.'

'When? I mean, how?'

'Shall I draw a diagram?' She laughed at him, squeezed his hand.

'Are you telling me you're pregnant? Really?'

'*Yes!* A Christmas baby. Isn't it marvellous?'

Julian extricated himself from the sofa and paced up and down. His hand ruffled his hair; he stopped a couple of times to offer a comment but was lost for words. He opened his mouth to speak and then almost ran to the drinks table, poured himself a large whisky, dispatched it, and refilled his glass. Then he strode over to the coffee table, grabbed Lotte's wine glass, threw the contents in the ice bucket. 'Bloody amazing news. You clever girl. What do you want? A girl? A boy? Are you sure? Are you okay? Have you been to the doctor and—'

'Yes. Dr Khan has confirmed it and has pronounced me fit and healthy. And so long as we are all healthy, I don't care whether it's a boy or a girl. Please tell me you're happy too.'

Julian joined his wife on the sofa and embraced her warmly before shouting for Annie and giving instructions for his wife's every need to be catered for. 'Have you heard? She's pregnant.'

'Been obvious these past few weeks, Master Julian. Should

have been clear even to you. *Men!* Having shared her reaction, she smiled broadly, drew him into a bear hug, and congratulated them.

'I didn't know she could smile,' said Lotte.

'Oh, yes. I saw one about five years ago.'

FOUR

2019

DI Arthur Hemming grabbed the case files, sighed, and left his orderly office to enter the half-deserted situation room. He dumped the files on the table in front of DS Ruth Dodds to join the others she had been asked to review. Ruth looked up expectantly, watched with a wry smile as the guv'nor tugged at his waistcoat and placed his suit jacket carefully on the back of his chair, adjusted the flowing red silk handkerchief from the top pocket of his navy-blue pinstriped suit jacket. He crossed his legs, flicked a speck of dust from his trousers, and looked approvingly at his shiny brown brogues.

'Where is everyone, guv?'

'This is it. You, me, and our young apprentice here,' he said as he reached over to tug out the earbuds of DC Tim Jenks. 'Not interrupting your leisure time, am I?'

'Sorry,' mumbled the callow DC.

'Sorry...?'

Tim looked with a frown at Ruth, who raised her eyebrows before mouthing the words to him. 'Oh. Sorry, *guv*,' said Tim.

'Apparently, we are a commando unit. Think SAS on a raid.'

'I like that idea,' said Tim with a grin.

'Without the fitness, the firepower, or the latitude to run the op as we see fit. Ours is not to reason why, but we have a handful of stale files to resurrect. Cold cases. Starting with a certain misper: Scott Banks. Did you look at the Banks file, Ruth?'

'It didn't take long,' she said, and grimaced her disapproval. 'Scott disappeared into thin air in September 2017. His son, Simon, is the last known person to meet with him on 24th September. His mobile phone's not been found, his bank account untouched since around this period, and the last known WhatsApp message was sent on 20th September to his son. After that – nothing. The case was investigated briefly before being consigned to a dusty drawer in spring 2018. Why resurrect it now, guv?' asked Ruth.

'Good question. It appears that Simon Banks—'

'Who?' asked Tim.

'Do stay awake, if you would be so good,' said Arthur, managing to embrace the two characteristics he was best known for: sarcasm and excessive politeness.

'Scott's son,' added Ruth.

'Simon's a reporter who's been running a series of articles on police ineffectiveness. Apparently, we are guilty of prioritising non-crime hate incidents over missing persons, burglary and, well, you get the gist. And the nationals have picked up on this. Our revered police commissioner appears to have come under pressure, so, here we are.'

'I heard him this morning on BBC Radio 4. It was quite a rant about police incompetence, which managed to link institutional racism, sexism, and soft woke tendencies with low conviction rates and rising crime. He said he was convinced his dad was no longer alive – probably murdered – but that all the police had done was slip it into the "Too difficult, doesn't matter" file,' said Ruth.

'Highbrow morning listening, DS? I'll speak with Simon Banks. Let's see if there's any substance behind these apparently baseless assertions. Either way, he's certainly stirred our hierarchy.'

'The file's pretty thin,' Ruth said.

'What do we know about Scott?' asked Arthur.

'Appears to be an unsavoury character. Divorced in 2010, lived on his own, not averse to frequenting the red-light areas.'

'Any previous?'

'Fined for ABH in 2013, cautioned for drunk and disorderly in 2015, and various complaints of threatening behaviour, all of which were dropped after cursory follow-up. He worked at a few pubs over the years. The dates aren't clear. The Yorkshire Belle, owned by a Terence Gerald Sinclair, and at The Golden Lion and a string of others, on and off. Sacked several times with various allegations of petty theft and offensive behaviour. The longest stint was at The Yorkshire Belle until a fallout with Terence Sinclair. Something similar also happened with a Baxter Hinds at The Golden Lion, but again, no dates are recorded,' said Ruth.

'Check all of that out, if you would, please, Ruth… and which pubs does he drink in? Who are his mates? When did they last see him?'

'Will do, guv. More recently, he was involved with a shady debt-collecting business owned by a lowlife called Fred Hughes. He bought debt, then chased it down. And he wasn't too squeamish in going about his pursuit.'

'Let's find him and see what he has to say for himself,' said Arthur.

'He died in 2018, I'm afraid,' said Ruth.

'Great. How was Scott involved? Let's get the details and follow up those leads.'

'The file has some detail in this area. Scott was working on four accounts: Zoya Patel, a single mum; Viktor Iliev, a Bulgarian plumber; Terence Sinclair, The Yorkshire Belle's owner; and Steve Yates, a pensioner with a gambling addiction.'

'Okay, will you—'

'On it, guv.'

'And, Tim, take a detailed look at the file and dig into Scott's background and movements. How did he get around? Driving licence? Passport? You know the drill.'

FIVE

2019

Julian's last sojourn as Cassandra's lodger was hard to dispel from his mind. The simplicity of her mountain retreat, the splendour of the Alps, their mountain hikes. And the moment when he had almost succumbed to powerful emotional forces that magnetically pulled him towards Cassandra. He dug deep, stopped his reflections, his meanderings, and forced himself to grapple with the realities of his home situation. France and Cassandra and home with Lotte were conflicting parallel universes.

His thoughts refocused on Lotte and the news that he was about to become a dad. There were still a few months to get used to the mind-blowing idea. He was excited at the prospect. But troubled. Their marriage was not exactly firing on all cylinders and the news had caught him by surprise. They had never spoken of being parents, and a bit of him found the prospect preposterous. Lotte could barely look after herself, they were not coping as a couple, and they had not enjoyed the physical side of marriage to any great extent over the last year. In fact, Lotte had effectively exiled him to the spare bedroom on the pretext of his persistent nightmares, so they must just have struck lucky. Their marriage spluttered despite the baby news. And why had Lotte not told him about earlier suspicions that she might be pregnant? Neither had she told him about her visits to the doctor. *You're never here, darling. You probably don't remember. You never pay any attention to what I say.* He would remember. How could he not? Instead, she had turned the tables on him and demanded to know if he would sell his business in France. He had shaken his head and taken refuge in his study, tuned into the retro *Deep Purple in Rock* album. But why was it going so wrong? She resented his business trips, quick to go on the attack despite knowing it was to be a feature of his business life before they married; he was fed up with her moods and petulance, but if he tried to broach the subject, he was given short shrift. The truth of it was, she only seemed happy when partying or socialising with so-called friends. It all seemed so shallow, so pointless. When he had asked her what she wanted out of life, how they might develop mutual interests, she dismissed his question with an acerbic comment and a sneer. Why did she not put any effort into making their marriage work? But was he equally guilty? What was he doing even allowing his mind to reside in France with Cassandra? It could be misconstrued. He was married, he was about to become a parent. He was confused, conflicted, condemned to be continually unhappy if he could not work all this out. But he knew what he had to do. He had made his vows, had made his bed, as his dad ungraciously described it, so had to do as instructed: *Bed made, now lie on it*. Parenthood would be a game changer. It was an unplanned irrefutable fact. And the thought of fatherhood thrilled him. And scared him. Before the baby was born there was time to rediscover their love for each other, locate the misplaced magic. But he was confused, surprised at a mishmash of feelings of despair with

Lotte, imminent fatherhood, growing fondness for Cassandra. Emotions had almost overwhelmed him in the Alps. He had felt a giddy happiness in contrast to life in Yorkshire.

Julian made sure he found time for Lotte over the summer months as she bloomed and glowed, managing a few day trips and occasional weekends away. In early September, they found themselves in a hotel in the Lakes, and over breakfast Julian suggested they go for a walk around Keswick.

'I'm not feeling so great today,' she said. 'Why don't you head for the fells? You know you're dying to. I spotted your boots in the car. I'll curl up with a book in the lounge and may have a snooze.'

He had not needed much persuasion, and relished the day to himself. Nothing was better for getting perspective on business issues – on any issue – than a hike to a hard-won summit. On the way back to their weekend hotel he had even managed to find a store to buy baby stuff Lotte had said she liked. It was a good job he had rented a four-by-four SUV for this break; his Aston would not have been up to the job. It dawned on him that they would need to buy a more practical vehicle.

Back at the hotel, he proudly showed her his purchases. Lotte's eyes narrowed, her brow furrowed, and she looked first at Julian and then to his purchases: cuddly toys including a green dog monstrosity, dummies, blue and pink baby clothes, a baby bath, decorations for the nursery, various toys, and children's books. He followed her gaze and took it all in with a fresh eye: an odd gallimaufry of baby stuff – some might be more relevant than others, he could now see. But he was pleased with himself nonetheless, and puzzled by Lotte's dark looks. He was about to comment further when her eyes locked back on his; they signalled danger.

'You did this on your own?'

'I did well, didn't I? Aren't you pleased?' he added as her face tightened.

'I can't believe you sometimes. You bought stuff for *our* baby without *me*? You didn't even discuss this with me. How could you be so utterly crass, so utterly thoughtless? Why did you not want to do this as a couple? Prospective parents pulling together, enjoying the moment as they set up their nest for their first baby?'

'Sorry, I didn't—'

'No, you never do.'

Julian let her comments settle, and as the evening wore on, they relaxed a little and spoke about the challenges ahead as they prepared for a fundamental change in their life.

'I know it's been difficult for you, Lotte. A big change from your previous life.'

'Oh, you noticed, did you?'

'Difficult for both of us, what with Dad's illness and business woes and… but are you happier these days? You seem to be. A bit, at least,' said Julian. 'A good idea to come away this weekend, don't you think?'

Lotte shot him a look he struggled to decode. It did not exude warmth. There was a pause before she grunted. He took it to be a positive sentiment.

'I'll put off my trip to France,' Julian ventured quietly.

'You don't have to for me… not yet anyway.'

'Nonetheless, I want to be around as we both plan our new lives together.'

'Married life's going to be transformed, is it?' Lotte scowled.

'Err… it's bound to be different, isn't it?'

'Very perceptive of you.'

'Life's full of surprises, I suppose. But married life isn't so bad, is it? A few wrinkles were inevitable. Big change for both of us. And now another chapter.'

'"Not so bad"? Seriously? Have you ever stopped to look at it from my viewpoint? Daft question. All me, me, me with you, isn't it?' It was as if he had jabbed her with a pointy stick. 'Well, let's just recap, shall we? And *no*, you can't suddenly stop me just because you may get an answer you won't like. Have you even considered what I gave up for you? For this life? I mean, *really* considered beyond a few trite words. I mean, are you really asking me this? Do you really need telling? I gave up my job, my home, France, my friends. And for what? A part-time husband who largely ignores me, is as cold as a dead fish, isn't even here half the time. And I'm holed up in a huge house in a hamlet with no civilisation remotely close, in a part of the country I don't know. And you think one break in the Lake District… then you embroil me in family politics and The Belle business shenanigans. To make matters worse, you always want your own way in full certainty of your rightness. All the family are opposed to what you propose. But you insist it's the only option and upset your dad as he fails in front of our very eyes. He's *dying*. Remember? A fact just filed along with your emotions. How could you? And what do you get up to in France? Why do you spend so much time there? Is there more than business to attract you?' She paused and glared at him.

Julian pressed himself back in his chair under the onslaught. He paled as the torrent assailed him. 'I know, I did say—'

'Words with no meaning. That's what your words amounted to. I'm lonely, Julian. Bored, lonely, neglected…' Lotte glared at him, shuffled her bulk in her seat.

He fiddled with his wedding ring and said nothing for a while. What could he say? Nothing he did or said seemed to be right. 'I'm so sorry,' he said eventually, and then lapsed into silence. It did not seem to be the moment to remind her about her own moods, hormone-driven, perhaps; she had implied as much on several occasions, but she would not take kindly to him bringing it all up now.

But she wasn't done just yet. 'And while we're being honest with each other at last, there are times when I just want to give up on you. You aren't here much of the time, and when you are... well, you aren't, really. Always in the office or in your study. And when we're together you simply don't talk. Where's the fun, where's the excitement? Nothing since... since the honeymoon. What I see is someone who's withdrawn, selfish, controlling, manipulative, thoughtless, cruel even – *yes*, you *are* cruel. To your dad, to Emily with the way you just dismiss her out of hand, but most of all to me. You take me for granted. I feel... I feel... imprisoned, your trinket, too thick to understand your business challenges. Where's the person I met on the continent? You were quiet but you still liked to enjoy yourself, to party—'

'Not really. Just not me, Lotte. Never has been.'

'Well, if this is the real you then I can't cope. I just can't cope. So, I'm destined to be the modern-day Eloise, am I?'

'What's Emily said now?'

'The truth, Julian. How you deserted the love of your teenage years despite declarations of mutual love and undying devotion while in absentia at university. But you soon forgot the poor girl, didn't you? You didn't even let her down lightly. What with all your sports, mountain hiking, beer. And girls – especially girls.'

The willowy figure of his teenage love, Eloise: teenage love and passion unleashed mainly at her farm, hayloft antics. And he had meant his declaration of undying love. At the time.

'I was young.'

'How long did you write for? A month? Two? How long before the first university fling?'

Julian winced at the memory. Embarrassing. Reprehensible, really. But worse things happen, and it's all about growing up.

'And then to be so bloody inconsiderate, so cruel as to show off your new girl, take her to the local pub at home only for poor Eloise to catch you in mid-embrace. You probably planned it that way. Cruel bastard,' said Lotte as she burst into tears, slammed her cup down, and stormed out.

Julian grimaced.

'Don't worry, Master Julian. Hormones,' said Annie, her interruption welcome as she cleared things away.

Josh had been born prematurely at just twenty-seven weeks. He weighed in at 2.1 pounds, less than a bag of sugar. Labour had been brought on by a urinary infection. An autumnal rather than a festive baby, then. They were not ready. Not ready in any sense. But nature took its course, and the new reality quickly established its hold. The first couple of months were spent in hospital: at first in the intensive care baby unit until Josh was strong enough to progress to the children's ward.

Preparations for Christmas were in full swing by the time they got him home. The nursery had been decorated and kitted out, and their chosen nanny employed. A traditional lunch had been arranged as the family gathered, Julian's dad undertaking the ritual carving of the turkey as Emily, Luke, and his wife Tina joined Julian and Lotte. Annie joined them at the table, and they all raised a glass to thank her for another spectacular meal.

'Merry Christmas,' they declared in unison.

Lotte soon excused herself, blaming a headache. And Julian's dad had a nasty coughing fit to further mar celebrations. He had become thinner and weaker; his frequent coughing bouts and spluttering were hard to witness.

SIX

2020

As January unfolded Julian tried to be attentive, but his wife repulsed his efforts. Nanny Barlow quickly became a godsend and often accompanied Julian to the hospital as the baby struggled in the early months of the New Year.

Julian sought out the main man. He needed to hear what his prognosis was, what he had to say.

'I need to remind you of the potential implications of prematurely born babies. Many develop complex problems quite quickly.' Julian's face clouded, and Dr Lloyd quickly recovered to say, 'Little Josh is faring well.' He smiled self-consciously. 'Most suffer from repeated bouts of bronchiolitis, as you are finding with Josh. But some develop disabilities – impossible to diagnose just yet.'

'What type of disabilities?' asked Julian.

'Various, and some may sound scary, but many children grow out of their early ailments as they gather strength and their systems develop. Very occasionally chronic ailments like cerebral palsy, mental retardation, chronic lung disease, blindness, and hearing loss… but the risk in Josh's case is small,' Dr Lloyd added quickly. 'We should also be alert to signs of attention deficit hyperactivity disorder or ADHD. Or autistic spectrum disorder.'

Dr Lloyd's sensitivity was questionable, so Julian was pleased Lotte had not heard the account directly from him. He tried to represent the conversation to her more tactfully, but she responded emotionally. Well, it was worrying. They needed to be on their guard, monitor Josh's progress, get him checked out regularly.

And more generally, Lotte became moody and withdrawn; post-baby blues, Julian supposed. On finding her sitting in a dark room with tears streaming, he summoned the doctor despite her protestations. The diagnosis was mild postnatal depression. She just needed love and time. Meanwhile Josh's trips to hospital became more frequent, and sometimes Lotte did not even seem to notice her son's absence.

Lockdown was the government's response to the Covid-19 pandemic in the spring of 2020, and necessitated Julian and Thomas meeting via Zoom conference calls. Thomas soon descended into loose-fitting leisurewear and became unshaven. Today they had a meeting with an immaculately groomed Faye Dunbarton, who wore a white blouse under a navy-blue suit. She was an elegant middle-aged woman who wore her natural grey hair with aplomb and displayed impressive self-assurance. Julian thought it suited her. After the initial introductions and discussion about the health crisis, they got down to business.

'I won't waste your time, gentlemen. We wish to reinstate our offer for The Yorkshire Belle,' said Faye. She had introduced herself as being an intermediary, a lawyer by profession.

'Who's "we"?' asked Thomas.

'My client wishes to remain anonymous.'

'Why?' Thomas again.

'It's not unusual. There can be all sorts of reasons. I've found it best not to speculate. It just clutters the mind and it's irrelevant anyway. I simply understand my brief and then represent my client's interests as best I can.'

'It may not be irrelevant,' said Thomas.

'I have no knowledge of it being in any way pertinent to the offer, and if I had reason to assume the intentions were anything other than genuine it would have been someone else before you today.'

'Okay. To your offer, then?'

Just then, Thomas's email pinged, as did Julian's.

'It's generous,' she said.

The offer had increased by fifteen per cent. Cash on completion.

'Why do you consider it generous? Just out of interest?'

'I think when you compare it to market valuations, you'll reach the same conclusion.'

'And why would you invest in hospitality right at the point when the industry's being closed down by government diktat?' said Thomas.

'The offer is for the *assets* of The Yorkshire Belle. My client has asked me to be explicit. The offer is for the freehold. The business remains under the ownership of Belle Hospitality: assets, debts, contractual and legal obligations. You can dispose of those as you choose prior to finalising our deal. And we can complete quickly. Once you agree, we can release draft heads of terms, and the sale and purchase agreement will swiftly follow. It should be straightforward. Diligence will be minimal other than verifying title. You're quiet, Julian. What do you think? A tempting offer?'

Julian remained quiet for a few moments longer before he responded. 'My view's irrelevant. Our principal shareholder and the board have rejected all previous offers. They won't sell. My hands are tied.'

'You strike me as being a persuasive man with a reputation for getting what you want. I'm sure you'll find a way forward.'

'I will indeed. But I don't do business through intermediaries, so I won't put this offer to them.'

'I wouldn't have thought you the squeamish type. Won't you reconsider?'

'No.'

'Are we done here?' she asked.

'How long's the offer open for?' Thomas.

'Ninety days.'

An emergency virtual shareholder meeting was convened in early April to consider the pandemic's impact on business. It would be interesting to see how the Zoom video conferencing system worked. Julian's dad had been sceptical, but Emily had decided to bubble with him as lockdown continued, oversee his medical regime, and become his primary carer. At least she would be able to set Zoom up for him. Thomas shuffled in his seat and coughed before delivering his gloomy report: income had dried up, bookings cancelled, the return of deposits for hotel rooms and functions demanded. The business had responded to this existential crisis by slashing costs: negotiated rent reductions, cancelled supplier orders, delayed payment of invoices.

'What about staff?' asked Terence.

'We fully participate in the government's furlough scheme; it's generous. A surprise. But we've let all our casual and part-time staff go.'

'Sacked them, you mean,' said Terence.

'And other government schemes?' asked Luke.

'We avail ourselves of those – VAT deferral and all the rest of it. And we've applied for the loans they've made available on attractive terms,' added Thomas.

'Will our applications be successful?' asked Luke. He sat forward, his brow furrowed.

'I remain hopeful, but...' Thomas paused and seemed to agonise over his choice of words.

'Two providers have already rejected our applications,' interjected Julian.

'Why?' asked his dad gruffly.

'I'm afraid we fail the balance sheet evaluation. Belle Hospitality is regarded as a failing business, but we continue to argue our case.'

'What's your assessment of the seriousness of our position?' asked Luke.

'The bank's called in our loan and our investors refuse to release the second tranche of their investment commitments. Again, we argue our case with vigour.'

Terence suddenly slammed his hands on the desk, uttered profanities, and struggled to his feet. Emily helped him out of the room and returned a few minutes later.

'He's terribly upset, made himself ill. I implore you to stop these onslaughts of yours, Julian. You too, Thomas. He's dying. You'll kill him prematurely at this rate. I just don't know what's the matter with you both. His message is to sort out the mess *you've* created. It's obvious where you're going with this, and the answer's the same,' said Emily as tears flowed.

'We're all desperately concerned about Dad, but we also need to hear the business realities we face.' Luke's words were expressed quietly. 'Let's get to the nub of it. How long do we have left if we don't get any of these loans? What are our options?'

'We all have the analysis in front of us, Luke: balance sheet, cash flow, our assumptions. What's *your* assessment?' asked Julian.

'*You're* the CEO; the executive must answer these questions. How dare you seek to—'

'And our advice has consistently been rejected by this board. And *you're* the accountant. What's your professional opinion, Luke?'

'Now you're sulking,' said Emily between sobs.

'Not at all. I ask my non-executive colleagues for their guidance. The shareholders and this board have rejected our proposed strategy – the strategy supported by our investors, who are losing patience. As are the bank. I'd appreciate your advice. What's your prognosis? What do you suggest?'

'You just don't accept anything other than the sale of The Yorkshire Belle. It's become a macho trial of strength. You trying to prove yours is bigger than our dad's. Pathetic. Destructive. Manipulative.'

'Spot on, Em,' said Lotte, who had sat impassively until now.

'You're wrong there,' intervened Thomas. He glanced anxiously at Julian. 'I've been specifically asked not to say this, but we've received an improved offer for The Belle. Julian has rejected it given the board's decision. His question is genuine. And I would also like to hear what you have to say. As Finance Director I have legal, fiduciary responsibilities. We can't continue down this path. We must find a solution, however unpalatable. Maybe we sell The Belle? Maybe we sell the other bits of the business. But who's going to buy now? It's impossible. If we choose to do nothing other than tinker, then we will find ourselves in the hands of the receiver.'

His words hung heavy in the air.

'So, I ask again. What advice can you offer, Luke? Prognosis and strategy,' said Julian.

'I suspect we can limp along until Christmas. Maybe a bit longer if this pandemic ends sooner than we all think. Not as long if we face more lockdowns.'

'We concur,' said Thomas.

'Strategy?' nudged Julian.

'I draw the line there. Strategic options are for the executive to present. Then we can make our decisions. Do your job.'

Zoom had also become Julian's go-to communication default with Hotel L'Angleterre, and he had both weekly calls with Lysander and monthly management meetings attended by the executive head chef and the accounts manager. He also introduced Thomas to the team so he could establish contact despite Lysander's wariness.

In one of the one-to-one sessions with key staff, Julian Zoomed Cassandra. 'How are you, Cassandra?'

'Fine.'

'Sorry I had to leave so suddenly last time.'

'You don't have to explain.'

'No, but I'd like to. A few complications at home, I'm afraid.'

'Yes, you said.'

'Did I? Of course. How are you coping with Covid restrictions at your end?'

'No problem, really. You know me. Happy in my own company, and my chalet isn't exactly buzzing. Occasional company was nice, though… more than nice.'

'Boris's road map seems to be holding up, so I hope to get over possibly in the summer.'

'Okay.'

'And Thomas is on the case. The building projects. Is the investigation going okay your end?'

'Thomas seems competent.'

'He's trustworthy.'

'Summer, then?'

'I'll look forward to it. To… if it's all right to resume as your lodger?'

'Of course. And… me too.'

The line was terminated, and he sat back in his chair and replayed the conversation in his head. It had been undeniably awkward. Most unusual. Their conversations were always a bit staccato with lots of pregnant pauses, but never awkward. Until now.

Julian coped with the wet nappy inexpertly but with gritted determination, smiled, and spoke softly. Nanny Barlow looked on, offered the occasional piece of advice, but was happy to retreat to the shadows as the morning routine unfolded. Always Julian, rarely Lotte, she told him pointedly. Julian frowned and mumbled something about his wife's mild depression. Satisfied with the result, Julian pulled on the toddler's little dungarees and twirled his son in the air to catalyse at least some reaction: first a little chuckle and then a rewarding smile, hard won. Nursing Josh in the crook of his arm, he coaxed him to his bottle with limited success. Nanny Barlow soon took over.

He decided to give his precious metallic-grey Aston Martin DB5 an outing. The iconic vehicle with the chrome wire wheels always stirred him. The thought provoked a smile. A little ostentatious perhaps, but it was a glorious early summer's day, so perfect for the hour it would take to get to York from his eighteenth-century stone house north of the pretty North Yorkshire village of Hutton-le-Hole. In the wake of his very first deal he had splashed out on the car, convinced himself it was a good investment. In fact, he had already turned down an offer of more than half a million pounds for it. Come the day it became worth a million, well, then maybe. He would take a circuitous route today to enjoy the sunshine, the scenery, the sensational sound of the four-litre engine as it burbled through the village and to York via the market towns of Pickering and Malton.

Julian drew into the car park of The Belle, parked alongside Thomas's Jaguar. He stood back and took in the monstrously ugly pub. The original had been destroyed by a stray Luftwaffe bomb in 1942 and its replacement had been completed in the early 1950s and then grown haphazardly in the '60s and '90s. How could he possibly regard it as sacrosanct? But his dad was determined to build on the legacy of his dad before him, who had owned the original Belle, together with a handful of other pubs nearby. Grandad had obviously had a flair for business, and had circulated a story about the Dean of York, the mayor, and several civic dignitaries who had been killed in the air strike. Julian had never been able to verify the story, but it had become something of a legend his grandad had perpetuated. He had even retained a part of the ruin and placed an information board around it: the original sixteenth-century front doorway and a little of the walling had survived and been maintained at one side of the plot. Various faded pictures of previous clerics adorned the walls of the pub even today. Originally situated close to a rural village, Tingford, this had gradually been swallowed by the urban sprawl as York grew. The main A64 was close, and the pub, the farm next to it, and a swathe of agricultural land behind it was a rural oasis in the suburbs.

Rather than head inside, he decided to walk around the perimeter of this large site, remind himself of the layout. The offer for the pub had resurfaced as a surprise with the UK economy in a pandemic-induced parlous state. The hospitality industry especially suffered. The Belle limped on, but only by virtue of the furlough scheme and other relaxations of the payment of taxes. Why was The Belle receiving interest from would-be buyers? His antennae twitched. He passed the old stone ruins and the graffiti-adorned information boards, now besmirched by mindless vandalism. Behind the new pub was a further car park, and a pub garden with dilapidated wooden picnic tables and benches sitting desolately in the middle of an overgrown lawned area where brambles, nettles, and weeds encroached. To the west and north of their grounds was the run-down farm: a mix of dairy and arable. He made a mental note to enquire as to its acreage and to learn who the farmer was. At the front of The Belle, he turned right and headed along the face of the farm. The farmer used a side entrance that bordered the pub rather than a small access onto the main road. Long ago the family had given the farmer access to his property from The Belle's land. It was hard to imagine how the farm would manage otherwise. Walking past the farm's one legal entrance, Julian reached a narrow lane beyond the farm, and a few hundred yards down it was a gate to more fields stretching into the distance. He estimated there must be sixty or seventy acres. Probably more. He would check it out.

Thomas slurped from a mug of coffee as he waited in the snug, pored over a sheaf of papers. He wore a lockdown stubble and was informally attired in jeans and woolly jumper, Julian in a smartly tailored suit, leather shoes, white shirt, tie, and cufflinks.

'How are you? How's your dad?'

'Not good,' acknowledged Julian, helping himself to coffee. 'How are the twins? Molly?'

'They're great, thanks. Josh? Is he coming on now? No concerns?'

'Fine... let's get to it, shall we?'

'The bottom line is—'

'Crunch time. Decision time...'

'You've seen the accounts, Julian. We simply can't go on like this. The whole business is failing, as we've pointed out to the board with increased urgency over the past year. Even Luke concurred with our prognosis. The Yorkshire Belle is a bottomless pit and now the rest of the pub chain struggles. Now the offer for the pub's back on the table...' While much of their hospitality group was now open, and with high hopes that the chancellor's scheme (Rishi's Dishes, or Eat Out to Help Out) would stimulate trade in the wake of the lockdown, they still operated on partial capacity because of continued restrictions. Thomas illustrated his points with graphs and tables of figures, punctuated his comments with exasperated sighs and the occasional ruffling of his curly hair as he rubbed a lined brow. 'And have you seen the state of this place? The kitchens, the toilets, the furnishings, and—'

Julian held up a hand. 'I know all this. I've read the accounts, I've walked through the pub, inspected the bedrooms. Been transported back to Victoriana. Any update on how long we've got?'

'Sorry. Just venting… it depends on our assumptions, how long this pandemic goes on for, how generous government will be, when we can reopen, and what costs we'll incur to make it Covid compliant,' said Thomas.

'Your gut feel?' said Julian.

'No change. Six months tops. Might get to Christmas if we're lucky. We need a plan urgently. If only they would listen to our proposals.'

They allowed themselves a few minutes to recall the strategy Julian's dad had agreed; it had diluted the family's equity by the injection of investment funds on the premise of a change in direction: away from pubs to high-quality hotels. The investment had reduced his dad's stake to sixty per cent, ten per cent to each of Luke, Emily and Julian, and ten per cent to SI. But the family had reneged on the deal nearly three years ago, decided to plough most of the investment into the ageing, underinvested pub chain Belle Hospitality, having bought just one hotel half-heartedly. It hardly qualified as the much-heralded high-end hotel strategy. Now they had a disgruntled investor on board and an impatient bank.

'Julian.' Thomas gently prodded him.

'Sorry. Miles away.'

'The game's nearly up,' pressed Thomas. 'They just *must* listen, *must* come on board with the strategy. But they seem steadfast in their opposition, in denial of the realities.'

'Everything's changed now,' said Julian.

'Your dad?'

Julian nodded and sat back, surveyed his surroundings, took in his FD's earnestness.

'Listen, Julian. I sort of ran into Luke and took the liberty to urge him to relent, asked for his support. I couldn't have been clearer. Know what he said?'

Julian stared intently but said nothing. Thomas and Luke lived in different parts of the county, had different interests, were not close. Clearly, he had sought him out, hoped to persuade him where Julian had repeatedly failed. Fair enough. A finance director had responsibilities to the board, which transcended personal loyalties or accountability to a CEO. It was a smart thing to do.

'He said he'd support any sensible plan we come up with – except for one thing.'

'Sale of The Yorkshire Belle.'

'Yes. Luke said something about a promise. Do you know what he referred to?'

Julian said nothing for a while, stared out of the window, lost in his own thoughts. Turning back to Thomas, he answered his FD's quizzical look. 'Yeah. The Belle.'

'What of it?'

'He won't sell it…'

'Ever?'

'That was probably his intention, which certainly seems to reflect his obdurate attitude to a sale.'

'And Emily?'

'Probably the same.'

'He said you'd promised too.'

'Did he?'

'Are you going to enlighten me?'

'Mm.'

'This is like pulling hen's teeth. What do you want me to do? What's the plan?'

Julian glanced at the slides again, rubbed the outline of his chin, and sat forward. 'Benjamin Franklin's advice is apt: failure to prepare is preparing to fail. We line our ducks up. You pull together a punchy presentation of the facts – yes, again – an analysis of likely future trading, set out our options. Meet with the bank, get their inevitable rejection of a deferral of interest payments on our current loans and flat refusal to extend us a new loan. Get it in writing. Get another bank to do likewise. Ask them to be blunt as to the repercussions. No punches pulled. Then we need to lay out the options and convey to the board our executive decision, seek their agreement. Let's get the investors behind us: we need to sell The Belle to raise funds to roll out the agreed hotel strategy undeterred and unimpeded. We probably need another tranche of investment too, so I'll speak with the head honcho there. He made a fortune on my first hotel venture in France. We get on.'

'Why will your family accept yet more dilution, all predicated on selling their beloved pub?'

'With the investors behind us and more vocal, they have to listen and accept the inevitable.'

'I don't know. What if they still won't budge? They can outvote you. With or without your dad.'

'True. If they do – well, what the hell, I've always got Hotel L'Angleterre.'

'Great. I'd better brush up my CV.'

'Look, I've got a hunch I'll follow up. If none of this works, then I could do with a good FD to oversee an expansion in the Alps if you're interested… but let's not give up. Luke may choose to go down with the ship, but he's got no balls; he's no great shakes as a businessman. His own business totters on the edge. And Emily's unpredictable. Leave them to me. Now, I've got some calls to make. Speak later.'

The two of them leaned on the fence. Julian pointed out the land as they turned their collars up to protect against an easterly wind as rain slanted in across the fields: the British summer performing to type. His suit was only partially protected by an anorak, his leather loafers soon muddy and sodden. In contrast, Henry was very much the country gent in his Hunter wellies, tweed jacket beneath a heavy waterproof, and a flat cap.

'Good to see you, Julian, but tell me why we need to brave the elements to look at cows and run-down farms? The wind's picked up too, decidedly chilly. Fancy something to warm the cockles?' he said as he proffered a hip flask extricated from an inside pocket.

Julian shook his head and set out for Henry the assignment he had in mind. The agent was well connected, knew how the planning system worked, knew the movers and shakers. It had been Henry who had found Julian his house off market; his tentacles reached far and wide in both the residential and commercial property sectors. 'Find out if the farmer has any legal rights of access over The Belle's land. If you can, get the low-down on the farmer: financial position, likely appetite to sell. You know the sort of thing.'

'And the land beyond his?'

'I heard a whisper from a usually reliable source. I want to know who owns it, acreage. Has planning permission been granted? I doubt it, but I suspect they'll have sounded out the planners. But let's keep this quiet. My name mustn't surface.'

'Got your drift,' Henry boomed, tapping his nose. 'But I'm puzzled. What's the game plan? Will you buy and sell it on? Or is this a new venture into the murky depths of property development?'

Julian gave him a half-smile.

SEVEN

MAY 2020

DI Arthur Hemming strode into the coffee shop, spotted Simon Banks with a drink, mobile glued to his ear. He grabbed himself a flat white and joined the reporter. He was met with a smug half-smile and a raised hand. His call would soon be over. Arthur sat back and tuned into the pugnacious style of this hack, took in his crumpled T-shirt, faded jeans, and trainers. Simon was short in stature, with a loud, booming voice, and a chip on his shoulder. Arthur guessed that he lived alone, from his appearance and from his roving eye that followed young women in the queue, admired acres of their youthful flesh and their boundless energy. Or perhaps he was just another midlife crisis of a married man with noisy, expensive kids and a mortgage he could not afford. Arthur made a mental note to check out the man's background.

'Yeah, get back to me pronto or I go to print. No – no more dilly-dallying. Pull your finger out or… up to you.'

The mobile was consigned to Simon's pocket. He smiled and turned to Arthur, who held up his warrant card for inspection. Simon proffered a hand for the DI to shake, took a slurp, and sat back expectantly.

'Good to meet you, Mr Banks.'

'Simon. About time we saw a response from the police.'

'I tuned into your radio interview. Seems you're rather miffed by our performance.'

'Miffed? The bloody understatement of the year… wherever you look there's corruption, incompetence, crimes meriting no more than a crime number. Any thought of detection? Pah. Fucking scandalous. And a thoroughly inadequate investigation into my dad's disappearance just speaks to the incompetence. Cast aside after six months. All your lot have been able to see is a man down on his luck, perhaps guilty of a bit of ducking and diving, cutting a few corners…'

'That's as may be, but I can assure you that whatever his background or problems or offences, we treat every misper in the same way.'

'Bollocks you do. Always pulling him in, accusing him of theft or antisocial behaviour, even drug-pushing. Especially drug-pushing. So, you just cast him aside. Another piece of shit to kick under the sofa.'

'Drugs? Tell me about it.'

'Unbelievable. You don't even know about that? And you wonder why I accuse you…'

Arthur looked around the coffee shop, sighed internally, and then turned his focus back on Simon. 'We don't appear to have covered ourselves in glory, but let me see if I can put that right.'

'Can I quote you on that? Local plod admits incompetence? Corruption? That sort of thing?' said Simon, his eyes glinting.

'Not my words. Let's not get off on the wrong foot. I've been assigned this case only recently—'

'Amazing what a bit of press pressure can do.'

'And I understand that you must be very concerned about the disappearance of your dad. I need you to help me uncover what's happened to him. I can only promise that we'll do everything we can to find his whereabouts or—'

'His grave?' said Simon, putting down his cup with a bang, coffee splashing on the table.

'Mind if I take a few notes?'

Simon shook his head.

'Good. So, fill me in. How close were you? How frequently did you meet or socialise? When and where did you last see your dad? When did you last hear of him? Then we can move on to why you're so confident that something malign has happened to Scott. Your dad.'

'I know what his name is… and I went through all this stuff—'

'Humour me. If you'd be so kind.'

Simon Banks's answers confirmed the scant information in the police file. He had last met with his dad on 24th September 2017, had last received a WhatsApp message dated 20th September agreeing the time of their meeting; they usually spoke once a week and met only occasionally. They had clearly not been especially close and did not socialise beyond the occasional beer.

'He divorced in 2010, didn't he? Can you tell me about that?' asked Arthur.

'You can't even get that right. God alive, you people. It was 2005.'

Arthur made his notes. 'Did he remarry?'

'Nah, but he had a partner. Reason he split up with my mum. Penny. Love of his life. Not that I approved. Well, you're not going to, are you?'

'Is your mum around?'

'Alive, you mean? No. Died a few years back.'

'And Penny?'

'Developed early onset dementia. Broke his heart. And his

bank account. Stuck her in a care home when it all got a bit much—'

'Which one? Where?'

'Oh, for God's sake, do your own police work. Yet more evidence of police incompetence. I might just use this in my next piece. No comment to make, DI Arthur Hemming?'

'I'll leave your general assertions for the crime commissioner and the chief constable to determine a response; it's above my pay grade. You've been very helpful. We will follow this up from here. But before I go, I'd be enormously grateful if you would share with me the information that leads you to conclude that your dad's been murdered.'

'I can find no evidence that he's alive… nor can you lot.'

'That's not the same thing. Might he not have gone abroad?'

'How? He lived from hand to mouth. I used to lend him a few quid to get him through every now and then. Does he even have a passport? I can't ever recall him going on a foreign holiday.'

'Perhaps he's just gone to ground? In debt and chased?'

'By whom? He'd have called me.'

'Perhaps, perhaps not.'

Simon reluctantly agreed to forward his dad's WhatsApp messages to Arthur, and the meeting concluded. As a parting shot, Simon turned on his heels and said, 'You lot have a one-dimensional view of my dad: down and out, petty thief, druggie, general bad lad. People are more complex than that, contradictory. He loved Penny, would never desert her. And you might like to ask yourself how he managed to find the fees that paid for her care. I don't suppose you've even found the other bank account, have you?'

'Please, Mr Banks, if you have information that you are withholding—'

'Go to hell. Do your worst. All I will say, DI Hemming, is you'd better nail this before me. Find his body first. But especially find and lock away his killer before I get to him.'

Back at the station, Arthur and his team of two reviewed progress.

'What have you got for me, Tim, if I may divert you from surfing the net? Tedious, isn't it?'

'Sorry, guv?'

'Work just gets in the way. But if you have a teensy-weensy bit of time, we're all ears.'

'Sorry, guv. But it was germane—'

'Germane, was it? Mm. Well, stun us with your insights, young man.'

Tim scrambled for his notebook.

'Well?' prompted Ruth.

'Scott Banks's passport was last stamped in 2010. Barcelona.'

'When does the passport expire?' asked Arthur.

'It expired in 2016.'

'Interesting. So, unless he has a false passport, we know he hasn't fled abroad,' said Ruth.

'And his son confirms that he was not a man of means either, so funding a false passport seems unlikely. Bank account? Did you check?' asked Arthur.

'A Barclays current account with a balance of £76.20.'

'Ruth, please check if he had other accounts. We might start with Barclays. And I want to see all the records. Get the necessary court orders.'

'Will do, guv.'

'On this Barclays account. The one with a balance of £76.20,' said Tim.

'Yes?' said Arthur.

'What's interesting is that the bank made a charge of £25 for issuing a cheque with insufficient funds to pay out.'

'Payee?' said Arthur.

'The Golden Lion, and it was for £6,500. September 2017,' said Tim, who sat back and looked pleased with himself.

'So… the payee was the pub and not the manager, Baxter Hinds,' Ruth said.

'That's what our Tim said, isn't it?' Arthur.

'Isn't it a bit strange that Scott apparently owed £6,500 to the *pub* – and it could have been much more, might have been a down payment – *but* the manager, this Baxter Hinds, had a *personal debt*, which was bought out by Scott and his oppo?' Ruth pointed out.

'So, we've got a debt collector in debt to a pub whose manager himself had a debt pursued by none other than our Scott Banks. What a tangled web. It could all be a coincidence of course, but you know what we think about them, don't you, Tim?'

'What? Dunno… dunno, guv.'

'DS Dodds, I wonder if you'd be so kind as to channel your inner Agatha Christie to educate Poirot here once we're done.'

Ruth grinned; Tim blushed.

'This Baxter Hinds also disappeared around the same time as Scott and was replaced by a Kate Pringle, who subsequently made attempts to pursue the debt owed by Scott, but her endeavours to locate Scott were no more successful than ours,' Ruth added.

'Good work, Ruth. Keep digging on both Baxter Hinds and Kate Pringle. See if it leads anywhere. Let me tell you a bit more about my interesting meeting with Simon Banks. We need to check all the so-called "facts". Nothing must be taken as read. He claims that Scott divorced in 2005, not 2010. Apparently, a relationship with a Penny was the cause – the love of his life. Sadly, she developed dementia and is in a care home. Or was. Who is she? Where is she? Which home? Cost? How are the fees being afforded? By whom? Is she still alive? And I'll speak with a couple of my contacts as Simon said his dad had a drug problem, that our lot frequently pulled him in on suspicion of being a drug pusher.'

'I've also wondered how Scott got around. The debts he was chasing were all over the place, many of them rural,' Ruth said.

'Good point. Let's find out, please, team.'

Tim suddenly perked up, leaned forward in his chair. 'Oh, yes. I can help there. No record of insurance or car tax payments in his bank account statements.'

'How did we access those?' asked Arthur.

'They were in the file. Anyway, he may not have bothered with such legal niceties, of course. And it appears he had a big fallout with a Terence Sinclair at The Yorkshire Belle.'

'I met with Terence yesterday,' Ruth said. 'He's not well. Terminal cancer. Quite weak and a bit vague. He said that Scott left after a few years. Reading between the lines, they had an argument, but Terence claimed there was nothing more than a general disagreement. It was time for Scott to move on. He also spoke of a big falling-out between his son Julian and Scott. Apparently, it was a long time ago when Julian was a teenager. But he gave no details, and a coughing fit brought his nurse into the room, who quickly banished me.'

'Let's dig into Baxter Hinds and Kate Pringle and the debt triangle, and The Yorkshire Belle's Terence and Julian Sinclair. It's something to explore, I suppose, but none of this seems like a smoking gun to me. And Tim, go through all the WhatsApp messages that Simon has sent us. Fine-tooth comb, please. Let's also dig into the other debtor files that Scott was pursuing. That's it for now. Let's get on with it, please.'

EIGHT

SUMMER 2020

Emily called as Julian was about to head home. 'We need to talk, Julian.'

With a sigh, he diverted to his dad's house to meet his sister.

'Hi, Emily. How are you?' he asked as they sat in the deckchairs outside, socially distanced, antibacterial gel at the ready.

'As you might expect. Daddy is so poorly. You do realise?' she said, and dabbed moist eyes. 'Why doesn't it get to you? And the police don't help with their questions about that Scott guy. I wish they'd leave him alone.'

'Yes, they buttonholed me too. It's a while ago now. I prefer not to think about that lowlife.'

On the brink of tears, her mood suddenly turned to anger, and she ranted at Julian, her silent target. He sat impassively and watched his sister's turmoil, waited for it to abate.

'I'm preoccupied with the thing he cares most about in the world: the business. Unless you back the sale of The Yorkshire Belle, the business will go bust. You do understand this reality, don't you?'

'Don't be so bloody condescending. Dad is at death's door, and you want to talk about business and demand what he forbids. Why can't *you* understand? I can't believe you really care: no tears, no sadness, no let-up.'

'We all deal with things differently. And what can we do about his health? He won't even accept medical intervention. The die is cast whatever we do.'

'Too bloody cold-hearted for me. Great son you are, some brother.'

'Feel better? I'll head off. You've had your say.'

'No. Stay where you are, or I swear... I've spent much of today with Lotte. She's hurting. Really hurting. And it's more than the baby blues.'

'They're behind her, but I know she isn't too happy.'

'She unburdened herself this morning. A heart-to-heart. Told me in no uncertain terms how she feels.'

'And you've taken it on yourself to enlighten me, have you?'

'I couldn't possibly breach her trust. She confided in me. I couldn't possibly... where are you going?' she said as he pulled himself out of the chair.

'I've got the message.'

'I've not really said anything yet. Hear me out, at least.'

'You just said—'

'Oh, don't be so literal.' Emily flung her hands up in the air. 'She feels lonely, neglected, unloved, and is stuck at home all day with a baby. Babies are hard work, you know.'

'We have a housekeeper and a nanny, and Lotte spends more time with a bottle of wine than with Josh,' he said through gritted teeth.

Emily looked surprised, taken aback. He relaxed his expression, let it go.

'But you're never there, so you can't know what she does in the day. Lotte tells me you're heartless and have no time for her or little

Josh, let alone display any affection. True to form, eh, Julian? You opt for your study in the evening and then go off to see Thomas, or whatever you do with yourself these days. And now you're off to the continent again. Do you want this marriage to work?'

'Are you done? I want to get home for bath time with my son.'

Julian was struck by how quiet it was as he wandered through a half-empty Manchester Airport. Masked zombies made exaggerated space for fellow travellers. None of the usual hubbub of families and loved ones excited in advance of a holiday, of self-important businessmen and -women speaking loudly into mobile phones, of groups of pint-swilling youths. Now it was primarily lone businesspeople who travelled. They went about their preparations in near silence as they showed evidence of test results, helped themselves to yet more antibacterial gel, and checked their Covid paperwork. Julian was rigorous about testing himself and insistent that others who saw Josh did likewise. As he awaited the announcement of his flight, he sipped a bottle of mineral water and asked himself for the umpteenth time what the answer was to Emily's question. *Do you want this marriage to work, Julian?*

Julian slipped his wedding ring into his pocket as he ventured through the sparsely peopled arrivals hall of Geneva Airport, found a taxi, and they sped towards the hotel in record time. At Hotel L'Angleterre he was welcomed by Lysander. Julian was interested to gauge Lysander's grasp of detail, having been debriefed by Thomas. He was met with generalisations and diversionary tales.

'Why are the project accounts presented at such a high level? Show me the detail, the supporting invoices. I'd like to see invoices matched to accounting codes to analyse both expenditure and revenue.'

He had been steered by Thomas and Cassandra. His intention was to probe only so far. Far enough for Lysander's mood to corrode from upbeat to moody to exasperated. Julian, irritated by his attitude, decided to push him further when he returned with incomplete information.

'Why is this supplier's invoice coded to both food and beverage and building materials?' asked Julian. He kept his voice low, but his eyes drilled into Lysander's.

'Dunno,' said Lysander with a sullen glower.

'And this same supplier number and invoice is also coded to wines and spirits, as well as to—'

'They must have delivered different things,' said Lysander with a shrug of the shoulders.

'This supplier delivers building materials. It clearly says as much on invoice J350012,' said Julian.

'Your point is?'

'Why is invoice J73976, from the same supplier, Jacques Durand, coded to food and beverage? It seems unlikely, would you not agree?'

'No idea.' Lysander crossed his arms across his chest.

'Have you got these invoices?' pressed Julian, bright eyes watching Lysander carefully.

'No.'

'Please get them.'

'All of them?'

'The invoices from Jacques Durand for this period.'

'Now?'

'Yes – the accounts department is just next door,' Julian said.

On returning, Lysander placed the folder on the table. Julian smiled and spent a few minutes rifling through the pile. He removed the relevant invoices, sorted in date order.

Lysander eased up from his chair and sighed. 'I'll leave you to it.'

'No, don't go.' Julian lifted his head, looked intently at his general manager, who sat back down in bad grace. 'Okay, this pile is all coded to the project account. All for building materials. This smaller pile is coded to food and beverage. All clearly for having supplied… *building materials*. Please explain.'

'There must be some sort of mistake. Let me see.' Lysander rummaged through the piles and scratched his head. 'It must be a coding error. A simple mistake.'

'I see,' said Julian in a quiet voice.

'I'll have words,' said Lysander.

Julian had caught sight of Cassandra during the afternoon. They exchanged glances, and he noticed the trademark raised eyebrow morph into the shadow of a smile before she lowered her head and returned to her books. But they had not spoken, and she had gone by the time he had finished sparring with Lysander: a few sharp jabs, but he held back a sucker punch, the knockout blow that would surely come.

Julian grabbed his overnight bag. He was looking forward to seeing Cassandra, but also wanted to stretch his legs, so opted for the longer route via two hamlets. As he slowed his pace to admire a historic cluster of houses, he had the sensation of being followed. He paused on the pretext of viewing the old well, and concentrated hard. Footsteps stopped a split second after he drew to a halt. He was sure of it. Almost sure. He wandered on, rounded a corner, darted into a gap between two houses. Footsteps quickened behind him, were almost on him. His heartbeat raced and his palms moistened. He held his breath, watched, and waited. Not one person, but two. Closing in. What could they want? Why follow him? He shrank deeper into the recess. Soon enough, two youths strode by, chatting amiably to each other. Farmers, by the look of them – not in the least bit interested in him or anyone else. Feeling faintly ridiculous, he emerged from his hiding place. As he pressed on, he calmed down to enjoy the rurality.

He knocked rather than use his key, not sure of the welcome he could expect. It had been a while – too long. As he waited, he felt anxious. She could not have heard him, so he knocked again, this time louder, and the door opened immediately.

'Sorry... I didn't think you could have—'

'I was upstairs.' She opened the door wider and smiled.

'Hi, Cass,' Julian said. He felt awkward.

'Cass, now, is it?' she said with arched eyebrow.

'Sorry...'

'Twice over...'

'I beg your... oh, I see.' He dumped his things in his room and joined Cassandra on the bench outside to enjoy the last of the evening sunshine, the nights beginning to draw in now. He had shrugged on a light jumper as the temperature dipped. They sat in companionable silence as he tuned into the scents and sounds of the Alpine evening: the clang of cowbells from a neighbouring farm as they roamed the pastures, the wild flowers providing a splash of colour in the fields, insects buzzing. 'Neither of us are great conversationalists, are we?' he said.

'You noticed.'

'It's good to see you,' Julian said, tearing his eyes away from the mountain landscape to look into her hazel eyes.

'You too, Julian.'

'I couldn't get away before now. The pandemic.'

'Life on hold.'

'A lot to sort out, too.'

'The family business?'

'Yeah, amongst other things. I'd like to tell you a bit more about—'

'Good. But we've got all weekend, and I've got something rustic ready to eat.'

Cassandra busied herself in the kitchen while he set the table and poured the local country wine into a small decanter. The whole set-up was functional, understated, informal. It was a delicious antidote to the Hotel L'Angleterre's opulence, to the formal dining room in Hutton-le-Hole. He heard her whistling as she went about her tasks – out of tune, but it seemed to signal contentment. When it stopped, he walked into the kitchen. He stopped short and watched as she just gazed out of the window. Cassandra was lost in thought. Was she happy? He hoped so.

They ate, toasted each other's survival of the virus, Cassandra grasping knife and fork in one hand to free up the other for her glass, a habit he had not seen elsewhere. Mopping their plates with chunks of crusty bread, they finished with raclette washed down with a glass of red wine.

'I suppose we should be socially distanced,' said Julian, looking across the small table at her.

She squinted at him, cocked her head to one side. 'A bit late now.'

'Have you had your jab yet?' he asked.

'No. You?'

'Yes. It seemed a prerequisite of travelling, although I met someone who said she hadn't had hers. Who knows? It's chaos back home.'

'No better here. The French are a stroppy lot, so the vaccination programme is met with resistance, as are lockdowns and restrictions.'

'For what reason? The vaccines, I mean. The science seems to remove all room for doubt.'

'Who knows? The French don't need good reasons to protest. It's just another on the list of excuses to march.'

'At least our government seem to have the vaccination programme sorted. On the law of averages, they had to get something right eventually.'

'Still waiting for the EC... they're content to politicise everything. And Macron is...' She pulled a face.

'Yes,' agreed Julian. 'Ursula von Whatever too.'

Having cleared the plates away, they lapsed into silence as if exhausted by conversation, until Cassandra announced it was time for bed. A long day's hike was planned for tomorrow. Would he like to join her? *Yes*.

'Tell me about your life in the UK tomorrow, then. I'd like to hear,' she said.

'Goodnight.'

Julian was up early after a good night's sleep. He never seemed to be troubled by nightmares when at the chalet. He pulled some clothes on and went outside, savoured the freshness, the chill on his bare arms. Rabbits scuttled for cover; a mountain hare loped across the landscape. He headed back inside contented – a rare phenomenon. Time for a shower before Cassandra surfaced. He kicked his shoes off, grabbed his towel and washbag, and crept barefoot up the stairs. Julian saw her bath towel draped over a rail in the corridor. Good. It meant the bathroom was unoccupied – their system to communicate in the absence of door locks. He quickened his pace, trod lightly to reach the landing. He was at the door when it suddenly opened.

And there she was.

Right in front of him.

Less than a foot away.

Her lithe body naked except for a simple silver locket dangling from her bare neck.

Utterly beautiful.

His mouth agape, he kept his gaze fixed on her widening hazel eyes. They both stood for a moment, transfixed like rabbits in the headlights. Cassandra smiled her apology and reached down to grab the towel. She pulled it around her, his eyes followed her movement, took in her shape; a momentary pause, and then he reacted: turned on his heels and shouted his apologies as he headed back downstairs. He heard the bathroom door close softly behind him.

By the time she had showered and dressed, he had thrown a few things in his case. He paced up and down; his suitcase sat patiently, symbolically, by the front door.

'I'm so… so…'

'It's all right,' Cassandra said.

'No, it's not all right. I've invaded your privacy. Please forgive me.'

'The fault's mine.' She rested a hand lightly on his arm, and he flinched. She nodded towards his bag. 'Going somewhere?'

'I can't stay here.'

'One sight of me and you're off. Too shocking, eh?'

'What? No. *No*. You're beautiful, stunning. I mean… oh, God.'

'I'm teasing. It's no big deal. Almost worth it to see your smooth exterior crumple. Didn't realise you flustered. But if you must go… I'm heading for the hills. Up to you. But I promise to keep my clothes on…'

She turned and completed the packing of her rucksack, and he was sure he could hear her chuckle. As he calmed down, he began to feel foolish. His head was a jumble of confused, conflicted thoughts; his emotions were shot through. Not like him at all. *Get a grip, man.* It was a severe overreaction he would have to ask forgiveness for. Yet another apology due. From teenage-like nerves to contentment to embarrassment to confusion via flustered. Quite a journey.

After an hour he lagged some way behind her, struggled today. Some days were more difficult than others. This was obviously not a day to cover himself in glory. He battled on, enjoyed the scenery when he could, the physical challenge. As Cassandra disappeared around a rocky corner, his mind wandered back to their last venture into the mountains. He had struggled then too. Not only with his limp and fitness but emotionally. Julian recalled his reaction to the scenery and an emotionally charged exchange with Cassandra back then, on another day, another mountain.

'Wow!' said Julian. The vista was spectacular.

'The Massifs des Bornes and Bauges, the Vuache mountain range, and Lakes Geneva and Annecy,' she said. Cassandra glowed from the exertion but seemed to be at home in the mountain terrain. And the weather had been kind to them so far. The waterproofs and most of the additional layers still reposed in their bags, and once they had eaten their lunch, they smothered themselves with sunscreen and simply took in the views. Their familiar cabin silence reasserted itself in this magnificent outdoor theatre, the air especially clean, thinner at altitude. Cassandra pointed to the quarrelling mountain choughs, and they were mesmerised by a soaring golden eagle, admired its wingspan, awestruck by its presence.

She turned towards Julian with a half-smile and her eyes locked on his.

'Cassandra?' he said, puzzled by her expression.

She smiled.

'You should smile more often.'

He wondered what her story was. How had the graffiti at her place come about? Why? Who? It had obviously spooked her given the security arrangements. But she never answered his questions, brushed them aside as unimportant. And why the animosity towards Lysander? And why had her marriage never happened? The man was a fool. Beneath her plain exterior could he not see her inner beauty? These were shared moments in the inspirational, spiritual mountain theatre and family woes seemed distant. But what was Cassandra thinking? Julian reached out to her, placed a hand tenderly on her arm. There was a moment before she swivelled back to him; she held his gaze with wide eyes, glanced down at his touch and smiled. Natural forces drew them physically towards each other. Julian tingled with anticipation, the danger enveloped him, the lure magnetic. In the films they would soon kiss, embrace, declare their undying love inspired by the grandeur of their surroundings. Julian breathed deeply, moved by the electricity of her touch.

'I so enjoy your company, my humble lodgings. We seem to get on, don't we?' he said.

She raised a single eyebrow. '*We?*'

'Err. I didn't mean to imply, you know… sorry.' Then he saw the hint of a smile play on her lips.

'It works,' she said simply, and held his eyes.

'Why didn't you marry? And what is it with Lysander? Why the hermit existence?'

Cassandra looked down; the smile replaced by a frown.

'So many questions, but I'd rather not…'

'Okay.' Why those questions? Why now? The moment was lost.

'What about your life back home? You never say,' she said after a pause.

So, it seemed he was to be dragged back to home realities as Julian described the family's travails, the intractable problems of Belle Hospitality. He was open about his dysfunctional family. He expressed regret at having taken on the family business, how emasculated he felt in the role. But he said nothing about his dad's terminal illness, nothing about Lotte. Nor about his imminent arrival into fatherhood. Instead, Julian spoke of his love of the business in the French alps, of the pursuit of his favourite activities, opening his arms wide in demonstration.

'The truth of the matter is I love it here, the serenity, the simplicity of your lifestyle. I really like being with you,' he said before he quickly looked away, gazed into the distance.

Cassandra nodded but kept her counsel, 'Why don't you give up on it then? The family business.'

'Families aren't so easy, are they?'

'They can be,' Cassandra countered.

His mind snapped back to the present, surrounded by a similar grandeur on a different mountain. He tried to focus his mind on what he wanted to say. He had to take this opportunity to speak with Cassandra, to level with her, to allow himself to express his innermost feelings. But the words would not form in his head. Rounding the bend, he joined her on a makeshift rocky seat, slightly out of breath. His limbs ached.

'Your leg troubling you?' she asked.

'A bit.'

'What happened?'

He looked sideways at her, sat forward, rested his head in his hands, and composed himself. Took himself back all those years to the pub yard.

'I've never told another living soul before…'

'Then don't if it's too painful.'

'There's much I want to say, explain, share with you. It just doesn't come easy, opening up.' He paused and glanced at her.

'I'd never have guessed,' she said, a half-smile reaching her eyes.

'Whereas it's second nature to you?'

'Touché.'

'I've something more important to tell you, so the long version will have to save for another day… if there is another day.'

'You've got my attention now.'

'The limp and this,' he said, touching the faint scar on his face, 'were the result of an altercation when I was fifteen. I was beaten up, knocked out for a while, woke up in hospital, then a couple of operations and a few months' rehabilitation at home.'

'Poor you. Who did it? How? Why?'

'In a nutshell, the scars are more mental than physical. My dad…'

'He didn't? Your own dad?'

'No. No… he just chose to believe my assailant rather than me. Knocked me for six. He tried to apologise to me, but it was too late.'

'You couldn't forgive?'

'Too late for *him*. He didn't mention it again, and now he's got terminal cancer. Quite close to the end point, we think.'

'Oh, Julian. I'm so sorry. Your emotions must be all over the place.'

'I don't seem to be wired like my siblings. They castigate me for being unable to express my emotions.' But Julian's voice cracked, could say no more. Why now? He fished his handkerchief out of his pocket, blew his nose noisily, surreptitiously wiped a tear away.

'I'm so sorry. The prospect of losing your dad…'

'We aren't close.'

'Did you tell your siblings about the teenage incident? Your mum?'

'My siblings hear only Dad's voice. Mum died a long time ago.' He offered no explanation as the tears flowed. Cassandra pulled him towards her, and he allowed his head to rest on her shoulder. He felt quite disoriented. Not since his teenage years had he cried. Except on Josh being born, of course. Oh, God – another story he had no idea how to broach. First things first. He gently pulled away and the two gazed into each other's eyes, and this time the magnetic forces could not be averted. They embraced, they kissed. Gently, softly, briefly.

'Turning out to be quite a day, isn't it?' Cassandra said.

'There's much more I want to share, *need* to share with you, Cass, but let's move on to the col you mentioned. But I just need you to know... whatever you think... I really want to find a way of being with you. I don't know... I mean, I'm telling you what I feel. I've not thought the implications through. I don't yet know how to make it happen. But whatever you think later, please know I never meant you any harm. Quite the reverse.'

'Now I'm worried. I only ask one thing, Julian. Please don't lie. I couldn't take another man's lies.'

'Never.'

'Come on, then, before those clouds dump on us.'

They reached the vantage point to take in the views, take a rest, refuel on fruit, bread, continental meats, slices of cheese. They exchanged glances, stole a brief kiss, and then set about their lunches as a mountain goat peered down at them and a bearded vulture made an appearance above.

'You wanted to say something?'

He gazed heavenwards as dark, tumescent clouds gathered. The storm clouds seemed ominous.

'I want to be with you, Cass. It's as if... we're just right together. It feels right.'

She gazed into the distance. Julian stayed quiet, let her take in what he had said. He needed to take it in himself. This had not been part of any plan. He had allowed his feelings to dominate and surface for once. At last, she said in a soft voice, 'I see.'

'Tell me if I'm misreading the signs.'

Cassandra looked away, declined her head, and paused. His heart missed a beat. Then she turned back to him, leant over, and kissed him lightly on the lips and smiled. 'No, you're not. We work. At least, I think we can.'

'Now I must tell you… it's not easy, Cass. I've agonised over this for ages. I don't normally do scared, but you can add it to the list of today's inadequacies. I'm scared of how you might react. Please just hear me out.'

She nodded. Her smile slipped away, her face tightened, she squinted. This time it seemed more threatening than mischievous.

'Just say it.'

'I met someone a while back. Charlotte. Lotte. You know her from—'

'Lotte from the hotel? *No*. You and Lotte? You're joking. You and *Lotte*?'

She was incredulous. And with good reason.

'She's, well, gorgeous, stunning. A party animal, isn't she? Sorry. Rude of me. I'm just taken aback.'

'The thing is. You see – a couple of years ago… well…' He paused and looked at her. Her mouth was wide open. He saw shock in her eyes. He took a deep breath. 'I married her. She's… my wife.'

And a gulf opened between them.

She was suddenly far away, distant, withdrawn.

'Cass—' he began. But she just held her hand up, turned fierce, confused eyes on him. The moment seemed to last forever as the dark clouds slowly enveloped them. Black clouds now masked the sunny uplands he had glimpsed just a few minutes ago. He shivered as fear gripped him and the elements began to rumble their disapproval.

'So, you *did* lie to me,' Cassandra said at last in a hushed voice.

'*No!* I've never lied to you.'

'You obscured the truth. A lie in my book. How dare you

deceive me?' Her nostrils flared; her eyes flashed as her face flushed. 'And what are you doing here with me? Why have you made advances? Why speak now? What is it… lust? Is lust the driver?'

'I see a beautiful young woman who means a great deal to me, a woman I'd like to spend the rest of my life with.'

'Beauty? You speak of beauty. The ugly duckling to Lotte's beautiful swan. You just wanted a bit on the side, did you?'

'No, never! You're upset and have every right to be. When I look at Lotte, I see an insanely pretty face and not much else. When I look at you, I see beauty from within: depth, character, goodness. You're authentic. I just wish you didn't so despise yourself. I can help you—'

'No, you can't. You're *married*. End of. I won't be a mistress. Sorry to dash your hopes,' she said with barely disguised bitterness.

'Mistress? Never. If I wanted you as my mistress, why would I tell you? My marriage is over.'

'Oh, is it? Does she know? When did you decide this?'

'We've both known there's no future for a long time. Only recently did I decide what I have to do about it.'

'This morning? Desire the catalyst?'

'Last year when we walked in the mountains was the first time I realised I had feelings. It overwhelmed me, confused me. It's preoccupied me ever since. I've missed you these last few months. And when I saw you yesterday, I realised I had to grasp the situation and do something about it. My marriage will end. It's already over, to all intents and purposes. Lotte has told me she feels trapped in my presence and she's not enjoying motherhood—'

'Are you… are you telling me she has a child? Yours?'

He blanched and his insides turned liquid. Julian bowed his head and spoke softly, 'Josh. He was born prematurely. He's been in and out of hospital.'

'It just gets better. So, you're not only walking out on your wife, but deserting your son? How could you? How wrong have I been about you? It's so utterly... utterly... *disgusting*.'

And the Gods rumbled and clapped thunderously in support of her sentiments as the first fat drops of rain spattered.

'I will *never* desert my son,' Julian said through gritted teeth. He forced himself to relax his jaw. 'Lotte and I will divorce. I'll always provide for him, be a dad to Josh. Do better than my dad did for me. You must believe me. Lotte will welcome an end to what has become a nightmare. She hates where we live, she hates the lifestyle, she's bored, lonely, misses her friends.'

Heavy black clouds now covered the surrounding peaks, visibility sharply reduced, and the drop in temperature demanded action. As the rain slanted into them, they pulled on their waterproofs and headed back to their chalet in silence. Nature filled the void with claps of thunder, snakes of lightning scorched the skyline, and the wind howled. It was as if the elements now punished him, reflected Cassandra's anger. He had seen in her eyes the sense of betrayal.

Their evening passed in sullen silence. Cassandra opted for an early night, taking a book and a glass of milk to bed. But she had a final thought for him. 'I won't be caught in marital crossfire. I won't be the other woman. You've hurt me, Julian. Go home and repair your marriage for the sake of your little boy. I won't have him or Lotte on my conscience.'

Bag packed, he waited for her to appear to say his goodbyes. She seemed brittle, bore dark circles under red-rimmed eyes. Her body language was defensive, guarded, almost hostile. She would have had as bad a night's sleep as he had.

'I thought I'd head off,' he said in a hushed tone.

'Good.'

'I'm so sorry, Cass.'

'You said.'

'I've got a lot to sort out with Lotte. There's also a business crisis, but I've got some ideas, the semblance of a plan. So, it's likely to be a couple of months before I return. Can we Zoom about the fraud thing at L'Angleterre with Thomas?'

'You expect me to think about work? After everything you've said?'

'Of course not. Sorry. I'll sort this out, Cass. Whatever conclusion you reach about me. Whether we can have a relationship or not, my marriage is over. The two things aren't linked. I never meant to hurt you. I'm so—'

'Sorry?'

'I won't give up on you. Will you be all right?'

Cassandra glared at him; her scowl deepened. 'Goodbye,' she said.

She closed the door to leave him on the threshold. He turned to walk away but paused. It cut him in two to hear the muffled sobs from within. What more could he say or do? After a few steps he he turned, saw her at the window and waved. She raised her hand as if to return the gesture, but it dropped disconsolately. She closed her shutters, banished daylight and the outside world - as if in grief, mourning for what might have been.

NINE

SUMMER 2020

DS Ruth Dodds settled into the proffered seat while Arthur gazed out at the coiffured lawns and watched the gardener attend the herbaceous border alongside the gleaming Aston Martin.

'Nice place, Mr Sinclair… may we call you Julian?'

'How can I help you?'

'Petrolhead?' asked Arthur. 'Nice motor… business has been good to you, I gather.'

'Sometimes, sometimes less so.'

'Storm clouds brewing?'

'Always a challenge to attend to.'

'Family businesses, eh?' said Arthur.

Julian smiled, said nothing.

'Warm day. Mind if I remove my jacket?' Arthur slid off his blazer, draped it on the back of the chair, adjusted his red braces and sat down, crossed his legs.

Ruth smiled at the dapper appearance of her guv'nor, who now displayed multicoloured socks above leather brogues.

Arthur turned his attention back on Julian, who sat quietly, perfectly at ease. He wore a bemused smile. All the time in the world.

'We're grateful to you for sparing your busy time. Aren't we, DS Dodds?'

Ruth frowned, flicked untidy hair strands back, sighed. She licked her pencil, now poised, notebook at the ready. She said nothing. Her body language betrayed irritation.

'Business problematic in the family firm, Julian?'

'I'm sure you don't want to hear about such things, Detective Inspector.'

'Warring families can jar, can't they? Family members can be driven to do the strangest things, don't you find?'

'I understood you had some questions for me?' Julian said.

'We do, we do. How well do you know Scott Banks?'

'Not seen him in years.'

'Are you sure about that, Julian?' Ruth.

'I think so. Yes.'

'But you used to know him well, didn't you?' she persisted.

'No.'

'You used to work for him,' she said.

'I wouldn't put it like that.'

'How would you put it, then?' said an exasperated Ruth.

'We'd be grateful for a few details,' Arthur prompted.

'As a teenager I worked at The Belle: odd jobs around the pub when Scott was the manager. But I worked for my dad. Never him.'

'Bad blood?' asked Ruth.

'Let's just say that Scott and I rarely saw eye to eye.'

'Ever fight with him?' Ruth interrogated.

'A fight would suggest two participants. No. But we did have an argument.'

'Tell us about it.' Ruth again.

'He was feisty, free with his fists. I was his punchbag,' Julian said.

'Over what?'

'I really don't recall.'

'Try.'

'It was a long time ago and your predecessors asked me about this a couple of years back.'

'Case reopened. Some repetition is inevitable. You've not seen him since?' Arthur enquired. He decided not to press Julian on the teenage incident. For now. He would rather do so once he had checked some of the background detail.

'As I said.'

'Very well. Thank you for being so helpful, Mr Sinclair. We've taken up enough of your valuable time. I bid you good day,' Arthur said, and they made their way towards the door of Julian's study.

'Oh, just one more thing. Where were you in the period 20th September to 7th October 2017?' Ruth asked.

'I'm sure I was asked that before.'

'And your answer was?' said Ruth.

'Testing me? I'll double-check but I'm pretty sure I was on the continent. My other business.'

'That is indeed what you said, sir. Perhaps you would be good enough to check?' Ruth's sarcasm to the fore. 'And if you were mistaken, please let us know at the station. Here's my card.' Ruth slapped her card on his desk, threw him a black look, and turned on her heels.

As they headed back towards the station, Ruth expressed her frustration. 'What a waste of bloody time. Smug bastard. We know the family are scratching each other's eyes out, the business is going to pot, and he pretends all's well. I don't trust a bloody thing he said.'

'You said that Terence also referred to an incident between Scott and your favourite businessman, didn't you?'

'He was vague too. Both recall it, neither acknowledges it was anything other than a spat.'

'Maybe it wasn't. Smug and complacent, yes, but that doesn't mean he's—'

'But there was a scribbled note in the file saying he was hospitalised.'

'Julian?'

'Yeah.'

'Difficult to see how this has much bearing on the disappearance of our Scott, but check it out. Let's do our groundwork, be professional. And let's hope young laddo turns something up from the Baxter and Kate inquiries. We need to check out the other debts Scott was chasing too.'

'This must be the coldest of cold cases. Nothing to go on. Hard not to despair.'

TEN

AUTUMN 2020

The taxi dropped Julian at the end of their private road. He walked up the drive, in need of fresh Yorkshire air after a day of travel punctuated by delays and bureaucratic tedium: the impact of Covid regulations and Brexit as the French continued their petty vindictiveness on travelling Brits. *Will they ever get over it?*

There was no sign of Lotte. Annie huffed and puffed her disapproval as she told him Lotte had gone out, 'yet again'. Julian declined anything to eat, dumped his bag in his bedroom – the spare bedroom. He was desperate to see little Josh, but first he needed to test himself to ensure that he did not inadvertently infect his son – the last thing that Josh would need.

Good. All clear.

Next stop: the nursery. He crept in, and all was peaceful as his son slept in near darkness with just a night light in the corner. Julian gazed at Josh, leant over, planted a kiss on his forehead, a snuffling noise his reward.

'What are we going to do, son? Any bright ideas? I'm all ears.'

Julian sat himself down and watched his child through the cot's bars, took in the menagerie of soft toys: bears, lions, a giraffe, an elephant. And Green Dog, Josh's favourite. They had even resorted to a backup Green Dog – just in case. Inevitably, his mind pondered the Lotte task ahead: how he might navigate it with minimum upset. Perhaps he should follow one of his business rules. Be certain of the reasons for radical change, be prepared, be swift in execution, be humane and as generous as circumstances allow. Not a bad doctrine. He tried it on for size. Did it fit the divorce challenge? Not perfectly. But it might have to do.

'But whatever happens, little man, you come first. Now and forever,' he said softly, just as the door opened to reveal Nanny Barlow. She smiled her greeting, mouthed, *Welcome home*, and left him to it. Julian's eyes alighted on a contraption on a side table near the cot: the baby listener.

Intent on a walk in the grounds, he pulled on jeans and a woolly jumper and ventured into the dark of the evening. The security lights detected his movement and lit the path ahead. He opted for the cloak of darkness and ventured across the lawns at the back, looping around towards the front gate. He enjoyed the serenity as the autumnal musty night's fragrances and country sounds played with his senses. The landscape was indistinct in the swirling mist. A distant branch had shed its leaves and drooped to resemble a hanged man in the fog. He shivered; it all seemed a threatening portent of danger, of troubles ahead. The tranquillity was quite different to what he experienced in the Alps, the near silence and peace tonight an English variant. Cassandra would be enjoying the authentic version on her own, a thought he found painful. Enjoying? Would she ever forgive and forget? He could only hope so while doing what he now knew to be right. He could live a lie no more than Cassandra would allow it. But Lotte was his wife.

The woman from whom he had to extricate himself. Lotte, oh, Lotte. Where was she tonight?

As he cogitated, headlights lit the road beyond his gate. He stepped into the pitch black afforded by the beech trees and rhododendron bushes at the side to observe. His movement provoked a shower of raindrops, cold rainwater coursing down his neck. The dense banks of dark clouds his plane had descended through had shed their contents earlier, and threatened to do so again. The car drove slowly towards their gate, used the turning circle. Julian stared intently as the rear lights pierced the mist. The headlights shone on the tarmac surface beyond, but then were doused. He could just make out two figures in the front. An owl hooted somewhere above; foxes screeched in the distance. Something scurried and scampered in dense, dank, damp undergrowth. The evening was now cold, and he felt the dampness on his clothes, shivered. A tear in the clouds revealed a gibbous moon, its light casting a silvery tint on the wet grass as the mists ebbed and swirled. He squinted at his watch: it was approaching ten o'clock. He felt like a voyeur intruding on others' privacy as his eyes, now well adjusted, fixed on the dark figures in the car, watched them move, merge into one. After what seemed an age, they pulled apart. One figure opened a door to activate the inside light. She leaned back in, met the other figure stretching towards her. They seemed to kiss briefly. A laugh, a wave, and the door slammed shut to break the night's silence. The engine started and the car moved forwards, a waving Lotte in its wake. Julian pressed himself deeper into the bushes, watched her struggle to open the gate, then totter up the drive. A light was activated after about fifty yards, and his wife was spotlighted in vertiginous heels and a short skirt as she meandered towards the house. She had no coat, carried a small clutch bag; dressed more for nightclubbing in Soho than anything on offer in this area. Suddenly she stopped, reached down and, one by one, removed her heels as she neared the house. He saw her falter, her hand shoot out to grab a nearby staked sapling to steady herself, thought he could hear a curse followed by a small giggle before she continued unsteadily towards the front door. Julian skirted around the back. He removed his wet shoes and sodden jumper and moved silently to the drawing room to find his favourite chair. He sat quietly in the dark. Watched and waited. As he expected, the door soon burst open, and a hand snaked around the door jamb to find the light switch.

'Oh, what are you doing here?' Her words slurred.

'An early flight. A good night?'

'Oh, here we go. "Why are you drinking? Why are your skirts so short? Why so late?" Blah, blah, blah. You enjoy being judgemental, don't you?'

'I just asked…'

'Well, it was good to get out for a change, good to live a little,' she said. She reached for an opened bottle of Sauvignon Blanc, sloshed wine into a half-empty glass. 'I thought you were gallivanting on the continent.'

'*Me* gallivanting? Not your usual accusation.'

'Never here for our little boy.'

'Let's talk tomorrow. Now would be bad timing, I can see.'

'And what about *your* timing?'

'What are you talking about, Lotte? And why the aggression?'

'Anger, not aggression. You forgot, didn't you?'

'Forgot what?' Julian fought to keep any intonation out of his voice, tried to hide his irritation.

'Josh. His assessment. Autism.'

'What assessment? The medics said it's much too early for a diagnosis. Let's talk tomorrow.' Julian hoisted himself out of his chair. As he reached the door, her words made him spin around.

'He's autistic. ADHD, most likely, but you go to bed. You've never worried before, so why now? You're just a selfish bastard, Julian. Not sure I can continue like this.'

'Nor I. Goodnight.'

Julian played with Josh for a couple of hours: the demolition of building-block towers pleased him most, the wooden train set interested dad more than son. Josh quickly lost interest in any story from the pile of books Julian delved into. He seemed almost self-contained and unresponsive to adults, eye contact rare, as was a shared smile. Left to his own devices, he crawled or toddled uncertainly from one thing to another. Were these the telltale early signs? And had the medics really given an early diagnosis, contrary to previous assertions? Lotte would not have made this up, but nor was she in talk mode this morning as she nursed a hangover, returning to her bed with paracetamols.

Julian took a light breakfast in Annie's domain as she busied herself with chores. The inane chatter was distracting. Local gossip: Julian invited to regard the vicar in an entirely unexpected light. Entertaining, though unlikely to bear much resemblance to reality. Complaints about the government's diktats on the pandemic while dispensing her own pearls of wisdom followed with barely a pause for breath. Julian did not have to say much as she droned on in her broad local dialect. Then she left her food preparation duties and, hands on hips, decided to dispense a few home truths.

'You know me, Master Julian: never one to gossip, never complain. Easy-going as they come, that's me. Hardly needs saying. Patient, too. Even served the old bugger for donkey's years – beg your pardon, being your dad and all that, but he's difficult. More than difficult. Cussed, stubborn, bad-tempered… not a patch on your missus, though. You've chosen a rum 'un there and no lie. Excuse my bluntness.'

Julian poured more coffee and settled back in his chair. If she needed a rant, it was probably best out. Lance the boil. And as she got into her rhythm, her accent became more pronounced.

'Always on my case. Nothing's good enough for her. Not sure I can put up with it much longer. And she never has time for little 'un. Poor little mite. And you might spend more time at home yourself, I'm bound to say. Truth's better out than in. If she's not having me entertain her friends, she's out partying. God knows where round here. Hangover most mornings. The thing is, Master Julian…' And she paused before leaning forward, planting her hands on the kitchen table. 'It can't go on. Now, what do you have to say about that?'

Julian took a final slurp of coffee and stood up. He went over to her, clasped her shoulders, and spoke quietly just inches from her face. 'You're a marvel to behold, Annie. I really don't know what we'd do without you. Bear with me. All will be sorted soon. I promise. Now, I don't suppose you could stretch to one of your apple pies tonight, could you? Unmatched in the universe.' He pulled her into a bear hug and, as they parted, planted a smacker on her cheek.

'Well, I never… but just you remember what I've said.'

'Every word, Annie.' As he reached the door he turned back and said, 'Thick custard as well. Bagsy me the skin.'

Annie smiled, recalled his childhood. 'Oh, be off with you.'

Thomas persuaded him to meet for what was billed a lads' night out. A gastropub was chosen, and both had arranged transport to allow them to drink. Julian liked Thomas, him being one of the few people in business he trusted without question. Thomas urged him to dress casually, banish the suit and tie, don jeans and a jumper. Julian entered The Broken Man in smart chinos, a button-down shirt, and a jacket. It was as close to the specification as he could manage. Thomas emerged from the shadows and smiled as he joined him with a pint of beer in hand. Settled down with his G&T, Julian took in the surroundings as his eyes adjusted to the subdued light: stone flag floors, dark wooden beams, low bowed ceilings all oozed history and, together with the hustle and bustle, created a convivial atmosphere. As they caught up on family news Thomas told him Molly had caught Covid but was recovering now and had just managed to stay out of hospital.

'It all seems so random,' Thomas said. 'Some catch it and never even know about it; some are hospitalised. But you wouldn't think man and wife could live in the same house, share the same bed, and one catches it but not the other.'

Julian listened and nodded, expressed concern for Molly.

'How about you, Julian?'

'I'm fine.'

'Despite scams in France and the Belle Hospitality family drama?'

'Let's not talk business for once in our lives.'

'Wow! Mr Business himself wants to opt for small talk?'

'Let's just say I need the practice.'

'Would never have guessed, mate.'

'More like it. Take the piss…' Julian smiled, allowed his body to relax as the mix of alcohol and camaraderie took its effect.

'Just one question on The Belle… I got a call to say the front gates had been padlocked, and the farmer's side entrance too. I know we've shut the place for a while, but why lock the gates?'

Julian shrugged.

'He'll go ape in the morning. Do you know anything about this? We aren't waging war on our neighbours as well as upsetting family shareholders, are we?'

'I never wage war. I'll investigate it tomorrow. Just one thing – I've stayed in touch with Faye. Yes, I know…' Julian said in response to Thomas's raised eyebrows. 'She's said she can keep the offer alive to the end of the year. Let's both stay in touch with her. End of business chat. Anyway, I get the feeling you have an agenda this evening,' he said, looking at his friend closely as Thomas took a deep slurp of his ale.

'As ever, you're right. It's delicate. We've known each other… how long? Since uni days – what, twenty-odd years now?'

'Guess so.'

'And you know I've never poked my nose into your personal life.'

'But now you're going to? Well, hold on while I get these in first. So, this is what a lads' night out's all about, is it? I'd rather got the impression it was a bit more raucous and earthy than an agony aunt session with beer.'

Julian threaded his way through the throng, placed his order, and returned to Thomas.

'What's it to be, then, mate? Shut up shop or ruin a habit of a lifetime and allow engagement?'

Julian raised his eyebrows, sat back, and surveyed the scene. A small group of beer-swilling youths getting louder and louder; two young women perched precariously on stools in their miniskirts pretended not to notice the leering men; two businessmen in animated conversation; an older couple sat quietly with their drinks, observing the revellers. 'What's on your mind, Thomas?'

'Engagement, then. I'm pleased. I really do need to say this. I promised Molly.'

Julian's eyes momentarily diverted to the nearby scene, observed the two young women and the young men merge into one group. He smiled. Turning back to Thomas, he said, 'Spit it out, then.'

'How are you and Lotte these days?'

Julian said nothing, but cocked his head.

'The thing is, we rather get the impression all's not well. You pulled out of lunch recently. You never mention her. None of our business, except we've known you a long time and, well, the thing is, you see—'

'*Thomas!*' Julian's eyes narrowed, his tone a warning.

'Molly's worried about you two. I mean, *worried*. Me too.'

'I see,' said Julian.

'Oh, look – here are our drinks and starters at last… Lotte made Molly promise not to say anything.'

'Then don't.'

'Lotte's unhappy; miserable. You're always away, and I must admit it surprises me you spend so much… she thinks you're having an affair.'

'Lotte or Molly?'

'I think Molly's putting two and two together—'

'And getting the wrong answer.'

'Sorry. I said it was awkward. But… you've got family now.'

'I noticed.'

'Tell me to mind my own business.'

'Yes, you should.' Julian leant forward and his eyes pleaded with Thomas. 'Things aren't great between us, and we need to find a solution. I'm working on it.'

'Can we help?'

'No. But tell Molly it's not all Lotte's fault—'

'Not sure she thought it was.'

'Fair enough. She's not settled in this area. Hates it. Misses her friends and her partying and…'

'Will you and Lotte…'

'Survive?'

They lapsed into silence before Thomas offered his and Molly's help. 'Have you thought about mediation or counselling?'

'No.'

'Might be worth considering.'

'Thanks for the advice. Now let's change the subject.'

'Okay, but you do seem troubled.'

'Yeah… You said it yourself: Belle Hospitality, scams in France. What do you expect? Now, let's eat, drink, be merry, and talk about football or whatever.'

'You know nothing about football, and given you've closed this door on me, what's your game with the farmer chap? And what are we going to do about The Belle?'

'On the latter, it's a familiar tune and you know how it goes. On the former, I've no idea what you're suggesting. I have the semblance of a plan I can't share with you, though.'

'Farmer or Belle?'

Julian raised his eyebrows and said nothing.

'You don't trust me?' said Thomas.

'Thomas the friend I trust implicitly; Thomas the FD is constrained by his professional code of conduct.'

'Now I'm worried.'

'Don't be. Nothing illegal. Nothing immoral. It's just a bit of sailing close to the wind. And so far, the breeze is barely a whisper. We're becalmed. Now, tell me about the twins.'

The door flung open, and an exasperated Annie complained that she was now expected to be doorman and general dogsbody. An amused Henry was shown in.

'I suppose you'd like coffee too,' shouted Annie as she retreated downstairs, later to return and plonk a cafetière on the table.

'You've finished your enquiries, then?' nudged Julian, anxious to get on with his day.

'Well, I've got much of it. Full story or abridged?'

'Abridged.'

'Okay. Bernard Archer is in his sixties, a widower these last ten years, two kids, neither of whom are interested in farming; the eldest emigrated to New Zealand a few years ago and the other works down south. It's a small farm with a bit of arable – wheat and oilseed rape – and dairy cattle. He employs just one other bloke, a bit of a simpleton. Barely scratching a living, I'd say.'

'Small farm?'

'Relatively speaking, yes, at 108 acres. But interestingly, he owns the land himself,' said Henry, pausing to finish his coffee and crunch a ginger biscuit.

'Why's that odd?'

'Most farms in these parts are rented and this one can't afford him more than a meagre existence. The whole place is run-down. He works every day, all hours, for bugger all and yet he's sitting on valuable land.'

'How valuable?'

'All depends on—'

'Spare me the ifs and buts.'

'As farming land, it has to be worth three quarters of a million upwards.'

'And with planning permission?'

'It doesn't have planning, a pal on the planning committee confided.'

'But if it did?'

'Not thought about it. Millions.'

'Have you reached out to him? Intimated an offer might be forthcoming?'

'He won't discuss anything with me. "Give me the organ grinder, not the monkey," he said. Bloody man is impossible. Nothing I said would persuade him. And he's an educated man: doesn't even sound like a farmer, let alone a Yorkshire farmer. He went to university to study agriculture.'

The land beyond the farm was about the same acreage, Henry now understood. And his mate at the council had said it had been earmarked as potential development for housing, although there seemed to be a query over access. However, only about half of the land could potentially be used for building for some obscure reason or another, all subject to public consultation and the usual planning processes. It would likely take years to navigate the arcane planning regulations, the inevitable not-in-my-backyard objections, the bureaucracy. As Julian had guessed, the owner was a property development company. He resolved to find out more about them.

Julian thanked Henry and took Bernard Archer's contact details. 'And right of way over The Belle's land?'

'It's entirely at your discretion. Custom and practice might count for something, I suppose.'

They sat in awkward silence, the screen blinking as they awaited her arrival. Thomas had tried to talk about first the scam and then general business matters, but Julian was monosyllabic. Julian sat and played with his wedding ring before slipping it off his finger; he surreptitiously dropped it into his pocket, shuffled his papers, repeatedly checked his watch. She finally appeared and nodded at Julian's greeting. Zoom meetings were rarely free-flowing but this one was faltering and staccato. Cassandra was distracted and occasionally her head ducked out of view.

'It's full-on fraud,' said Thomas without preamble.

Cassandra nodded. The finance director then set out the details, and Cassandra added to his commentary where she could.

Julian listened and made notes. 'Okay, let's marshal the data, line up our facts, get a corroborating statement. Will the company play ball, Cassandra?'

Pause. 'Yes.' She was deadpan.

'Why so confident?' asked Julian.

'Because I know them, and they worry that the accounts suggest malpractice on their part. They're keen to clear their name,' she said. Her tones were hushed, her hair hung like curtains either side of her face, and she mainly looked down at her papers. 'But we can't keep this quiet for long.'

'No. I shall have to get over there sooner than planned. A few things to line up first, though. I need a couple of weeks. Can you keep them at bay?'

Pause.

'Cassandra?'

'Yes... have we finished?' She itched to escape.

'Can you hang fire for a moment? There's something I'd like to ask you.'

'I'll leave you to it, then,' said Thomas. He waved to Cassandra and, as he gathered his papers together, raised his eyebrows to Julian.

'How are you, Cass?' asked Julian once they were alone. His eyes pleaded with her, searched her for signs of encouragement, but her head remained bowed, the curtains closed.

She turned away and gazed into the distance, lost in her own thoughts. 'Okay, I suppose,' she said after a while, and glanced up.

'I've missed you. I can't stop thinking about how I've upset you.'

She frowned. 'Quite.'

'I never intended to,' he said.

Pause. 'No?'

'Lotte and I are—'

'I don't want to know.'

'I plan to speak with her soon. Our marriage is doomed... just a question of timing,' said Julian, now searching, pleading, gazing into her sad eyes. They had been reluctant to meet his and soon turned downwards, too heavy to hold steady, too painful.

Pause. 'Leave me alone, Julian. Make your marriage work for the good of your son.'

'I thought we had something special, something—'

'Me too. You know… oh, leave it.'

'Please go on.'

And she met his eyes; hers flashed warning signals. 'You know, I thought we communicated at… oh, I don't know – an almost spiritual level. From early on I thought we shared the same airwaves, enjoyed the same simple things in life, treasured peace and tranquillity. We didn't need lots of noise, emotion, and debate. We connected. Then I found out you shared my interest in the outdoor life too, so important to me…'

Julian watched her become animated, felt her emotion, and did not want to stop her flow.

'The attraction came from nowhere and was a powerful force. But it's spent, Julian. Gone. You can't reignite the flame your deceit doused. Leave it alone. Stay home with your wife. I don't want to see you again.'

'Please don't—'

'Leave me alone, Julian.'

'My marriage is over whatever you say.'

'Goodbye.'

And she was gone.

Cassandra bowed to the inevitable, had realised his intentions had always been honourable – they were destined to be together, had succumbed to love. And little Josh seemed to thrive on the Alpine air, on the love and attention of Mummy and Daddy. His plaintive cries disrupted the peace, and Cassandra nudged Julian.

'Your turn,' she said sleepily.

He unfurled reluctantly, leaving the warmth of her body to minister to his son's needs. He felt the cool air on his skin as he made his way to Josh's bedroom. His son had been having a dream and was soon reassured and lulled back to sleep, so Julian was able to make his way back to Cassandra, back to her warm embrace. And she was now awake, welcomed him back with a gleam in her eye.

'Not quite time to get up,' he said.

'No?' And she turned her sleepy but now bright hazel eyes on him, smiled, and reached for him. Their kiss was passionate, hungry tongues urgently explored, shudders of pleasure and expectation coursed through him, and soon he felt himself being pulled into her: Cass the instigator, Julian the only-too-willing lover. Their movements became insistent as desire surged, ecstasy flowed, an explosion of delight. Man and woman entwined, engaged, enjoined as if one, before their movements slowed and morphed to a gentler rhythm that prolonged, enriched. He was suffused with satisfaction, love, warmth, and wanted to shout for joy. Then a sense of well-being enveloped him as they lay and smiled before nodding off in each other's arms.

The alarm sounded like a klaxon to rudely awaken him, brought him back to reality. And it had seemed so vivid, so real, so perfect. Julian rubbed his eyes and checked his watch. Five o'clock. He splashed water on his face, pulled on trousers, shirt, and a jumper. He grabbed his car keys and faced the cold, wet Yorkshire morning. He made his way towards The Yorkshire Belle, parked the Land Rover at the end of the road, found a vantage point, settled down unseen to await the action. He was intrigued. How would the educated farmer react this morning? Twice padlocks had been removed with bolt cutters. Angry telephone messages followed. He pulled his coat tight around him, dragged his beanie over his head, and donned gloves as he raised the binoculars to his eyes. It was still dark, but the sky was lightening. In the fields behind him cows chewed the cud, birds called in the hedgerows, and a territorial robin made his presence felt. Julian unscrewed the cap of his small flask and poured strong coffee. The caffeine kick was slow to impact but the warmth was welcome.

He caught movement in the distance and soon a red tractor emerged from the farm entrance with a burly figure at the helm. Lights shone on the wet tarmac as it made its way on its morning journey towards The Belle. This time not only was the farmer met with padlocked gates, but by barriers. The tractor turned into the gates and stopped. The farmer alighted and inspected the obstructions. He snatched off his flat cap and scratched his head as he surveyed the scene, throwing his arms wide as if in exasperation, and then turned a full circle, looking for signs of other human life. Julian watched intently. The farmer seemed to be unsure of his next actions. How to deal with the obstacles in front of the gates? Then he replaced his cap, leapt back in his cab, turned his tractor around, and disappeared back into the farmyard. Less than ten minutes later the tractor re-emerged, and this time it had an attachment on the front: a rock bucket. Julian watched the farmer head for The Belle's gates, and the attachment was skilfully manipulated and scooped the three huge boulders one by one. Each was removed and subsequently dropped over the wall of the pub a few feet away to land haphazardly in the pub's car park. The farmer only took care to ensure they did not impede his intended route. He was purposeful and determined, characteristics Julian could admire despite their destructive application today. With the last of the boulders cleared, the farmer kept the rock bucket low and backed up before then unleashing the full force of the tractor, with its attachment, as an effective battering ram to demolish first the outer gate and then the inner gate to his own fields. Bolt cutters had been deemed surplus to requirements today. Clearly, Julian's farmer neighbour needed and valued access via The Belle. Interesting.

Then a little later his loyal sidekick lumbered through the gap, herding the black-and-white Friesians, full udders swinging, trampling the wooden gates underfoot as they made their way to the milking shed on the other side of the road: a journey they made twice daily. The farmer was last to materialise on his tractor, completing the destruction of The Belle's attempts to thwart his living.

Julian joined Lotte for breakfast to reassert some sort of routine, to share time together. Lotte's body language was defensive. She questioned how long it might be before one of his jaunts on the continent; her eyes flashed danger but she was otherwise quiet and withdrawn after her outburst the other evening. Perhaps she carried guilt over her transgressions? A hangover? The latter seemed more likely. But Julian had nothing to be proud of either. He knew what he had to do, however difficult. He was clear. But he was not yet sure how to go about it, how to lessen the blow for her, how to serve Josh's best interests. He had once read about the challenges of writing novels: he knew what the outcome needed to be, knew where they were, but needed to work out the *how*, the plot, the strategy. How to get from point A to point B. Strategising was easy, execution difficult in the business world as well. So, it seemed, was how to dissolve a marriage without undue hurt, anger, collateral damage. He mused on all this as he pushed a Cumberland sausage around his plate.

'Please, Lotte. We need to talk.'

'A bit late for talk,' she muttered.

Munching on a piece of toast, he enquired about her plans.

'Today? No idea. The rest of my life? Even less,' she said disconsolately.

'You said yourself—'

'I know.'

'It's not your fault, you know, not—'

'It certainly isn't,' she interjected. Her dander rose immediately.

Julian lapsed into silence. Perhaps later in the day would be a better time to broach the subject. And the silence became all-embracing. A brooding atmosphere pervaded, both lost in their thoughts.

Just then the door burst open, and a bustling Annie began to clear the pots. She noticed the food waste and tutted her censure. Even Annie must have noticed the charged atmosphere. She piled the plates onto her tray and made her way, huffing and puffing, to the door. She suddenly turned on her heels, plopped the tray down with a crash on the sideboard, not noticing, not caring as the milk jug discharged its contents. She walked over to them, now centre stage. 'I won't stay silent a moment longer. This isn't right, isn't good for either of you. You both should be ashamed of yourselves. Neither of you are happy, not that it's any of my business.'

'No, it isn't,' said Lotte, who glared at her housekeeper.

'Don't much care what you think, but I care about that little mite. A disgrace. A mother needs to be with her child, and you aren't. You never are. And you need to stop your fannying around with other blokes and boozing and whatnot—'

'How dare you?'

'Sack me if you like, but—'

'You're *sacked*.'

'No, she's not,' said Julian.

'And you, Master Julian… Well, you need to stay home more. For God's sake, you're supposed to be a family. Live in a grand house, the life of Riley, got everything anyone could want, and yet you leave little Josh to his own devices. Oh, I know you have Nanny Barlow. And a fine woman she is, thank the Lord...'

'Are you going to listen to this drivel any longer? Have you got nothing to say? I don't see you leaping to your wife's defence. Call yourself a man? Pah!' said Lotte, throwing her serviette in Julian's direction. 'You're *sacked*!' she screamed at Annie.

'Shut up, the pair of you. Annie, your care and concern is touching, and you've made your point. And, Lotte, I've known this woman all my life. She speaks more sense than I've heard in a long time. She's right. We need to sort ourselves out. Make it work or put the marriage behind us. And decide fast.'

Lotte jumped to her feet and stormed towards the door, pushed past Annie, who watched, open-mouthed. She stopped just short of the threshold, turned, and said through gritted teeth, her face devoid of colour as a white heat of rage absorbed her, 'There's no future for us like this, Julian, no future. End of.'

ELEVEN

AUTUMN 2020

DC Tim Jenks plonked two mugs of coffee on the desk and returned with a cafetière for Arthur.

'Thanks, Poirot. Right, what have we got?'

'Square root of bugger all, guv,' said Ruth, receiving a thin smile and raised eyebrows from her DI. 'We're getting nowhere fast with Terence and Julian Sinclair and The Yorkshire Belle angle. As for The Golden Lion, that changed hands a year back.'

'Baxter Hinds?'

'Serving time September to December 2017, so we can scratch him out.'

'Kate Pringle?'

'She – *he* calls himself Ron Pringle now—'

'Trendy,' ventured Tim, who received glares from his superiors.

'Kate, aka Ron, denies any knowledge of debts owed to Scott by Baxter Hinds or anyone else. She claimed that she didn't even know Scott. Remember that Baxter Hinds allegedly owed money to an unidentified person, a debt that Scott's debt collection business had bought out. Scott was just a name on a list to chase for debt on behalf of the pub. Never got anywhere,' said Ruth.

'How much debt?' asked Arthur.

'Over £10K, she – he – thought.'

'For what?'

'For Scott helping himself to cash and booze over the period of his employment. But Ron, aka Kate, didn't get anywhere, didn't pursue it through the courts. Waste of time, no chance of recovering it, and he disappeared so that was the end of that,' Ruth said. 'I also spoke with other pubs he'd worked at, but nothing there. Managers had either changed or the pubs had closed, and those who did have a vague recollection of our man just said he was a petty crook, unreliable, drank the profits... that sort of thing. A few speculated that he may have fled the country—'

'His expired passport was in the box of possessions, we know he didn't renew it,' interjected Tim.

'It's unlikely he could have got a false ID, guv: no money, no mates. In fact, most people who admit to knowing him just said good riddance.'

'What about the other debts Scott was pursuing in his ironic role of debt collector?' Arthur said.

'I can help there, guv,' piped up Tim. 'Zoya Patel settled her debt with a deal. She just shuddered when asked to recall Scott and was pleased to have seen the back of him. Viktor Iliev went back to Bulgaria before Scott and his oppo could lay their fists on him again. And Steve Yates claims he was beaten up by Scott and some "heavy", shelled out a few quid, and scarpered. He's a drug addict, alcoholic, and now he's homeless... not exactly a reliable witness, and anyway, claims he knows nothing.'

'Good work, Poirot. But it leaves us precisely... nowhere. How did you get on with the bank, Tim?'

'He had a second account with Barclays. The balance is only £10.65. But the interesting bit is that there were loads of transactions. All the deposits in cash, the last in September 2017.'

'What was the pattern? Similar amounts each month?' asked Ruth.

'Completely the opposite. Some months there would be little deposited, sometimes multiple entries from £50 to £6,500. I've summarised all the deposits and the outgoings,' Tim said, and handed the list to Ruth. 'But the outgoings were regular as clockwork, and for the same amount each month: £900.'

'To whom?' asked Arthur.

'Pastures New Care Home. I've got an appointment tomorrow.'

'Interesting.' Arthur.

'Oh, almost forgot—'

'What, Tim?' said Ruth through clenched teeth.

'Within the box of his stuff was a copy of an email to Terence. It's a diatribe about The Yorkshire Belle. Threats to get even. Mentions his "git of a son, Julian".'

'There was a similar threat to Baxter too,' said Arthur. 'Obviously his modus operandi. Check it through, Tim. I thought we were likely to shelve this case and move on, but we need to check these lines of inquiry through.'

'Still amount to—'

'I know, Ruth. But let's do our homework. I need answers for the top brass.'

TWELVE

AUTUMN 2020

With a heavy heart, Julian and his trusty FD entered the boardroom. Emily and Luke were assembled, Zoe too. The dark, moody atmosphere soon foiled Thomas's valiant attempts at breezy small talk.

'Daddy's too poorly to attend,' said Emily.

Julian nodded.

'But we all know what his views are,' said Luke. His tone was sombre. 'I hope you have solutions for us, and we aren't to be subjected to a replay of the same old tune.'

'I've only got half an hour,' said Emily. 'Someone has to care for him.'

'What's the bank's position?' asked Zoe.

'No change. They've called in our loans and cancelled our overdraft facilities. All our submissions for other loans from elsewhere have been rejected,' said Thomas. 'We have nowhere else to go.'

'Except into administration,' said Julian quietly.

'*Nooo*,' wailed Emily.

'When?' asked Luke.

'We will struggle to survive beyond January,' said Thomas.

'SI could save the day by releasing the second tranche of investment, couldn't you?' Julian said to Zoe.

Luke scoffed his surprise; Emily swore.

'Our position remains unchanged,' said Zoe.

'You mean you could, but you won't,' said Luke.

'I see no point in repeating previous explanations.'

'And *if* this board supported the execs' proposed sale of The Belle? If we sought additional investment from SI beyond the second tranche?' interjected Julian, raising his voice above Emily's objections.

'Then of course the changed position would be met with a positive review of your proposals. *Have* things changed?' said Zoe.

'No,' said Luke. 'We won't renege on our promise while our dad is on his deathbed.'

He was resigned to having to settle for his hotel suite. Julian dumped his bags and joined Thomas in the conference room. They studied the papers to rehearse their line of attack, marshal the supporting evidence before they then asked Cassandra to join them. She came armed with files and notebooks, her PC, and a dour expression.

'How are you, Cassandra?' Julian asked. Always Cassandra when on business.

'Okay, thanks.' And she patted her files, indicated her preparedness for the work ahead.

'Good to see you.'

Thomas received a nervous smile from her, Julian barely a glance from dull, dead eyes. Her head was bent over papers, her PC, her pens – her attention on anything other than her boss. Cassandra's hair was even longer and dropped straight. A veil. Julian sat back, and for once his thoughts were of anything other than business. But Cassandra would allow no conversation *other* than business. Thomas looked quizzically at each of them in turn, took in the awkwardness, the strained atmosphere.

Time to get down to business. Thomas led; Cassandra offered input at a level of detail. Julian's role was reserved for the end phase. He felt prepared on the wider front, knew what the outcome would be, had a clear grasp of the strategy. But the foundation blocks were the data, the facts – irrefutable facts for the case to result in acceptance of an outcome without question. Preparation now would save stress and additional work further down the track. He would not fail to prepare. He had learnt his lesson. In the final hour they choreographed the scenes planned for tomorrow. Julian focused on the parts where Thomas and Cassandra would be pivotal, ensured they were meticulously planned. The final act he kept to himself, the poker player with secreted aces. Satisfied with progress, they called it a day and Thomas left the two of them to cover other operational matters.

Cassandra shuffled nervously with her papers, reordered her files, turned off her PC, then sat with her hands in front of her before making eye contact. She had no smiles, no laughing eyes, just awkward body language.

'Can we talk, Cass?'

'I'd rather not.'

'No. I know. But you need to know—'

'No, I don't,' she added quickly in a stage whisper.

'Very well. I need to tell you – I *want* to tell you – where I am, having made a promise to you about my marriage.'

'You have no obligation to me. No need to account or explain. Better if you don't.'

'My marriage was a huge mistake, a sham. It makes Lotte unhappy. Neither of us are the people we thought we were.

She doesn't like the real me; I don't understand or like the real Lotte. She deserves someone who can give her what she wants – a free spirit. We're over. Done and dusted.'

'It's sad to hear, and criminal for your son. I feel sorry for Josh, but none of this concerns me. All I want is to do my job, live my life, find peace.'

'And happiness too, Cass?'

Silence.

'Cass?'

She looked sad, downcast. 'Perhaps too much to ask. Contentment, maybe.'

'But we could be happy as well.'

'I once harboured the dream. But there is no "we"; there can't be. Even if you and Lotte find separate futures, what about Josh?'

'I will never desert Josh. Whatever the outcome, whatever happens—'

'To us?'

'Josh will always be a huge part of my life. I want you to be as well.'

Cassandra shook her head slowly but said nothing.

'I'm going to be here for a week or so. Can I resume my lodger status? Can I?'

She shook her head, brushed away an errant tear from the corner of her eye. 'Not a good idea. You're a married man.'

'Lotte and I have spoken. She's told me our marriage is over. Dead. No future.'

'So, you have a divorce certificate or whatever, do you?'

'No… no, not yet. But we will.'

'Then there's nothing more to be said.'

Thomas called Julian early to suggest he read his emails.

'What is it?'

'Your siblings.'

Julian groaned as he skipped over the dross. Sighing, he opened Emily's email first.

From: Emily
To: Julian
CC: Luke, Thomas, Lotte
Re: YOUR Daddy... OUR Daddy!

He's so weak. I don't know how much longer he can hang on. Why won't you come round? Daddy needs to hear good news. You need to sort out the bank... for God's sake, Julian, pull your bloody finger out, leave your TART alone, and give him some good news before... why are you soooo bloody cruel?
   Emily

Julian sighed and deleted the email, and then turned to Luke's:

From: Luke
To: Julian
CC: Emily, Thomas, Lotte
Re: Business Crisis

I urge you to press SI on extending their loan, Julian. If they are so keen to back your wider plan, then I'm sure the family will support a change of strategy. But it can't be funded by the sale of The Belle. You know why. We've all promised. It's the heartbeat of the family business. I implore you to use your influence. Let me know if I can help...
   Luke

Julian swore and typed a sharp response:

From: Julian
To: Luke
CC: Emily, Thomas, Lotte
Re: Business Crisis

You offer warm words to imply support. It's nothing of the sort. We've trod this ground so many times. You know why this isn't possible without the sale of The Belle or the release of funds from elsewhere. The banks won't lend to us; private equity won't invest. We've run out of options. Sell The Belle or go under. Your choice, Luke! If you have any other ideas or the funds, then we can talk. If not…
   Julian

Lysander joined Julian and Thomas in the conference room with a grim expression, a sour mood. Julian skipped the pleasantries in favour of clipped business efficiency. Lysander looked from one to the other: the grave faces, the ordered files, the formality of Julian's language. Lysander's arrogance drained away; he became grey and lined.

'Let me tell you what the outcome of this meeting will be. Your future will change. You get to choose the path: one easy, the other a much harder, official route. Both end up in the same place,' said Julian.

Lysander looked from one to the other. His mouth opened and closed before he sat forward and said loudly, 'I don't have time for riddles. I've visiting dignitaries to welcome, a special luncheon for the mayor…' The words were delivered in a wavering voice.

'Lunch is being taken care of by your successor,' said Julian.

Lysander stared at him, aghast. Thomas too.

'As of ten minutes ago, your successor, Philippe Deveroux, began his duties. Even now he is meeting the senior team and staff. So please don't worry about operational matters. Your time at Hotel L'Angleterre is over. I feel it's always best to give the outcome first, then you know with clarity where we're headed.'

Lysander spluttered incoherently, threw his arms around, and then sat back.

They met in a corner of the dining room screened from the public to assess the day's work.

'Happy with the outcome?' asked Thomas.

'Yeah.'

'You were a bit brutal, weren't you?'

'It became personal on top of everything else. He didn't deserve more. But he did okay. Had we gone to the police he'd have faced a custodial sentence. And we did all right too. I cut a deal with the property developer so we can expect another half-million to come back in this direction. Had we gone the official route we'd have had to wait years to get any money back, and by the time his lawyers had their teeth into it…'

'And Cassandra?'

Julian looked at his colleague with a deadpan expression.

'What is it about you two? One moment you could cut the atmosphere with a knife, the next you're filleting someone for being rude to her.'

'He was cruel… wouldn't have mattered who it was,' said Julian, almost as an afterthought as he replayed Lysander's spiteful words.

'*Bitch*,' his GM had spluttered.

'The cost of your insult is an extra €100,000. Any further insults to offer? Care to add to the pot?'

The fraud was clear, and Lysander only had barefaced lies, denials, and a smokescreen to offer. Now he had to return €3 million by the end of next week. Plus, the €100,000 for the abuse of Cassandra, and additionally another €200,000 for his subsequent threats. Julian had lined up a property developer to buy two of his overseas properties to fund the sums involved.

'What's the game plan for the next few days?' Thomas asked.

'I want to spend time with Philippe and Gabin. The two are critically important figures to build the future around. I suggest you head back home.'

'You're up to something back home too, aren't you? Are you going to tell me?'

Julian smiled, then said, 'Come on, my friend, eat up and have another glass of wine. Well earned today.'

There was a spring in his step as he walked through the hamlet, his mood cheered as Cassandra had relented on his lodger status. She shyly thanked him for his words when she'd been under Lysander's attack. *So, if you'd like to stay over for a few days?* Would he ever. But her stance on their relationship had not changed: she hoped they could be friends, but needed to learn again how to trust him. Fair enough, a starting point, but their futures were destined to be shared – he was certain of it. He paused to look inside a quaint shop with local produce and once more had a feeling of being watched, felt the weight of eyes on him, heard sounds from behind quietening a moment after he stopped. The thought would not go away. He quickened his pace, rounded a corner just short of the end of the hamlet, and darted behind a tree. Julian paused and then walked briskly back in the direction he had come from. And straight into someone headed in his direction. The figure diverted slightly to one side; Julian stepped into his path.

'Can I help you?'

He was faced with a small, dumpy guy wearing jeans and a hiking coat with a black beanie pulled over his head. The man was out of breath. His eyes exuded panic, and his right hand thrust deep into his pocket. '*Non, Monsieur*,' he stammered in a bad accent. He hopped from one foot to another, piggy eyes darting hither and thither, jowls assuming their own momentum.

'You were following me. What do you want?'

'You're mistaken. Now I bid you good day,' the man said, the pretence of French nationality cast aside. He drew himself up to his full height. But the gesture neither impressed nor disguised his lack of inches.

Julian put a restraining hand on his chest. 'Not so fast. Let's have some answers.'

'I need to get home. Please excuse me.'

'Where's home? There's nowhere beyond those two glass palaces there,' Julian said, and nodded towards the new houses at the end of the village. 'What's in there?' He grabbed the man's hand and wrenched it out of his pocket, extricated a notebook, an inhaler, and a small digital camera.

Julian rifled through the notes: dates and times. Scanning his mental recall, they were likely to correlate with his visits to Cassandra. The portly guy seemed to be on the verge of a panic attack as his breathing laboured, his brow beading with perspiration.

'Here – it looks as if you need this.'

The man grabbed the inhaler, took two deep puffs, pushed Julian aside, and ran for it. Julian let him go. He would peruse the contents of the notebook and see what the camera revealed. He allowed himself a few minutes to have a cursory look at the notes and quickly flicked through the images on the camera; some were of him.

Cassandra opened the door wide. She wore jeans, a large woolly polo-necked jumper, and a wary look. Her half-smile did not reach her eyes. The two of them were like nervous adolescents: unsure what to say or do. Julian dumped his bag in his downstairs bedroom and offered to do the cooking. She gratefully accepted, busied herself with the table, stoked the fire, and selected classical background music. Dinner passed without argument, but conversation was stilted.

Settled either side of the fire, they soon shed their jumpers as the chalet became toasty warm. The second glass of wine helped them to relax a little.

'I hope we can become friends again,' said Cassandra.

Julian nodded and watched her struggle to add to the sentiment. He stayed quiet as she seemed to have more to say, her expression one of intense concentration with a slice of angst.

'But it can't be...'

'I understand,' he said. 'I'm more optimistic, though, Cass.'

'No, it can't be.' Cassandra picked up her crochet and put it back down again, took a sip of her wine and then another. 'I promised myself I'd say this to you.' Her eyes implored him to understand.

Be patient, Julian, allow her to have her say. 'Yes, Cass?'

'The thing is, my life's a bit of a mess. My family disowned me years ago. I was a nightmare teenager, and they just didn't bother to support me through a difficult time. I gave up on them, walked out. And more recently, my partner...' Her words dried up and she sighed.

'Your partner, Cass?'

'He constantly undermined my confidence, controlled me, bullied me. A nasty piece of work. He turned me into a victim. Beneath the bonhomie, showman exterior... and Lysander's not dissimilar. I'd rather not say too much, but your ex-GM is behind the daubed messages on my walls. I'm sure of it...' Cassandra sat back and drew a deep breath. The outpouring had exhausted her.

'We owe you a big debt of gratitude. I meant what I said in there,' Julian said.

'Thank you, it means a lot. Someone who believed in me, was prepared to stand up for me, was… was… almost overwhelming. But as I said to you in the mountains, I can't afford the risk of being hurt again, lied to, abused. It's easier to live the life of a recluse.'

'Not necessary, we can take our time. We're meant to be together,' Julian said, sitting forward. He reached out to take her hands in his, but she pulled back.

She gazed out of the window. Julian doubted she saw anything, wondered what she thought.

'Cass?'

'We can't be together. Not now, not ever. And why would you want to be with a perpetual victim, damaged goods? It's impossible.' She spoke in barely more than a whisper.

'No. No, it's not. We can become friends, Cass. Take it from there.'

'How can I ever trust you, Julian? I don't know you. All I now know about your life is you're married and have a son. I've seen companionship, rapport, and… kindness today, to be fair. But I also feel betrayed. It's what I *feel*. I've experienced your lies, and experienced pain from your actions. Then I witnessed a chilling, almost callous ruthlessness… towards *him*…'

'He deserved it. Hurt me or those I *love*…' There, he had said it. He had articulated what was in his heart, what imbued his whole being. He loved Cassandra. He'd thought he had loved Lotte, but never had he experienced with her the emotional wringer he was going through now: the urge to love and protect, a need to be with Cassandra. She had become the centre of his universe. And yet something snagged at the back of his mind. His desire for something, his need to make something happen sometimes grew into an obsession when denied him. It was his nature. But this was different. This *must* be different. It *felt* different. Cassandra was not Eloise. And nor was it a business parallel to his fight over Belle Hospitality, or the shabby deals he had cut in his early business ventures.

The music had long since finished, and they sat quietly for a long time. The fire glowed, spat and crackled as it died. Cassandra seemed exhausted, emotionally drained. And Julian's mind reeled with some of her observations: *You can't reignite the flame your deceit doused*; *utterly… utterly… disgusting*; *lies, deceit, betrayal*. To the litany could be added callousness, ruthlessness, cruelty. Lotte's unwelcome words also leapt into his mind: *selfish, controlling, manipulative, thoughtless, cruel even – yes, you are cruel. To your dad, to Emily, but most of all to me.* Unfair accusations. Mostly. Suddenly all his transgressions, misjudgements, frailties seemed prominent. It hurt. But he had to show character. He knew his own feelings. He needed to be with this woman for the rest of his life. He was sure of it. But how?

Cassandra stared into the fire and said nothing.

'I do love you. Genuinely, wholeheartedly. But I know I need to earn your trust and sort my home situation out. Let's embark on a journey of discovery. Uncover each other's backgrounds. Get to really know each other, if you like. Neither of us is naturally open or loquacious. It won't be easy.'

She seemed lost in thought before she turned towards him. 'Maybe. But I've had more than I can take for one day. It's getting late. I'm bushed… by the way, I don't want to know *everything* about you, and I won't share everything with you either. We both deserve some privacy, our private spaces. But I *would* like to know the essence, what makes you tick, makes you what you are, who you are, because I'm confused, bewildered. There are too many conflicting values, too much I don't understand, too much I don't trust. Let's take a picnic tomorrow up the valley; a lazy day ambling, chatting, and picnicking. What do you say?'

'Perfect.'

'Goodnight, then. And don't worry about the shower: I've had locks installed to spare your blushes,' Cassandra said, and threw him a smile, and this time it did reach her now-bright hazel eyes as the evening ended in hope.

THIRTEEN

AUTUMN 2020

Dinner was a sombre affair. Lotte was morose and withdrawn. She had a glass of wine, but only the one. Julian imbibed more heavily. He had put it off for too long, but no matter how often he told himself it would be all right; it was what Lotte wanted… she could be volatile, difficult to anticipate. And on getting home earlier he had been thrown by the sight of mother and son at play; they'd both seemed engaged and happy. Josh had even smiled and giggled, responded to the stimulus of playing with his mother. It lifted Julian's heart, but it also confused him, played with his conscience, seeded unexpected doubt. It wasn't normal, though, was it? Had Nanny Barlow and Annie exaggerated? *Goodness knows Annie likes a bit of drama, is prone to exaggeration, extrapolation, exuberance, and tends to get carried away with her stories.* He prodded at his meal and Lotte kept sparse conversation light and superficial, non-controversial: the weather was depressing; the meal was one of Annie's better efforts; no plans for the weekend.

In the drawing room they refreshed their glasses: Lotte opted for Chardonnay as Julian reached for a Dalwhinnie ten-year-old malt whisky with a cube of ice. She sat on the sofa with her legs curled beneath her; he sat in an armchair, the distance between them symbolic. Lotte grabbed the TV controls and flicked through the channels but found nothing to take her fancy.

'Can we talk, Lotte?'

'You want to talk?' Her tone was world-weary rather than hectoring. As if she had been worn down, was at the end of her tether, defeated.

'I never thought it would come to this,' he began, and he could see her attention had been grabbed. She looked sharply at him with those beautiful green eyes. They had once enraptured him – now they narrowed as tension seeped into her features. 'I once thought our future was assured. Envisaged growing old together, wrinkly and arthritic, but happy in our dotage…'

'And now?' she asked, Lotte on her guard, wary, alert.

'As you yourself said, we've reached the end of the road—'

'Oh, no! Don't. I never said any such thing. Maybe if you listened to my *actual* words. God knows things aren't right between us. Things need to change. We can't go on like this. But I've never spoken of the end.'

Julian gulped. His Adam's apple bobbed up and down. 'I know you're unhappy. I know you gave up everything to marry me and live here. I understand. I know I'm a disappointment to you. You've already said you don't like who I am. We can't live like this, Lotte. I know it's tough, it hurts like hell, but let's stay friends and call it a day. You won't—'

'The bimbo in France wins, then?'

He sat back heavily and stared at her, his mind in overdrive. Cassandra? What did she know? How much did she know? How did she know? Maybe the dumpy little man? 'What are you talking about? This has nothing to do with anyone other than you and me.'

'You deny she exists? Remember I have friends in France who keep an eye out for me. Anyway, I know her. I don't suppose she's told you how she disgraced herself, failed her family who threw her out? She's no angel, not who she pretends to be. You've been duped, taken for a mug. As for your relationship with her, do you need photographic evidence?'

Lotte rummaged around in her handbag and extricated her mobile. Julian sat, transfixed. The dumpy man in France must have been employed by her. But Julian had taken the camera, and the images all seemed innocent. Okay, they were of him in the wrong place with someone he had not mentioned to Lotte, but they were not incriminating. His mind was in turmoil, but he was also intrigued, so he stayed quiet as she searched her phone. She scrolled through various images until she found what she was looking for. Lotte shuffled over to the edge of the sofa closest to where he sat and showed him: Julian striding through the hamlet; Julian in snowshoes with another figure; Julian and Cassandra on the bench outside the chalet; Julian and Cassandra in hiking boots and rucksacks.

'Look, I should have told you about my lodgings. But it didn't seem important. I lodged with one of our staff in a remote chalet. It was perfectly innocent.'

'Would you say this is innocent too?' She flicked to a photograph of him and Cassandra on the mountains – kissing, embracing.

How on earth? Dumpy only had a small camera. The porcine asthmatic was surely incapable of hiking to such an altitude. And the confiscated camera could not possibly have taken this photograph. This was a long-range shot from a similar altitude on an opposite ridge. Impossible to imagine Dumpy's ascending such heights. So how? Julian had not expected this.

'It's not what it seems there. We have a platonic relationship—'

'I've heard it called some things.'

'This isn't about her, about France—'

But Lotte was razor sharp now, her hackles up, and she interrupted him again, her tone scathing. 'Yes, it is. It's always been about your absence, about your failure to commit to this marriage.'

'That's unfair. What about you? Your behaviour hasn't exactly been exemplary.'

'True enough, but I've not been shacked up with anyone while my husband galivants.'

'So, explain the other night? The car at the end of the drive, your escort home, the lingering and mauling taking place before you tottered up the drive. Pissed, of course. Again.'

'So now you're a peeping Tom hiding in the bushes? You're unreal. You play the superior, smart businessman with the big house, the Aston Martin, servants, trophy wife, but you're squalid, manipulative—'

'Oh, please, not again. Play another record. Answer the question. Who was it? The guy you clinched and slobbered over?'

'My long-lost brother, Jonathan. Satisfied?' Lotte sat back, poured herself another glass of wine, took a deep slurp, and stood up. Peering down at him, she said, 'You've got some explaining to do. Let's pick up when you've had a chance to reflect. But try the truth next time.'

This was not how it was supposed to have played out.

Julian had at least reached one decision on the home front earlier this morning while giving Josh his breakfast. His departure was delayed so he could spend more time with his son. A quick message to Henry deferred their meeting with the farmer. Let him stew a little longer. As they played with the wooden train set and bricks, Julian studied his son's image and frowned. It would not matter, whatever the result. Josh was his son. Chemistry could never change how he felt. He just needed to know, needed the certainty for reassurance. Or moral leverage.

As Josh played with the assembled towers of bricks, the door creaked open and Lotte shuffled in. She ignored Julian and lifted Josh, who complained at the intrusion on his demolition duties. Josh writhed, wriggled, and wailed until she gave up her struggle with a sigh. She looked daggers at Julian as he took in her dishevelled appearance, the dark rims under bloodshot eyes.

'Did you see Jonathan?'

'Yes.'

'Can I meet him? I'm intrigued, I'd love to get to know him.'

'I doubt it,' she said vaguely.

'I must press on,' he said. 'Perhaps we can talk about your brother tonight. Tell me all about him. Dig into the family archives. There must be old photos of you all.' He made to give her a peck on the cheek, but she moved away.

As they walked up the path to the farmhouse, Julian wondered what sort of reception lay in store, but a snarling Alsatian dog strained at the extremity of its leash and seemed an ill omen. Henry hammered on the door, but there was no answer until a gruff voice called out to them. The owner emerged from the side of the house preceded by two collies who excitedly bounded towards Julian and Henry before being called to heel. Bernard Archer shook their hands, Julian's near crushed in the bearlike paw. He wore a dirty flat cap and muck-stained overalls, was brusque, but not hostile. They followed him into the farm kitchen as he kicked his wellies off. They sat at the large table in the centre of the stone-flagged floor, the farmer's flat cap still in place. A kettle was placed on the Aga as he threw teabags into a brown earthenware teapot, rinsed mugs, and scolded the dogs; they lay down instantly with a sigh and mournful eyes. He made tea, assaulted the fire with a poker, and threw on logs as Julian took in his surroundings. The kitchen was huge and as rustic as expected: whitewashed walls in need of a lick of paint; shoes, wellies, and coats piled into one corner. Dirty pots and pans and mugs scattered around the kitchen. Two battered chairs sat either side of the fireplace on a threadbare, scorch-marked rug.

'I get to speak to the organ grinder after all, then.'

Henry winced.

'You'll start with an apology, no doubt?'

'The gates?' said Julian. 'I'll have words. We should have discussed our plans with you rather than act precipitately. I hope you'll accept my apology.'

'Mm.' Farmer Archer did not seem impressed.

'I'll get to the point of my visit—'

'Wish you would. No time to spend socialising on a farm. Tough life, you know.'

'We have a proposition to put to you—' began Henry, before being silenced by Bernard Archer. He wanted to hear from the main man, with all respect.

'We have plans to share with you, and a proposition to outline. Bad news, good news, if you like. As to our plans, I'm afraid you won't be able to access your fields via The Belle's land in future, although we can give you a little time to sort out alternative arrangements. I realise you've been using the access for a long time—'

'An agreement with your dad. An honourable man, Terry.'

'Indeed, but time marches on, circumstances change. We need to develop our site. You know how run-down The Belle has become. So, this will result in building work on the boundary between our property and your farm.'

'The agreement we have counts for nothing, then. Shame you've not inherited your dad's traits. Perhaps I should speak with him.'

'He's very ill.'

'The reason I haven't sought him out. Out of respect…'

'We understand the dilemma it will cause you, and I have a proposition, one to your advantage. Ever thought about selling?'

'No.'

'I can offer you a quick sale on generous terms.'

'This is my livelihood. Why would I sell up? I don't know any other life, and anyway, I don't have to explain myself to you.'

'True.'

'Now, if you'd bugger off…'

'Don't you want to know what the offer is?' asked Henry.

'If I'm not up for sale, why would I?'

'We estimate the market price as being around £700,000 for a farm with your acreage. My client,' Henry said, nodding to Julian, 'is prepared to offer you £800,000.'

Bernard grabbed his flat cap in his huge paw and scratched his head absent-mindedly.

'The building works I spoke of need not affect you,' Julian said. 'And you can obviously take your livestock and machinery and relocate. We're not buying it as a going concern, you understand.'

Bernard glared at him, pulled himself out of his chair, stood tall. 'I'd rather speak to the monkey after all.' Turning to Henry, he added, 'Tell your client to go to hell. I don't take kindly to threats; tell him to remove his smugness from my house before I let the Alsatian finish this conversation.'

Having regrouped in The Belle, Julian told Henry he was not surprised at the farmer's reaction. At least they had his attention, and he still had the problem of access to resolve.

Henry looked doubtful, but asked, 'When will your building work start?'

Julian allowed a half-smile and paused briefly. 'Leave it a week, then go back and negotiate a conclusion, Henry.' He gave him a generous budget to work with, and an incentive: the lower the price, the more Henry would be paid. 'For no one else's ears.'

Julian was troubled as he settled into his study to think things through. Time for some heavy rock: Metallica, AC/DC, Guns N' Roses. Nothing was going to plan, so it was time to review, reassess. *If things aren't going to plan, change the plan.* But some things he would not change. Despite Farmer Archer's obstinacy, the acquisition of the farm lay at the cornerstone of Julian's Belle Hospitality turnaround strategy. He would persist, increase the budget, grease a few palms. The success of his strategy for the ailing business depended on it. Then he would need to run a few risks, but even the downside of a negative outcome was better than the status quo.

The other key to his plans was Lotte, and here things were going seriously awry. Not only had she managed to turn the tables on him, but she had sown doubts about Cassandra he could not entirely dispel. He had thought Lotte would bite his hand off at the offer of a generous divorce. How wrong could he be? A different approach was needed. As the rock music thumped, he mulled and cogitated. And his brain ramped up a gear as the synapses went into overdrive, linking neurons to allow a speedy revamp of the plan, one he was confident would lead to success. What mattered was the outcome, and he knew just what was needed in respect of Cassandra, Josh, Lotte, and Belle Hospitality. For him. It would all come together just as the painstakingly detailed plan in France had come up trumps to condemn Lysander to a wholly justified fall from grace.

He poured himself a glass of an excellent peaty, twenty-year-old malt whisky and joined Lotte in the lounge with a spring in his step. She nursed a mug of coffee as she flicked through a magazine. Lotte grunted as he tried to engage her in small talk: always an effort, but one he had to make. Roles seemed to have turned as he was met with monosyllabic answers: no, she had been nowhere today; no, she had no plans for tomorrow or for the weekend.

'Tell me about your brother, Lotte. I know so little about your family. You must have told me, but I can't remember anything. I'm sorry. Not good enough. But I'd like to hear about him, meet him, get to know him.'

Lotte looked at him askance and sighed. 'What are you up to now? More of your games?'

'Okay, I understand why you're suspicious. I owe you an explanation. You demanded one the other night. You were right.' Julian moved onto the sofa, where he tried to take her hand. She snatched it away. 'You're upset with me. I get it. I truly get it. Time for mea culpa. Okay, let's park Jonathan and start with Cassandra.'

Lotte shuffled away from him, grabbed a cushion, hugged it tight to her chest. She looked blankly at Julian; disbelief clouded her pretty features. Julian had resolved to play this out, had anticipated her reaction, did not expect to win her over straight away. But one way or another he would have his say and see where the cards landed by the end of the evening. He recounted how he had met Cassandra, her work for his first hotel venture as a trainee, his subsequent surprise to find her employed at Hotel L'Angleterre, alluded to the abuse he was sure she had endured. He shared his speculation that Lysander was responsible.

'Why?' Lotte scoffed.

'Cassandra had uncovered his fraudulent practice, had asked questions, and he had warned her off. But she persisted, albeit driven undercover as she attempted to cover her tracks. She was discreet and chose not to speak to other staff members. Unfortunately, he still found out. Then the intimidation started. First, he tried to buy her off, then he threatened to sack her, but he had no pretext. She told him she would simply fight him, cry foul, go to the authorities as well as to the owner – me. I assume he thought better of it as it would provoke a more public row. It became personal, sinister. He cornered her one day, assaulted her. Sexually—'

'No.'

It seemed a credible sequence of events to Julian, and Cassandra had hinted as much. The extrapolation was logical.

'But she was strong mentally.'

'How did you get drawn into this? When did you shack up with her?' Lotte's tone was bitter, but he had drawn her in, captured her interest.

'I genuinely wanted to lodge somewhere away from the hotel. Oh, I lived in style, my every need catered for, but living above the shop has its drawbacks. I craved somewhere quiet. She had a spare room on the ground floor of her chalet. It was perfect: tranquil, simple living with the mountains on the doorstep. And she was as talkative as I am,' he said, smiling at Lotte. His irony did not move her: the frown permanently etched, her eyes narrowing. 'I'm sorry I didn't say anything to you. It was wrong of me. It's led to mistrust and mistaken motives. We just read, worked, enjoyed companionship. It was wholly platonic.'

'Until it wasn't. You can't deny the photographic evidence,' Lotte said.

'Just think about it, Lotte. You've had your spies watch me for how long? And what's the most incriminating evidence you can find? A solitary clinch on the mountains. The photo makes it look worse than it was. We were just caught up in the moment on a glorious day. It shocked both of us. There's no romantic relationship. Just friendship. I've not slept with her. I've not been unfaithful to you, Lotte… can you say the same?'

Lotte turned away from him and stayed quiet, clasped the cushion tighter.

'Does Jonathan really exist? And what about Jeremy Brash? I know you've had nights out with him. How often? How many times did you not come home, Lotte? Who's really the unfaithful one?'

'I'm not going to answer your allegations. What do you want, Julian? I don't buy this mea culpa crap. What's your manipulative, devious game? Just come out and say it.'

'I want a divorce.'

'Go to hell.' Her words were spoken quietly.

'Why resist? You hate it here; you miss your friends and family. You've made it clear you don't like me – the real me. It hasn't worked. You said so yourself. Why continue in purgatory?'

'And why tell me all this about… about *her*? What's the point? Why not hit me with the punchline up front?' she said. Lotte was calm when he might have expected fireworks. She seemed thoughtful, contemplative.

'You said I owed you an explanation and you were right. I just wanted you to know how it is. I can't make you believe me, but I can tell you the truth. For peace of mind, if you like.'

'Sounds a bit more like you: self-serving.'

'I see. What do you say? Will you think about it? Why don't you level with me? Tell me about Jonathan. Tell me about Jeremy. I've levelled with you. Your turn.'

'Goodnight, Julian.'

Farmer Archer extracted a price of £1,450,000 – about double the farm's market value as a going concern. Furthermore, he had extracted from Julian an agreement for him to continue to run the farm and live there for up to six months after deal completion. In return, Julian had extracted a legally binding non-disclosure agreement or NDA: a gagging order. Now he could make his move.

'I'll come straight to the point, Faye. I'm ready to do a deal at the right price,' said Julian on their Zoom call.

'I always had confidence you would hold sway with your board,' Faye said, allowing a smile. But she was on her guard. She would have conducted many such negotiations, and her mind was razor sharp, a legal brain, a savvy operator. She deserved his respect.

'Before we get to price, I need you to agree special terms. I have in mind a two-stage deal.'

'We have other options, you know…'

He paused, a little surprised at her warning shot. He took in her quizzical expression as he allowed the pause to linger. But she made no attempt to fill the silence. An experienced negotiator. 'I don't think you do, actually,' Julian said quietly.

'Yours isn't the only land abutting the acreage my client owns.'

'Mm… are you sure?' He fell silent, watched intently, allowed his words to sink in, gave her time to think. Julian smiled and thought he detected a slight change of expression, but it was fleeting. Perhaps he had sown doubt, undermined her confidence. His certainty would come across to her. 'Let's be frank. You wanted The Belle to give you access to your development land,' he said.

'We have access already. Have you not surveyed the area?' she countered. She spoke quietly, her mouth tight, her eyebrows knitting together.

'True enough, but it simply won't allow the traffic 750 houses would generate. You would have to restrict your building to perhaps fifty. Not economic. Your client wouldn't make the killing he envisages.'

'You seem overly confident in your numbers and they're simply incorrect. But I repeat – we have an alternative to buying The Belle, although I will concede the pub's my client's preferred option.'

'The only other land next to yours is the farm.'

'And?'

'Why not buy both? The three plots, even given county council and local restrictions, would easily accommodate 1,200 houses and all the additional services needed: green areas, community centres, retail areas, maybe a school. A conservative estimate. Over five hundred houses on just the farm and The Belle. The total acreage of The Belle and the farm is 118 acres. We estimate the retail value as being over £140 million,' said Julian. He had been told this by Henry, who'd made the total sale value calculation from industry metrics.

'You don't own the farm, though. We are in negotiations with the farmer, although I can't discuss details with you.'

Julian said nothing. He simply raised his eyebrows.

'I see... I need to make a quick call. Can I come back to you in an hour?' said Faye. She stood, straightened her skirt, and ended the call.

Three hours later she reappeared onscreen. Her face was stern, her demeanour businesslike, brisk.

'Very well. We assume you've managed to buy the farm. Can you confirm?'

'Yes. But you don't have my permission to divulge this to anyone, and I must ask you to sign this NDA before I can possibly say more. And your client, too.'

'A bit OTT, isn't it?'

'I have my reasons. I'll enter negotiations with you and your client in good faith once it's signed. If you choose not to then, alas, our negotiations can't even begin. I have options myself.'

Julian sent the NDA via email and showed Faye into another room for her to speak with her client and obtain the necessary authority to proceed. Within the hour she pinged the signed documents to Julian's private email address.

'I've been asked to remove our offer for The Belle. Furthermore, we need to hear about the shape of the deal you have in mind.'

'Okay. We estimate the market value of the two properties is around £2 million.' Julian paused and took a sip of water.

'We'd probably accept—'

'I bet you would. Let's talk about the farm first. A conservative estimate of the value as development is £9.5 million. So, each of the houses you build would have a land value of only around £23,000, assuming you only build fifteen houses per acre. The economics would be highly advantageous. But given the strategic importance of this to your client and the position we find ourselves in, I place the market value at £12 million.'

'I bet you do, but my client is unlikely to accept. Just for completeness, what are you seeking for The Belle?'

'£5 million. It's a smaller plot, but critical to your project.'

'I'll get back to you.'

'Of course. But you need to move quickly. We need to conclude a deal by the end of the week, signed and sealed. My professional advisers are on hand to meet as soon as you're ready. In the interests of timeliness, let me outline the shape of the two-stage deal I envisage. The first is the sale of the pub under the cover of NDA by the end of the month. But there is one complication you need to know about. The farmer has a tenancy for six months post-completion. Again, this is all tied up legally. As for The Belle, the deal must be signed with the funds placed in escrow. I envisage needing up to six months prior to completing and drawing down the funds.'

'Why the complicated structure?'

'I've a few things to tie up, a board and shareholders to manage.'

'I'll take instructions.'

FOURTEEN

AUTUMN 2020

Storm Agnes unleashed its wrath on large swathes of the country as Ruth scurried from the car park to the station. She was rarely late, hated it. She was soaked, and a towelling of her hair did little for her unkempt appearance. 'Sorry, guv. Rosie was a nightmare this morning… terrible twos and all that. Armageddon out there.'

'I'd like us to up the pace on the Banks case, guys. There seems to be something in the assertion that Scott was involved in drugs. Or at least, that we thought he was. Let's check that out, and go back to 2000, please. Is it of significance or a red herring? A good reason to press on. That and the pressure from above. His son's been on to the commissioner with none-too-subtle threats.'

'But this misper is going nowhere. And we've shelved it twice to solve other cold cases. Surely, it's time to admit defeat?' pressed Ruth.

'That's not how the senior brass sees it. Anyway, I hate failure, so I've reread earlier statements. Seems to me that Terence Sinclair and your favourite businessman are withholding. And the archive has magically revealed more for us to go on... just how bad can an investigation and archiving of files get? An unpresented cheque has been unearthed.'

'To be fair, guv, the DI, Bobby Digger, had cancer. He was a good detective but retired on ill health; died soon afterwards. I worked with him once. He was all right,' said Ruth.

'Okay. Enough of the past investigation. It's ours now.'

'I thought we'd covered this cheque business ground, guv?' said Tim.

'Another pub. The Black Anvil.'

'That shut down, didn't it?' Tim again.

'Good knowledge, Poirot. Pub sold up for development, manager moved on. The cheque was found in Scott Banks's bedside table in his flat. Dated August 2017 and signed. But here's the thing. Our first glimmer of hope: another cheque for £5K was written and signed. To Terence Sinclair. Dated and signed 28th October 2017. Found in the original investigating DI's desk drawer.'

'So, Scott was obviously still around then. Probably,' said Tim with a youthful grin.

'Brilliant analysis, Kojak.'

'Who?'

'Poirot was too subtle for you – our '80s lollipop-sucking, bald American super sleuth is more apt.'

'A bit before his time, guv,' said Ruth, smiling. 'Mine too.'

'I love the classics. I considered Starsky and Hutch, but they were all action, Columbo just too slovenly. Could never accuse you of that, could I, Kojak? Back to October 2017. Yes, he could well have been around then. That's significant news.'

'I don't wish to throw out a dampener, but he could have post-dated the cheque, guv,' said Ruth.

'Also possible. But let's look further into this. How much was the debt? For what? Did Terence or Julian know a payment was being made? Why haven't they declared this? And we also found a notepad with angry doodles and a note: "YB 10th." Did the meeting take place? 10th November, or maybe even December?' said Arthur.

'He didn't seem to go in for long-term planning—'

'No, but we investigate, please. October and January too. And if this meeting took place, how did he get there?'

'He had a clapped-out Ford Mondeo, guv. Scrapped 25th November 2017, or around that date. The scrap metal guy's paperwork wasn't totally reliable,' said Tim.

'Scrapped by whom?' asked Ruth.

'Police found it burnt out; no insurance, no tax,' said Tim.

'Good. At least police records should nail down that date. Get on it, if you would be so kind.'

'Yes, guv.'

'And check out all travel records, flights, ferries for Terence, Julian, and The Golden Lion woman. And Baxter Hinds. Nail down where they all were in November and December 2017,' Arthur said.

'Baxter Hinds died in February 2018,' said Tim.

'Then he could still have been around and involved in some way with Scott Banks's disappearance in November 2017, guv. But involved in what beyond low-level criminality by shady characters, none of whom we can directly link with Scott's disappearance? We don't even know if he's alive or dead.'

'All true, Ruth, but now we have something to go on, and I need something – anything – to deflect the heat from above right now. You and I'll meet with Terence. Keep digging, Tim. For now, the working hypothesis is that Scott was still around in October and may have met with Terence or Julian on 10th November 2017. Let's get to it.'

'You wanted me to look at that bank account, guv. Track the payments to the care home.' Ruth.

Arthur signalled for her to continue.

'Regular payments were made to Pastures New Care Home of £900. Every month from 2010 onwards.'

'Every month? Until when?' Arthur said.

'They stopped in June 2017, by which time the account was virtually empty. The home says they were for his partner, Penny Crummock, who had contracted early onset dementia. Scott evidently doted on her, visited at least once a week from 2010 onwards. In June 2017 she was transferred to hospital, and soon thereafter to a hospice for end-of-life care. I've checked and Scott was with her most days until she died on 20th August 2017.'

'So, our lowlife was also a caring, loving human being. Not quite the image that everyone other than Simon Banks has portrayed. Interesting,' said Arthur.

Ruth opted for the toilet to compose herself as she studied her image in the mirror. She sighed at her appearance: bags under the eyes betrayed sleepless nights. She pulled a comb through her unruly hair, tugged a cardigan around a crumpled blouse worn over blue trousers. And now she had to face the smug persona of her least favourite businessman.

Julian greeted DS Dodds, smiled fleetingly, and, as an afterthought, offered her coffee.

'I have a few questions.'

Julian nodded.

'Please tell me of your whereabouts between 8th and 15th November 2017. The period when Scott Banks—'

'Went missing. Yes, I recall.'

'And? If you would be so kind,' she added.

His raised eyebrows acknowledged her sarcasm. 'I was probably on the continent,' Julian said.

'We need to be sure. Please check.'

'Of course.'

'Did you meet with Scott in the period between September 2017 and February 2018?'

'No. I've not seen him for years. Dad may have done, I guess.'

'We've not been able to see him.'

'He's fading fast, I'm afraid.'

'Why might Scott have met with your dad?'

'I don't know that he did.'

'You aren't being very helpful, sir.'

'I can't tell you what I don't know. Look, Dad and I weren't close. We still aren't.'

Ruth frowned, made a few notes, and then leant forward. 'Tell me about your fallout with Scott Banks when you were a teenager, please, sir.'

'I already have,' Julian said. His demeanour was calm, his voice quiet.

'But you weren't entirely honest with us, were you?'

'Wasn't I? In what way?'

'Sir, with respect, this is like pulling hen's teeth. You incurred extensive injuries, which necessitated hospitalisation. May I remind you that this is a serious inquiry about a missing person who his son insists has perished?'

'Murdered?' asked Julian. His eyes had narrowed, and the corners of his mouth twitched, but he remained quiet, composed.

'That's the claim. So, you see, anything that sheds light on this situation, that provides some context or enables us to understand this character, is important. No stone left unturned and all that. Yes?'

Julian nodded.

Julian had been hard at it since mid-morning, and as the busy evening period approached, he took a break. As he made his way to the back, he caught sight of Sidney, the dodgy youth used by Scott to do odd jobs for him, slinking around the corner and into a storeroom. Julian was intrigued, convinced he would be up to no good. Sidney called out to someone and received a muffled response from within. Julian pressed himself into the shadows and watched as a couple of crates were passed out to the callow youth, followed by a tattooed, hairy arm handing out bottles of gin, Scotch, vodka. Hunkering down, Julian watched Scott emerge with two heavy crates; he then helped Sidney transfer their booty through the pub yard to the side street at the back. Julian imagined Sidney's clapped-out Capri being loaded up. He did not dare dart out to catch them for fear of another beating. A car coughed into life, and Julian ventured out and retraced his steps to the bar. As he entered, there was Scott with the till drawer open, pocketing some of the day's takings. Julian crept forwards to get a better look, creaking floorboards announced his approach. Scott turned round sharply, his face thunderous, bristling aggression.

'Hi, Scott,' said Julian as lightly as possible. 'Okay if I take a break?'

'I already said yes. What you up to?' Scott followed Julian out, trapped him in the yard. 'Well? Snooping again? Putting your smart nose where it ain't wanted?' he said, and jabbed his finger into Julian's chest.

'Of course not.' But Julian coloured up, beads of perspiration broke out on his forehead, his voice wavered.

'Nosy, lazy little oik, ain't you?'

Julian said nothing but looked at his boss with wide eyes. Just then, the back gate opened and in breezed Sidney. Scott nodded to the youth and flicked his head in Julian's direction. Sidney grabbed Julian and pinned him up against the brick wall.

'You know what you've got coming, don't you?'

Julian stared at him. Had spotted Sidney's knife. News had reached him of the weekend's fracas in town, two teenagers hospitalised with knife wounds to the abdomen; one was critically ill.

'You didn't answer me,' said Scott, now inches away, his head thrust forwards.

'I saw you,' Julian said. He immediately wished he had said nothing. It would sound like a challenge to his assailant, a provocation.

'Oh, did you? Saw me what? Always quick to criticise, quick to accuse, aren't you? Well? What do you think you saw?'

Julian glared at him, breathed heavily. Sidney's hand dangled above his knife and his eyes glanced from Julian to the weapon. His eyebrows rose, he grinned wickedly.

'Please don't—'

The first punch was a body blow. Julian collapsed to the floor, doubled up in pain, struggled to breathe.

'Hand in the till, thieving stock… bloody thieves.' Winded, he hardly recognised the high-pitched squeak as his own voice. And the sentiments of bravado were inauthentic.

The feckless Sidney landed another huge ham of a fist and followed it with a boot.

'Okay, lad, I'll deal with this,' said Scott.

Sidney disappeared through the back gate after having the satisfaction of landing another boot, this one between Julian's legs. Julian saw stars, felt sick, then puked vigorously over Scott's blue suede shoes. He must have fainted until brought to by a cold-water drenching.

'You were mistaken. What you saw was nothing of the sort. This is a well-run establishment. Your story for your dad. Isn't it?'

'You're a crook…'

Julian finished his account, and a finger traced a faint scar on his face.

'The result of your encounter with Scott and Sidney, I take it?'

Julian nodded.

'And you woke up in hospital?'

'Yes.'

'Thank you. We have the report of your injuries. What was your dad's reaction? Our records indicate that Scott continued in his employ immediately after the incident.'

'He chose to believe the word of a crook rather than his own son.'

'The source of your disaffection with your dad?' asked Ruth. She watched intently, but still Julian betrayed no emotion.

'You could say that. Not the only reason. We just don't get on… most families have their tensions and conflicts, don't they?'

'What can you tell us about this note from your dad? A demand for £5,000.'

'I've never seen it before. It's not dated either, I see.'

'Our inquiries tell us it's money owed by Scott for cash and booze stolen from your dad's business going back to the time of your altercation with Scott.'

'I told Dad he was a crook years ago. As ever, he just wouldn't listen. Always knows best. But if this is a debt then the FD may be able to shed light on the matter. Thomas.'

'Thank you, sir… and you won't forget to get back to us on those dates?'

'No.'

'Oh, just one last thing. Was Scott a drug user?'

'No idea. I never saw him partake.'

'A pusher?'

'Who knows? Wouldn't surprise me.'
'And your dad. Did he ever take anything?'
'Not to my knowledge.'

FIFTEEN

EARLY DECEMBER 2020

Julian was summoned to his dad's house along with his siblings. The old man was failing; the end seemed close. He had gathered with Luke and Emily as a nurse hovered, fussed with Terence's bedclothes and pillows until gruffly told to leave well alone. His skin was papery thin, his watery, unblinking eyes barely open. His mouth was parted as he fought to form his words. Julian soon realised this was to be a deathbed conversation with an agenda: his dad's agenda. Fair enough. Dying must confer certain rights. His dad deserved a fair hearing. He would cut him some slack.

'Promise me,' he had pleaded with each of them. His weak voice was cracked, croaky, cancerous. No longer the dominant, booming tones reminiscent of their childhood. Come to think of it, the tone was not the issue: it was more the bullying, hectoring demands, and the intransigence. Not a man for intellectual discourse or the sharing of perspectives. Not a man to listen attentively to alternative views. Not a man for compromise. No shades of grey, no colour. Black or white, right or wrong, acceptable or unacceptable, tolerable or intolerable.

A man of absolutes. Whatever the topic. But especially when it came to The Yorkshire Belle.

Luke promised faithfully in a grave voice, and no one would deny his sincerity. He would be expected to obey his dad's dying wishes to the letter. But might circumstances render it more difficult than he could envisage? Luke was the sensible one, the son imbued with common sense, a logical, pragmatic man. If a little dull. Emily blubbed and hugged her dad, provoking a coughing fit and the intervention of his nurse. She would have every intention of doing as expected.

'Julian…' Terence's demeanour was almost pleading. 'The Belle… never, ever…'

His meaning was clear. His steadfast refusal to contemplate the sale of the so-called jewel in the crown was Julian's dying dad's preoccupation. Not him, not even Luke or Emily. His legacy, his beloved Belle – otherwise identified as the run-down, underinvested, cash-draining dump: a business in decline.

Julian looked at his dad and struggled to find the words, took a few moments while the tension in the room pulsated as the temperature rose. He made his promise. His tone was sombre, respectful, and considered.

This time it was his dad who stayed quiet for a while. He never took his eyes off Julian. At last, he found the strength to move on to a topic dredged up from their past. It clearly pained him to do so.

'What is it, Dad?'

'Julian… I'm so, so sor…'

But he descended into a coughing fit, turned puce. The nurse shooed them out of the room as Luke and Emily exchanged surprised looks. What had he tried to say? As Julian reached the door to follow his siblings out, his dad beckoned him back.

'Hang on,' he said in barely a whisper.

'Yes, Dad? Can I get you something?'

'About… you know… the pub…when a teenager…'

He could not continue, and this time the nurse was insistent, and Julian was banished from the room.

The funeral was not only the sad affair one might expect, but a lightning rod for family recrimination and reflection. Julian looked forward to his escape to the continent. Before his flight left, he checked his inbox. Two emails threatened legal action in the pursuit of outstanding debts and were forwarded to his FD. Dross was deleted, important emails flagged, and he tapped a quick note to Henry. Then he noticed an email from his sister. *What does she want now?* He sighed as he scanned the contents of the email from Emily:

From: Emily
To: Julian
CC: Luke, Lotte
Re: Daddy

Really, Julian? REALLY? Daddy barely cold in his grave and you bugger off on your jaunts yet again? Have you no shame? Thought I'd seen the worst of you, but you still surprise on the downside, don't you?!!! I always knew you were calculating, thoughtless, selfish, but this… this… I HATE what you've become… so cold, so heartless.
Em

'Love you too, Emily. Hey-ho. Hope you feel better now,' he said aloud. More importantly, there was still no message from Faye, with two days left before the deal timed out. He had been so confident they would party. It was still the most likely outcome, but time slipped away.

As Julian made his way over to Cassandra's all his senses were alert to a tail. He had read somewhere about so-called 'tradecraft' and recalled some of the techniques deployed. While there were no train carriages to dash into at the last minute, or public buildings with multiple exits, or buses to leap onto, he was circuitous in his routing. The village square was circumnavigated, he holed up in dark alleys, dodged behind trees. And he felt a little foolish as there were no signs he could detect, just the occasional bewildered child. His various Zoom sessions with Cassandra had gone reasonably well in recent days and he'd detected a gradual thaw in her demeanour. This would be a make-or-break visit.

He was welcomed with a smile and a peck on the cheek, and as they brushed past each other while setting the table, she gently squeezed his arm. The innocent touch conveyed warmth, proximity, a relaxation in her attitude. The format of their evening was pleasantly familiar. Conversation was sparse but the atmosphere devoid of tension. He watched her transfer her knife and fork to her left hand, freeing up her right to grasp her wine glass.

She glanced across, noticed his smile. 'What?' she asked, one eyebrow raised.

Julian pointed to her hand clutching both utensils. She shrugged.

As they pushed their plates away and opted for the armchairs, Cassandra looked away as if trying to dredge something up. 'You promised to finish your story… your teenage work experience.'

'Are you sure you want to hear this? It may seem… I don't know… petty compared to your…' His voice trailed off, and she smiled weakly.

'It mattered a great deal to you, I can tell.'

'Okay… where did I get to?'

'The pub.'

'Oh yes. I'd worked there for a few months and never got on with Dad's partner, a strange guy called Scott. He was a foul-mouthed, brawny ex-navy guy with heavily tattooed arms and a penchant for fancy shoes.'

'Fancy shoes?'

'His work clothes were typically denim jeans, a T-shirt to show off his pecs, his biceps. And blue suede shoes.'

'You didn't like him.'

'He didn't like me either. I'd seen him pocket money from the till, he watered down the drinks, drank the profits, bullied remorselessly…'

'And there was a youth a few years older than you, also on the make,' she recalled.

Julian sighed inwardly, and then he told Cassandra what he had witnessed, recalled Sidney's role, his fear on spotting a knife, Scott's brutality.

'When I woke up, I was in a hospital bed on a drip, black and blue, with cracked ribs, a punctured lung, and concussion. A deep cut on my cheek had been stitched and my leg was in a plaster cast…'

'Your limp?'

'Yeah, and I still have a small scar on my cheek. Anyway, by the time I was conscious Scott had told my dad a pack of lies. I was idle, on drugs, often drunk, and I thieved. He blamed Sidney, who was nowhere to be found.'

'Your dad wouldn't believe you?' said Cassandra.

'No… he even accused me of being in cahoots with Sidney, of sharing the spoils. Scott apparently told him he'd separated the two of us after an unseemly row, but not before Sidney had launched into me.'

'How did you feel?'

'Betrayed… sick… angry. I vowed to get my own back on

Scott. As for my dad… let's just say it destroyed all trust and respect. Our relationship became toxic.'

'You can't forgive him?'

'Too late.'

'Never too late, is it?'

'It is now.'

'You mean…?'

'We buried him five days ago.'

'Oh, I'm sorry, Julian.'

'Perhaps I should forgive. But somehow… I don't know. Might things have been different had Dad believed me, trusted me? Perhaps the family would have been more at ease with itself. But such is life. There's no turning back the clock, no reinvention of history. Perhaps the cancel culture attempts to rewrite history have a point after all? If only we could deny our past, shut out the blips, the shameful bits, reimagine it all. You've had your family problems too, haven't you, Cass? What happened?'

She cocked her head to one side, and for a moment he thought she was going to tell her story. He could see an internal debate rage in her eyes.

'One day, perhaps.'

So, it was too difficult. He wanted to press her but there was no point. The sharing of their pasts was a bit one-sided. But he owed her, and she was entitled to her own privacy. He no longer was. Not if he wanted to win her over. They both resumed their tasks in front of the dying embers of the log fire. Julian sipped a whisky and studied new menus to take the hotel to the next culinary level. Cassandra worked on a crocheted blanket. The chalet was warm and cosy and the atmosphere convivial. She seemed to have overcome her reluctance to be close to him, and he hoped the invisible line between them could be erased in time.

'I have some news on the home front, Cass.'

She looked up from her work and raised an eyebrow. She suddenly seemed pensive; her body tensed. 'Oh, yes?' she said, her head bent back to her work.

'Lotte and I have discussed divorce.'

'I see.'

'My feelings haven't changed. Lotte and I will divorce whatever happens to us. And I've taken steps to clarify the biological paternity of Josh.'

She looked up sharply. 'You have doubt? Wow. How come? Why? If not you, then who? I'm shocked… do you really think you're not his dad?'

'I've wondered for a while. People comment on how alike he and Lotte are, then look at me and say nothing. I see puzzlement in their eyes. And I've often wondered about Lotte and what she gets up to…' Julian paused and shrugged, taking in Cassandra's wide-eyed look. And then a cloud passed over her features.

'You're trying to detach yourself from wife *and son*—'

'No—'

'How can you believe I'd find your news reassuring?' Cassandra said, her expression one of abhorrence.

Her response stung him. Julian sat forward in his seat. He was on edge. His heart hammered in his chest. Their relationship and his future seemed to hang in the balance. 'Please hear me out. I'm Josh's dad and always, *always* will be. But I want to know definitively if I'm the biological dad or not. Don't you think he has a right to know? Don't you think he'll demand to know one day? Would you have me put my head in the sand? How can you think me capable of disowning him? Your rebuke's shocking. It all boils down to three extraordinarily simple facts. One, I love and will always be there for Josh. Two, Lotte and I have no future, and our divorce will be to her benefit as well as mine. Three, I love *you* and want to be with you for the rest of my life.'

He slumped back in the chair, emotionally exhausted. He looked intently at her, hoping for encouraging signs. At last, she reached over for his hand and turned her hazel eyes to him. They bored into his soul, seemed to read his sincerity, his intent, his desperate need for her understanding.

'Not for the first time, you've given me a lot to think about. I'm exhausted. Let's just put this matter to one side tomorrow and enjoy our day. Let's see if we can find peace cocooned from the rest of the world. If we can, then maybe we can find a way to deal with all this. *If…*'

A perfect December morning greeted Julian as he ventured outside, having donned multiple layers, padded coat, and beanie. It was crisp and bright as the sun slanted through the surrounding peaks onto frosty fields that glistened. The earlier dusting of snow had cleared. Perfect for a hike. A day to savour, but they needed to respect the elements. They would be well prepared: first aid kit, extra layers, water, snacks, spare gloves and hats, walking poles, crampons just in case. As they made their way up to the head of the valley, they chatted intermittently about Julian's background and business track record. Cassandra was not so much interested in his successes and failures as in what drove him, what his motivation was founded on.

'Oh, who knows? Some negative stuff like proving my dad wrong and the fear of failure. Both were quite powerful drivers. But much of it is innate. I think our actions and aptitudes, our characters, personalities, and inclinations are mainly in our genes… modified by our life experiences.'

Cassandra squinted at him. 'Isn't it about control? You do like to control, don't you?'

He thought for a moment or two but then admitted there was some truth in that.

'And you manipulate?'

Julian sighed. A familiar charge. 'Sometimes, perhaps. Maybe it's a side product of control. Lotte accused me as well...' He stole a look at Cassandra, but she did not react. 'But I don't think I do so in a malign way. Sure, I seek to influence or steer things in a certain direction. All businesspeople do.'

'Just a question of where you draw the line. A question of degrees...'

They toiled higher. The sun had long since been masked by darkening clouds and they had reached the snow line, but it was only a thin covering and posed no problem. His leg ached, so they took a break, reached for the flask of coffee and the chocolate snacks.

'I suggest we head back after this,' Cassandra suggested as the clouds gathered and snow began falling softly, visibility reduced.

Julian nodded and reloaded his rucksack. He struggled to his feet and stopped in front of her. They looked raptly at each other, Cassandra with her telltale squint. *What now?*

She stood on tiptoe and reached up to him, planted a gentle kiss on his cheek before she pulled back, smiling. 'It's good to spend time with you, Julian. Just a shame...'

'Yes.' Then he pulled her into a warm embrace, padded and entwined, to enjoy a moment as snow swirled around them. His heart thudded and he tingled with pleasure, hugely relieved to bridge a chasm. But he knew he had to tread carefully, go slowly, be patient. Life's path ahead was as treacherous as the mountain tracks had become.

They made their way back cautiously, their pace slowed by the elements as the wind picked up, the temperature dropped, and the snow thickened. It was now perilous underfoot.

Clambering down the rocks, Cassandra lost her footing on the icy surface and stumbled, but Julian spotted it, and she grasped his proffered hand. The change in weather conditions transformed the mountains: peaks and ridges were masked by low cloud; easy routes were rendered challenging; low visibility; footpaths vanished under a white blanket, and temperatures plummeted to threaten well-being. Their progress became laboured. Julian's leg also troubled him today, his limp now pronounced. They continued in silence, saved their breath, and focused on each precarious step.

Eventually they emerged onto the lower path. They could breathe more easily. Nearly there. Julian's mind drifted away from their immediate environment as he tried to imagine how his relationships with Lotte and Cassandra might change over the coming months. He knew what he wanted. It was just a matter of encouraging events and relationships in the right direction. Encourage? Manipulate? And he had yet to hear from Faye about his proposition to the property developer. Another day lost. The time window was closing. Just one day left. Mm. This was not what he had expected, and he might have to bring his contingency plan into play. What a shame. It would still facilitate the necessary outcome on the Belle Hospitality front, but it would leave him with much less headroom for manoeuvre. It would leave negotiations with his siblings and Lotte on a knife-edge. What was Faye playing at? Perhaps it was all part of their negotiation stance: let him sweat, then hit him with a lower price. Maybe they would not allow him to call all the shots on the two-stage methodology, the time frame, and the price.

Perhaps it was a freak patch of ice, perhaps it was his distracted mind, but in the next minute he was flat on his back. His rucksack saved him from serious head injury, but he was winded, and his ankle hurt like hell. Cassandra was a few paces ahead and it took his shouted entreaties for her to realise there was a problem. Close inspection suggested it was not too serious: perhaps a sprain, as the ankle swelled in front of their eyes. After a short break to recuperate and gather themselves they finished off the remainder of the coffee, chose a sugary snack for energy, checked their walking poles. He disliked these and had chosen not to use them – an error of judgement; they would be a key aid now. Cassandra helped him, and bit by bit they made their way in the snow to eventually reach the chalet as dusk fell.

She helped him into a chair by the fire, already laid and soon alight. He plunged his foot into a bowl of ice. They were sure it was nothing more than a sprain, though painful. The fire now roared, and they sipped sweet hot chocolate as Cassandra sat on a cushion at his feet. Julian enjoyed her closeness and touch as she draped an arm over his legs, occasionally reaching down to check on his ankle. After a while she knelt in front of him, stretched up, and they kissed, gently at first, then longingly. As the evening wore on all the doubts and challenges dissolved like ice in his whisky. Julian knew she would not forget but he hoped she may have started the process of forgiveness. Cassandra spoke a little about her past, her difficult teenage years, but only in general terms. He did not press her, and tried to suppress Lotte's accusations: *She disgraced herself, failed her family... she's no angel.* But one day he hoped to find out what happened. It was only human to transgress, to disappoint, to fail. Perhaps she had something to be ashamed of, perhaps not. It would not change how he felt about her. Anyway, they had agreed to see if they could find peace cocooned from the world, and neither of them wanted to let too much of the real world in. Not today. The ankle injury was unfortunate, but it seemed to have brought Cassandra's tenderness to the fore: she was attentive, poured his whisky, made supper, then applied a compress to his ankle. And the tenderness extended to another kiss, this one prolonged, passionate, pulsating.

It had been quite a day. As the fire died down the temperature began to fall off. Cassandra helped him to his feet and into his downstairs bedroom.

And she stayed.

They both sat on the bed and his heart fluttered. Even now he did not want to ruin anything by presuming. They spoke softly, but words soon gave way to a more physical expression of their love as they kissed, embraced, held on to each other tightly.

'Cass—' he began to say, but she shushed him, eased him down onto the bed. A gentle hand on his chest nudged him flat on his back as she took charge.

'Just promise me, *promise* me I can trust you.'

'I love you; I absolutely promise.'

Rarely did Julian cede control so easily, so willingly, so hopefully. His senses were on high alert as he watched her pull away to reach for the light, flick it off. Stood before him, she slipped out of her clothes in the black of the night; a faint red glow from the fire next door seeped into the room to produce a silhouette of beauty, the silver locket glinting in shards of light.

She called the shots as they consummated their intense love for each other. As they became one.

It surpassed his dream.

This was for real.

She was back.

They were back.

All would be well.

SIXTEEN

DEAL DEADLINE DAY

His early departure from Cassandra's warm embrace was a wrench. The flight got him back into Manchester around lunchtime, and the first thing he did was check his emails. Julian frowned at the absence of anything from Faye or the property developer, Optimum. Today was the last day, the last chance to secure the two-stage deal. He needed to put in place the contingency arrangement with another of Henry's contacts, PJZ Holdings. He picked up his mobile and made a call to the lawyer handling both the Optimum and the PJZ Holdings deals, Francis.

'Are you sure about this? The timing? The process?'

'Yes.'

'You do realise PJZ will demand you meet their costs? You could elongate the timescales to give your preferred buyer a chance to come good... even a week might help, and then we could line up your contingency arrangement to complete over the course of the following month. It would reduce costs substantially.'

'Understood, but set it up for PJZ to complete at half-past midnight if Optimum don't.'

The contract would be signed, sealed, and placed in escrow pending Julian's instructions. A half-hour's grace would give him time to pull the deal or trigger its conclusion. But he remained hopeful for plan A. He rooted for Faye and Optimum. It would represent the magic wand he yearned for. A great strategy, inspired, creative. But would it work? It promised to be a tense evening.

15.00, Deadline Day

Julian was greeted frostily by Lotte, warmly by Annie and Nanny Barlow. Josh was in the main lounge, attended by Nanny, with Lotte curled up on a sofa with a magazine. Julian dumped his bags and made a beeline for Josh, ignored Lotte's sarcastic barbs. It took a deal of patience before Julian had a direct response from his son and a hard-won smile. The months had slipped by, and it must soon be time to get a diagnosis. Lotte looked on as he discussed it with Nanny. She put her magazine down but did not engage in the conversation, just stared at Julian.

'What do you think?' Julian asked of the nanny.

'All children develop at different paces. Some are just late developers. I can tell you about one little chap I had—'

But Julian cut in, not keen for one of her tales. 'I'll arrange an assessment.'

'I *told* you,' Lotte said. 'ADHD… but of course you didn't listen.'

'I spoke with Dr Lloyd. He didn't tell you Josh had ADHD. It's possible but not certain. It's still too early for a reliable diagnosis.'

'As I said.'

Julian was agitated with her obdurate attitude, her hostility. It was not like him to let her get to him like this, but today… 'No, it wasn't. There was a clear qualification about the possibility of autism; none of your certainty.' He spoke through thin lips, his tone quiet, his annoyance manifest.

Lotte glared at him, and Nanny Barlow swept up Josh as he toddled aimlessly; she took him away from the poisonous atmosphere.

'Home five minutes and causing a row already, Julian. How was France? How was your mistress?'

He sighed and looked heavenwards, said a busy work agenda beckoned. But he remained seated. He felt guilty. He had consummated his relationship with Cassandra, had breached his vows. What had he said about it previously when challenged by Lotte? *Wholly platonic*. He looked down as he rubbed his wedding-ring finger, noticed the missing ring, which languished in his pocket. It no longer seemed warranted; he would feel hypocritical. *I've not slept with her.* Now he was guilty of the betrayal Lotte had accused him of. *I've not been unfaithful.* At the time he could not have expected the relationship with Cassandra to develop. He had been given no reason to even harbour hope. But he had wanted this outcome since their very first walk on the mountains when they had both resisted their urge to kiss. Whether or not this had been inevitable, he knew deep down that he had always hoped.

'I'm sorry, Lotte. You're right to be angry. What I said previously—'

'Oh, do spare me the gory details. You and the harlot shagging in your love nest.'

'We must sort this out. Let's not prolong the pain.'

'Go to hell.'

'I really don't have time to argue today. I want a divorce; you need a divorce. I'll be generous, but I really have business stuff… it simply won't wait. Let's talk tomorrow.'

Lotte threw her magazine at him, and he held his hands up in surrender.

16.15, Deadline Day

He checked his emails and compiled a list of the most urgent things he needed to do.

'Nothing much to report of any major consequence, Julian,' said Thomas. 'Trading's no better. The Belle's still closed. Your siblings have both been in touch to ask what's happening. It's a fair question, to be honest. Unless we have some answers soon.'

'I know.'

'They said they'd be in touch with you. At least they seem to have accepted the gravity of the situation. Time's running out. I suggest we arrange a shareholders' meeting—'

'Next week.'

'But what do we have to tell them that we haven't said before?'

'I'm working on it,' said Julian.

as CJulian said they would sort things out within the week.

His FD was intrigued and frustrated. 'I'm trying my best to stand by you in the bleakest of possible circumstances, but if my CEO won't confide in me, won't let me in on his plans...' His voice tailed off. Thomas's irritation was too bad. This was no time to assuage hurt feelings. There would be plenty of time to lick their wounds later.

Julian had two emails from Francis – his next port of call. Francis spoke urgently about the legal challenges. On both options.

'Is there a solution?' asked Julian.

'Yes, we can either—'

'Then get on with it.'

'I'm not sure we'll be able to do either by midnight. They're really pressing me for a deferment of a week. Maybe if we gave them three or four days?'

'No.'

'You might have to intervene. They won't take it from me.'

'Then arrange the call. Remember, neither knows of the other.'

'Of course, rest assured we've been discreet – different lawyers on the two deals. PJZ are also mumbling about price now as well,' said Francis.

'Mm.' The line went quiet as Julian thought for a moment or two. He was exposed, and the risk of ending up without a deal loomed large. Should he relent on the time frame? Would it really matter if he lost another week? But to relent now would weaken his negotiating position. What to do? 'Stand firm. They've had their pound of flesh. I'm in touch with Faye on Optimum's price and will let you know what she says. They get this done within the time at the price we've agreed, or the deal is off. And you'll miss out on your fat win bonus. Make it happen.'

Francis was curt in wrapping up the conversation. But he was a seasoned operator and would have experienced worse than Julian's sharp tongue. He would understand the pressure cauldron. He had his instructions, was being paid well, with a handsome win bonus the incentive. Julian would not waste time worrying about his lawyer's feelings.

17.00, Deadline Day

Julian glanced at his watch as the clock in the hall chimed. Just seven hours remaining. Then his email pinged, and he smiled for the first time since landing back home. Faye. At last. He skimmed the email. A frown replaced the smile.

From: Faye
To: Julian
Re: The Deal

We need to speak, Julian, but the essence is, the deal won't fly. My client regards the time limit as ridiculous, the price as much too high. Unless you're prepared to renegotiate, then he says it's off. Let's talk.
Faye

Julian curbed an inclination to bounce back immediately. He needed to think, and decided to grab some air to clear his head. Pulling a coat on, he ventured out into the frosty, foggy evening. The air was still. It was eerily silent. It was as if the animal kingdom had hunkered down on this inhospitable Yorkshire evening, although, lost in his own thoughts, he would probably not have noticed even if a deer had ventured close as he circumnavigated the house. He suddenly came to a halt, seized by a need to act. It was not Faye he rang, but Francis.

'How're you getting on?' he enquired, trying to keep the tension out of his voice.

'Making some progress, but both buyers' legal teams remain sceptical it can be done tonight.'

Julian meandered on and cogitated.

'Julian? Are you there?'

'Yes. Just thinking. Look, the time frame's mandated by reasons I can't control. We must finalise the legal documents by midnight. We need to be ready for completion of PJZ on my trigger half an hour later if Optimum back out, or it dies. PJZ has already extracted a heavily discounted price. If they are squeezing to find out where my bottom line is, well, they've found it. If we do the deal then they make a substantial profit and, Francis, they bloody well know it. And you—'

'I know. We get our bonus too.'

'The only question is whether they want it or not.'
'So, you're doubling down.'
Julian grimaced, rubbed his throbbing forehead.
'Julian?'
'Yeah. Trust me, they want this deal. Let's make it happen.'
Now he knew what the message for Faye was to be.

From: Julian
To: Faye
Re: The Deal

Then there's nothing to talk about. I'll sell to my reserve buyer if our deal isn't concluded by midnight. We've talked about this for long enough. You could have spoken with me about timing a week ago, but you decided to squeeze me, see if I was bluffing. I'll entertain a discussion on price, although there isn't much scope for movement. My final word. But the conditions won't change whatever your side say. If they don't want to do it, then so be it. On the other hand, if they wish to have a price-based discussion then ring me within the hour. There's no time to waste. I'm not bluffing. Let me know.
Julian

18.10, Deadline Day

He reread the note. It was a risky strategy to double down on both deals. But if it all went belly up, he would still own the farm. There would be other buyers. In time. Time Belle Hospitality did not have. He could consider going into property development. Not the future he wanted for himself, though. Another glance at his watch – less than six hours. Would Faye come good? Julian reached for the decanter of whisky, but stayed his hand. He hoped to see Josh before his bedtime and preferred not to import alcoholic fumes to the nursery.

He pressed return and watched the read receipt message ping into his inbox two minutes later. The die was cast. Julian felt better for having played his card. Time would tell whether he would come to regret his decision, but now seemed the time to retain his nerve. A break from all this would be good, and he might just be in time to help with Josh's bath and read him a bedtime story.

In the event, Nanny Barlow was ahead of the normal routine this evening; Josh had been challenging today. He had a runny nose and a cough, and was whingey. 'Needs his bed tonight. His mum gave up on him hours ago. A disturbed night in prospect. For me, anyway,' she complained.

Julian listened to her without really taking it in. It was not like her to complain, so she would have due cause, what with Lotte in a bad mood and a poorly toddler… what they would do without the nanny he did not like to think. He did not have long with his son, but it was the highlight of his day as he read *Room on the Broom* to Josh, embellishing the story as he went along, momentarily forgetting the business drama. He was just getting towards the end when the door swung open and Lotte entered, wine glass in hand.

'Wow, what a revelation. Have you taken a photo, Nanny? A rare moment: father and son.'

'Not so rare,' Nanny Barlow said. Her tone was sharp.

Julian had never heard her answer Lotte back, whatever the provocation. Annie, yes; Nanny Barlow, never. Lotte would know how reliant she was upon her, whereas her housekeeper was easily replaceable, or so she thought. Lotte ignored her with a toss of the head. She reached for Josh, but he complained when she tried to lift him as he snuggled in the crook of his dad's arm. Julian encouraged Josh to go to Mummy. However bad his relationship with Lotte, his son needed his mother, would need her in the future. But Josh whinged and whimpered until

Lotte relented and made do with a kiss on his forehead and departed in a huff. Julian looked at Nanny Barlow, who smiled nervously and shrugged her shoulders. For almost the first time he felt sorry for Lotte. She just seemed to get everything wrong. The pain of rejection was etched on her face, the shock wave moistening her eyes as she fled.

SEVENTEEN

DECEMBER 2020

Sleep had proved elusive as his heart raced, he broke out in a cold sweat, his head hammered sounds of torture. A cold shower, two mugs of strong coffee, two paracetamols, and a pint of water later, he crept into the lounge, where Lotte bickered with a tired Nanny Barlow who tried to entertain a bad-tempered Josh. Annie bounced in and out on her various chores and grumbled incessantly. The atmosphere was fragile, with Lotte dismissive of the nanny and half-hearted and ineffective with Josh as she sniped at Annie.

'And what the hell's the matter with you?' Lotte said, spitting out venomous words.

Julian ignored her as he knelt to play with Josh, his head thumping its objections. His son's nose streamed, his temperature spiked, he whined continuously. Nothing engaged him, and he tottered past his parents to Nanny Barlow with arms outstretched.

'Well?' demanded Lotte.

Julian jumped to his feet, straightened himself, and glared at her with bloodshot eyes. Without a word he grabbed her hand

and virtually dragged her into the dining room. He slammed the door behind them. Lotte looked at him in astonishment. Her emerald-green eyes morphed from surprise to anger, and flashed warning signals.

'I refuse to argue in front of our son, and you should get your maternal act together. What's the matter with you? You're an ineffectual, inconsistent, inept parent. All the things you criticise me of are *your* sins. You're obnoxious to Annie, rude to Nanny Barlow, and bloody impossible with me.'

'Hardly a surprise, given what you're doing over there…' She gesticulated and tossed her head. 'Shacked up and shagging, and then you trot home on your high horse. How do you expect me to be? We took vows. You said you'd look after me and love me and all that shit, and yet what do you do? Can't you see I'm unhappy? You're a selfish bastard, Julian. Never a thought for me.'

'Enough. How many times do I have to say this? It's not working, you're unhappy, you don't like living here, you don't like me, and you have your own love life. Don't pretend otherwise. Let's call it a day. Get divorced, but do it in a civil way for the benefit of Josh if no one else. We can agree a settlement and try to be good parents despite all this acrimony.'

'Same old record, same old, same old. All talk.'

'I'll see a solicitor next week and start the ball rolling. Are you going to work with me on this?'

'*Never!*' Lotte turned on her heels and strode to the door with Julian close behind. She suddenly spun around and slapped him hard across his face.

As he headed to Hutton Ridge, low, dark clouds scudded by as the biting wind assailed him; it carried with it the scent of dashed hopes. The slanting rain needled his face, a stinging rebuke as sharp as Lotte's strike. Nonetheless, he needed to walk out his anger, his frustration, his disappointment. And he walked hard to clear his head and recover composure when his mobile rang out. Even on this wet, miserable Saturday he was not to be left in peace. Business would seek him out. *What now?*

'What do you want, Henry?' he snapped into his mobile.

'Hey, steady now. I'm on your side.' Henry's tone was emollient and reassuring.

'Sorry. Please excuse me, not feeling myself today. You're a good man, Henry, and about the only one who had any decent news for me yesterday. I'm afraid it didn't go to plan. They ran me to the line and—'

'We need to talk, Julian. Let's meet.'

'I'm on the hills.'

'Tell me where and I'll pick you up. In fact, you may need a pick-me-up so let's find a hostelry.'

'Please don't tell me Raven have pulled out too?' Henry had lined up Raven as another option, a plan C should Optimum and PJZ fail to deliver.

'They will. You should regard it as dead. I've put out feelers, called in a few favours, and I know what happened. I'll brief you. I'm afraid we've been outgunned and outsmarted, my friend. But we live to fight another day. See you soon.'

Julian groaned and sat down heavily on a rock in the middle of the moor. Darker, heavier clouds gathered to press claustrophobically, further dampening his spirits. This was not his week. He wearily pulled himself upright to hike across the heather moor to rendezvous with Henry in a pull-in on a lane. *Pull yourself together, man.*

Settled into a corner of a tiny, old-fashioned pub, they set about their soup of the day and Henry pulled on his pint of bitter; Julian opted for a lemonade and soda.

'What's going on?' asked Julian.

'You're not going to like it.'

'Hit me.'

'Optimum are seasoned, cut-throat operators with great contacts and influence. They didn't like your price and objected to your conditions – particularly the timescales. So, they pulled a few tricks, flexed their muscles to strike a side deal with PJZ and warn off Raven. They know you're in over your head on this, in hock to the bank. They know The Belle will go bust if they just wait. Then they can pick it up for diddly-squat. Playing the long game is why there's so much land banking. It drives government mad. You might try and find another buyer but it's unlikely anyone will go against them, and anyway, without planning permission the risk's too great. It only works for them because of the access to their own land, as you rightly surmised.'

'Belle Hospitality isn't bust yet. What about the farm? Surely, they would want that as well?' said Julian, his eyebrows knitting in consternation.

'Maybe.'

'What should I do? I've obviously made a royal Horlicks of it.'

'Sit tight for a while, let this blow over, then try to sell the farm.'

'But if I sell it as a farm, I won't cover my outlay, let alone the costs incurred. It needs to be as land with planning permission. Familiar territory for those guys.'

'They aren't alone. I know some people in planning and some of the political figures. Why don't we make tentative enquiries? Mind you, this can take years. How's your patience?' asked Henry.

Julian grimaced. It was the antithesis of his strategy. Julian pondered as Henry went for another pint. It all rang true. They had played him and taken advantage of his need for a quick deal. He had been overly confident, had miscalculated. Big time. But he wondered whether Optimum would just wait for Belle Hospitality to go to the wall. The more he thought about it, the more he thought they would want to cut a deal for the farm at least. He quizzed Henry on the point when he sat back down, and he shrugged.

'Maybe. But one thing's for certain: you can't go to them. They must come to you. And if they do, they'll want a cut-price deal. You can bet your life on it. The best thing you can do is work out your real bottom line, suck it up, and party if it's worth it to you. Sometimes in life we must accept defeat. Accept we've got it wrong, take the pain, learn the lesson, and salvage what we can. Sit tight, Julian, and work the numbers.'

The events of the last few days had been as dark and forbidding as the weather, and now the tumult of a shareholder meeting had to be faced. Julian reflected on Henry's news. He had a lot to thank him for: his steadfast support, honesty, insight, and wise counsel. But his news had laid bare the harsh reality. Julian's entire strategy lay in tatters, the worst defeat of his career. And it hurt like hell. He was suddenly imbued with a heightened sense of vulnerability. He had endured setbacks and disappointments but never had he experienced acute failure; yet now he faced terminal catastrophe on the Belle Hospitality front. He bore this burden alone. Now he had to brave a meeting devoid of answers, devoid of optimism. What would he say? What *could* he say? The business was doomed. How much worse could things get? He had tried to defer the meeting by a week but even Thomas would not support him, and his siblings were scathing of his attempt to keep them in the dark. He had shared some details with Zoe Madden of SI to elicit her support, but not the entire game plan. In response she had promised to remain silent about the strategy until the right moment. Now he had to endure more pain in a conversation with Zoe prior to the meeting. At least she was professional in her reaction.

The one thing he did manage to find time for was a Zoom call with Cassandra. He lifted himself out of his torpor to reach out to her. He had to be more attentive, had to make the effort. And it was rewarded. She was bright, cheerful, and welcoming, her words caressing.

'When are you coming back, Julian? I… I miss you.'

His heart sang; it was the first time she had said as much. His mood lifted like the veil of a dutiful mourner now ready to face the world. He felt a visceral need to be with her, to hold her, to love her. 'I'll be with you as soon as I can. I miss you too, Cass. I love you. We need to be together.'

Cassandra nodded and her face broke into a warm smile; not the china-doll beauty of Lotte, but something more grounded, more authentic, more empathetic.

'I have chronic problems over here I must see through, though. Not good. Whatever I do, it just seems to get worse. Sorry, I mustn't burden you. I just need you to know… I won't be a moment longer than necessary.'

'I'm here for you when you need me, Julian.'

At least their relationship had turned a corner; the knowledge strengthened his resolve to navigate this difficult patch with Lotte and with Belle Hospitality. Something to latch on to as he marched into the dining room.

As he entered the ring, Thomas demanded to see Julian privately. His manner was terse. Julian sighed inwardly. This was likely to be an opening skirmish in a day of inevitable battles, acrimony, virtual bloodshed. Thomas paced up and down, demanded to know what was going on.

'You've ignored email after email over the last week, you make vague references to a deal – without any board or shareholder authorisation – and your FD knows nothing about it…'

Julian allowed him to let off steam, saw Thomas's face flush as he ran his fingers through his thick curls, his eyes flaring. He ranted about the position Julian had placed him in, said he was out on a limb, and it made it impossible to support him. He had received call after call from the investors, from Luke, from Emily. And he was under constant pressure to pay their creditors, fielding hostile calls, and was also in receipt of legal demands, threats of court action.

'Well?' Thomas shouted at him.

'There's no deal.'

'And?'

Julian looked at Thomas but offered nothing more than a mumbled acknowledgement of the difficult position his FD found himself in.

'And what line do we take this morning? What do you plan to say?'

'All we can do is tell it as it is.' Julian spoke quietly, more calmly than he felt.

'They'll want *solutions*!'

'Yes.'

'You do realise we've almost run out of time?' said Thomas. He slumped in a chair, his energy drained. 'And you still haven't told me what deal you tried to stitch together. Are you going to?'

'It's private. I'd hoped the ramifications would be positive for Belle Hospitality and the shareholders. I can't say more.'

'It's dead?'

'For now.'

As he pushed open the dining-room door to enter the gladiatorial arena, the tense atmosphere hit Julian like a wave. He was confronted by his dad's recently installed portrait and a fragile, resentful silence. Terence Sinclair wore a grave expression, his fluffy eyebrows knitted together in a frown. It was intended to demonstrate the gravitas of a business titan, Julian supposed. Sitting before their ex-chairman were his fellow directors and shareholders. They were silent. Not the usual irreverent, disrespectful, immature gossiping of Emily and Lotte, but instead sour, accusatory expressions. Luke wore a furrowed brow and tapped a pencil on his pad. Julian's siblings wore black as a mark of respect to their dad, Julian a black tie. Lotte made no such nod to their dad's recent death other than a black expression. Zoe Madden expressed her condolences and received acknowledgement from Julian and Luke, while Emily glowered at her.

'As a mark of respect, I suggest we observe a minute's silence to mark the passing of our dad, Terence Gerald Sinclair,' said Julian.

They all nodded and bowed their heads.

'Dad would have expected us to engage with the business despite our grief. Life goes on. We need to face the grave position of Belle Hospitality,' Julian said. He glanced around the room and received open hostility from Emily, wide eyes from Luke, while Lotte cast her eyes skywards. He then asked Thomas to present a summary of the company's financial position, and he subsequently fielded questions from Luke and Zoe. The pulled no punches. The situation was grim. He shared the lawyers' letters demanding instant payment, took them through the list of both debtors and creditors (the latter longer than the former), and presented the cash flow projections. The cash position was due to turn red in less than seven weeks' time, with substantial debt remaining, the largest to the bank and to SI.

'Will the bank extend more credit?' asked Luke.

By way of answer, Thomas handed out copies of letters from three banks; all had rejected requests for loans, and a further letter from their own bank threatened foreclosure of the various properties in the portfolio, including The Yorkshire Belle.

'And what about SI – our supposed partner and friendly investor? Why don't you inject funds?' asked Emily.

'Why would we loan more funds? They would simply be absorbed by debt repayment. Why would we?' said Zoe.

'What are you doing about it, Julian?' Luke demanded to know.

Julian sat back and stared intently at his brother before saying, 'You know very well what we advised the board and shareholders a long time ago. Do you really want me to remind you?'

'I didn't ask what it was you *previously* wanted to do. I asked what you are *doing* about it *now*,' said Luke through gritted teeth, tapping his pencil furiously.

'What would you have us do? We've taken advantage of every government payment relaxation available to us through the emergency Covid measures; we've shut those premises making a loss; we've furloughed where possible; we've laid staff off.'

'There must be something else. You seem so calm, emotionless.'

'Would it help if I ranted or wailed or cried? I repeat – what would *you* have us do? I'm all ears.'

'Sell The Belle,' said Emily abruptly, drawing exclamation and shock from all around her.

'*Emily!*' said a stunned Luke.

Julian sat back again and raised his hands in despair. And then Luke, Lotte and Emily spoke heatedly, shouting over each other until exhausted.

In a temporary lull, it was Thomas who spoke. 'Nearly two years ago we proposed a sale. We've set out the reasons for such an approach repeatedly. We identified a strategic buyer who would have paid a princely sum. It would have allowed us to restructure the company, draw down the second SI loan, and we would today be in a completely different place. And yet Julian's family failed to support him despite SI being keen on the plan. The board threw out the proposed strategy time after time despite our – *my* – warnings of the implications.'

'Then do it,' said Lotte and Emily in unison.

'It's too *late*,' said Thomas, who flushed and gesticulated his despair. The room fell silent before Thomas added in a softer voice, 'Our buyer has withdrawn their interest. And anyway, we don't have time to sell. I can't see how we can avoid going into voluntary liquidation unless something radical changes in the next three weeks. The board will have to take the legal decision when we cannot fulfil our financial obligations.'

'Luke reminded you, Julian, of the need for options to address our predicament. What are these? You're the CEO, you're supposed to have the Midas touch. You're the one who always knows best,' Lotte said. She slammed her hand on the table. Her tone was withering, caustic, derisory.

'All true,' agreed Emily. 'You're an arrogant—'

'This isn't helping, and it isn't fair either,' Thomas said.

'But the ship's about to go down on your watch, Julian. You're the captain. Have you no answers? Can you offer no hope?' said Luke.

'No,' said Julian. His tone was flat, his face expressionless.

'The business our grandad built from nothing and was then taken on by Dad, whom you criticised endlessly. Have you no shame? No remorse?' Luke persisted, snapping his pencil in two.

'I understand your feelings,' said Julian.

'And again, this simply doesn't help,' said Thomas. 'Each and every one of us must shoulder the burden and share the responsibility. Zoe? You look as if you want to say something.'

'I'm going to break a golden rule and enter this fray; I'll give you a professional shareholder's analysis. I sit on eight boards, and in my time I've been a member of perhaps fifty. I've seen businesses struggle and go under; I've seen flotations, mergers, successful exits. It's also been my misfortune to witness all manner of turmoil in family-run businesses…' Zoe said, looking around her. She spoke quietly, authoritatively, and commanded attention. 'The family has constantly thwarted Julian's and Thomas's plans. You're besotted with your dad's version of events. With due respect, you are attempting to rewrite history; it belies what you witnessed unfold in front of your very eyes. This business has been underinvested, poorly led, and its value has declined. SI supported the investment as we saw the potential for a turnaround, a new strategy, and we admired the leadership skills and track record of Julian. And all you do is throw insults and barbs as you realise you've left it too late. Perhaps you should all reflect on how it came to this.'

The siblings and Lotte exchanged angst-filled glances as silence descended, until it was eventually broken by Luke with a plaintive, 'So what now?'

'Thomas will advise when the board must make a final decision. Meanwhile, I'll continue to explore options. But every avenue I've explored has thus far been a dead end. I can't offer any optimism.'

'What options?' asked Luke.

'There's no point saying – they're leading nowhere, and anyway, they're private.'

'What the hell do you mean, "private"? You have a duty to share anything and everything with us,' demanded Luke, now drawing aggressive, angular shapes on his pad.

'It's private, nothing to do with the business.'

'Then how can it help?' asked Emily, who screwed her notes into a tight ball and threw it towards the bin in the corner.

'It can't now,' said Julian.

'Just tell us. At least it would help to know you're trying to do *something*,' snapped Luke.

'No, I can't.'

'*Typical*,' blustered Lotte. 'And if the family outvote your proposal to enter administration?'

'Then Thomas and I will immediately tender our resignations at the point where the company is unable to fulfil its obligations. It would be illegal to continue. As directors, you would leave yourselves personally exposed.' Julian spoke calmly and quietly.

'There is one other option,' said Zoe. 'We could enter a pre-pack.'

'What the hell's a pre-pack?' asked Emily.

'The short version is, the sale of the company by working with a specialist insolvency practitioner who would negotiate on its behalf,' Thomas explained.

'And we'd do this via a "Newco" arrangement backed by SI,' said Zoe.

'So, Newco would pay off our debts with the proceeds from Belle Hospitality, presumably a small percentage of each debt. And the slate would effectively be wiped clean to allow the company to continue to run the operation,' said Luke thoughtfully. He directed his comments to Emily and Lotte.

'I don't get it. If we can do this, what are we waiting for? It sounds perfect,' Emily said with renewed hope.

'Newco would not be owned by the current shareholders and the board would be differently constituted. Current shareholders would receive nothing for their shares,' said Thomas.

A deflated Emily shrank back in her chair.

'SI will support this outcome with Julian as CEO and Thomas as FD. All other board members and shareholders will be new,' Zoe said.

Julian retreated to his study and sipped a malt whisky. It took him back to France, to the chalet where he had sipped the same malt in front of Cassandra's blazing log fire. In the privacy of his study he was overcome with tiredness, by emotion as he tasted salty tears, his cheeks damp from the course they tracked from itchy, liquid eyes. Perhaps he should just accept defeat, retreat to the Alps, and suffuse himself with the love of Cassandra; settle for a simpler life. If only he could. He would not walk away from his obligations: to Thomas, his loyal friend and business compatriot; to Henry, to repay his friendship and expertise; but most of all to Josh. He reached to his inside jacket pocket to extricate an envelope. He held it reverentially, tinged with a sense of foreboding. What might the results be? He had carried it around with him for days now. He sighed and returned it to his pocket unopened; better left to a more positive day.

The meeting earlier had been as grim as he had feared, although Zoe's tabling of a pre-pack option was a huge compliment. Was this the only way out? It seemed likely. And despite his siblings' accusations, he bore the responsibility and took Luke's point about the ship falling asunder on his watch. Catastrophic failure. He was appalled, ashamed, angry. And how had he been so wrong on those property deals? He had been hopelessly mistaken.

There was a knock on the door and Thomas walked in. 'I figured you might need company. And I need to hear about the deal you've tried to push through. You owe me – as a friend, not as FD. Don't sigh – you don't have an option. I've booked a table at The Broken Man.'

'Thomas, please, I'm really not—'

'I'm not taking no for an answer. For once you can work to my agenda.'

Julian nodded, reached inside his jacket pocket, removed the letter, and locked it in his desk drawer.

He told Thomas about his failed deal as his friend drove. Settled into a dark corner on a busy evening, they were soon engaged in deep conversation. Thomas grilled him about every aspect of the thwarted deal, and they mulled over Belle Hospitality's limited options. They dissected in detail Zoe's offer – the only constructive way forward on the table.

'If you were to buy The Belle, then, together with the farm, wouldn't it stymie Optimum's development? Bring them back to the table? And if not Optimum, why don't you go up a league, find one of the big boys? They could then make a mint, perhaps even force Optimum to sell out their position for next to nothing. You'd get what you need and bloody Optimum's nose into the bargain,' said Thomas.

The thought tantalised. But time was Julian's enemy. It would all take months, and more likely years, he pointed out.

'Why don't you put it to the test? See what Henry has to say. What can you lose? And maybe all you need is the threat of such a deal to bring them back to the table.'

'You have your uses, don't you, my friend?'

Having ordered their food, Julian went in search of the gents'. He pushed his way through the people circulating, some wearing masks, some not. He was waylaid by someone he had once employed, and they exchanged pleasantries. Then in his eyeline he caught sight of a figure he recognised. How could he not? She attracted attention from the men around her as she sashayed through a group of young people, mask in hand, and headed for a corner of the pub, where a guy welcomed her. He wore a look of expectation and a broad smile. Julian found a vantage spot where he could observe, dissolving into the shadows in the dimly, atmospherically lit hostelry. The man embraced her, and Julian watched as they settled closely on the padded leather bench in their booth. The man poured champagne, they chinked glasses, and sipped. Moments later their greeting developed into something more passionate as they lost themselves in each other's arms. Julian felt like a voyeur and was open-eyed, rooted to the spot as the scene unfolded. And suddenly, without having made any conscious decision, he found himself in front of them. He looked down at the lovers. They were completely oblivious. He cleared his throat, coughed loudly.

They abruptly parted, the man irritated by the intrusion. 'What the hell, man?'

Julian gave him an icy stare and then turned his attention to the woman. 'So, at last I get to meet Jonathan, do I?'

'*Oh!* Julian. I… I… what the hell… what are you doing here?'

'Aren't you going to introduce your husband to your lover, Lotte?'

'Oh my God,' said the man, turning ashen.

'Jonathan? Your name?' Julian enquired with a raised eyebrow.

The man opened his mouth as if to speak, but then clamped it shut and nodded. He seemed to have physically diminished as he looked disconsolately first at Julian, then at Lotte.

'So, unless you've taken a liking to incest, my dear wife… but don't let me interrupt you a moment longer. Have a wonderful evening, both of you.' Julian smiled at Lotte, turned, and walked away.

Julian awoke to a foul, wet day. The rain lashed down the moors rendered invisible behind a blanket of greyness. But he felt better. The uncovering of Jonathan had laid bare Lotte's lies. It was time to shrug off the hair shirt, cease the self-flagellation; goodness knows his siblings needed no help to inflict painful abuse. Time to recover his trademark 'can-do' attitude. Time to make things happen rather than passively endure.

In his office, the first thing he did was unlock the drawer and extricate *the* envelope. It was time. He took a deep breath, slit it open with a shaky hand. He surveyed the contents, took in the results, and sat back to think. The smile was replaced by a thoughtful frown. A conclusive paternity test. All doubts dismissed. Stark reality stared him in the face. But Josh was his son, always would be. It begged yet another question, though.

The next call was to Henry. Julian asked him to identify other parties who might be interested in a proposition along the lines Thomas had suggested. Henry threw two names at him straight away and promised to make enquiries.

Julian turned to his PC, trawled through the long list of unopened emails, and highlighted the urgent ones, put aside others, and binned the rest. He then pulled up the latest spreadsheet from his FD. There was a faint glimmer of hope. The day of execution might yet be deferred with good news about some cash receipts and lower-than-forecast costs. With certain other measures, the day of reckoning might be delayed by a further four or five weeks. More time was important. Immensely important.

His thoughts were suddenly interrupted by a shrill tone on his mobile. Cassandra. He was astonished. She rarely called. He hit the green phone icon, and an emotional Cassandra told him her news: her dad had just died. While she was estranged from her family, the news had nonetheless hit her hard. She had not even known he was ill, but he had suffered from a cancerous brain tumour these last two years, she was told. The funeral was to be held at the church close to the family home in Hertfordshire tomorrow: a small affair, partly due to Covid restrictions on the size of funeral gatherings, partly due to family fissures. Her brother had also fallen out with his dad and did not plan to attend. Or see Cassandra. She was ringing from Heathrow, having just landed. Would Julian meet her while she was over here? Bet your life.

EIGHTEEN

DECEMBER 2020

Arthur rubbed his face as he reflected on the meeting with the hierarchy. They had been pleased with the clearing-up of two of the cold cases, damning of his failure to find Scott Banks. Arthur was hugely frustrated with the Scott Banks misper case, had paused it twice, and was nonplussed by the insistence that he give it one last push.

'We need this one sorted, Arthur. It shouldn't be beyond a man of your track record, waning though your success rate is. You don't want a transfer to the sticks, now, do you?' said Ted Beech, the chief superintendent.

Arthur glared, and communicated his contempt for the sentiment silently. They knew each other well, had worked together frequently.

'Arthur… this is more than important. It transcends our long-standing relationship.'

'Understood, sir.' Arthur looked Ted Beech in the eye, raising his eyebrows questioningly.

'Look, off the record, there's more to this than meets the eye.'

'And off the record, Ted, this is all bollocks. You know it, I know it. We've been chasing our tail around with nothing to go on but chicken feed. What the hell's going on?'

'You have your job to do, I have mine. We're both under pressure. That goes right up the line and beyond the force. I'm told it's highly likely your misper will, let's say, be in possession of government property. I don't know much in the way of detail, but I can put two and two together.'

'And?'

'Two things I can say – all that I know. Firstly, your job is to find our misper. Secondly, retrieve a document from his person or find out where it might be and report back. The first objective is for you and your team; the second is for you only.'

'Is he dead?'

'That I don't know. His son seems to think so.'

'What's this document?'

'I've no idea, and nor should either of us wish to know,' said Ted.

'What answer do you get to your two-and-two sum?'

'I've not said this. It's pure conjecture and I may be miles wide of the mark.'

'I'm all ears.'

'I recall a recent Home Secretary's career consigned to the bin. Hastily cast aside, rubbished by innuendo and rumour. A few nasty social media posts, salacious photos she claimed were AI generated. A smear job. You know how it goes. And she was moved out, along with her security minister, in the middle of the worst Covid news of the year. Death toll was rising, as was pressure from the doom-laden press. The government dumped loads of bad news in that period as the whole country was scared half to death. Then a quick reshuffle, and hey presto: Home Secretary one day, pariah the next. She resigned her seat and retired to the hills to lick her wounds. There were a few rumblings of spies and leaked documents and security breaches, all denied. The story ran out of steam. My hypothesis is that this was linked with our missing government property, which in turn was linked to your misper,' said Ted, who sat back heavily in his seat, puffed out his cheeks.

'How on earth could our lowlife be implicated? And surely the security services were all over this?' said a disbelieving Arthur.

'Bet your life they were. I'm betting they turned over every stone, nailed every suspected Russian or Chinese spy, did whatever those guys do. GCHQ would have been involved, tuned into the airwaves, as it were: electronic eavesdropping. Maybe there were multiple documents. Perhaps they thought they'd retrieved them all. Who knows? No one will ever know, I suspect.'

'And our Scott Banks?' prompted Arthur.

'Someone way up the chain... as close to God as... anyway, there's been a whisper channelled down to us that Scott inadvertently came across a stray, heavily redacted document. He probably had no idea what it was but smelt a value attached to it. We know he thieves and scavenges, and we suspect him of burglaries around that time,' said Ted.

'I struggle to buy that.'

'It's all I've been able to come up with. We have no choice other than to pursue this. Find him first. I'm guessing this last document is relatively benign, but it might hold the key for someone to piece this story together and nail the sequence of events. Perhaps an investigator, or...'

'Or an investigative journalist,' suggested Arthur.

Ted looked sharply at him and raised his eyebrows.

'Simon Banks,' said Arthur quietly.

'I didn't believe all this at first, but his son obviously thinks something's up, and I don't buy that he's showing latent familial love. Perhaps Simon Banks had sight of the document but couldn't lay his hands on it before his dad disappeared.'

'Or perhaps he used it to blackmail the perpetrator, the civil servant,' mused Arthur. 'Blackmail could even be a motive to do harm to Scott Banks.'

'Maybe, maybe not. I understand the civil servant was relatively junior and probably had no idea what he had. And, surprise, surprise – he's disappeared too. Emigrated, I'm told. Find Scott Banks, and find him soon. I doubt that his son gives a toss about his dad. But he can smell a big story. And he's stirred this up to see what happens. Shake the tree, see what falls out. Find your misper and don't give anyone else access to him until you have that piece of property.'

Arthur rubbed his brow and tried to press Ted for more details, but he had said as much as he was going to. As they shook hands, Arthur was reminded of the off-the-record status of their meeting.

'One last thing, Arthur... don't be tempted to play the moral crusader. Yes, this whole thing stinks, but it's bigger than either of us. It'll destroy us in the blink of an eye. Be warned. Just do your job.'

The small team gathered to review progress, to pool their knowledge.

'What do you think, Ruth? You've interviewed the key players around The Yorkshire Belle,' said Arthur as Tim Jenks tuned in.

'Frustrating. We never got to speak in any detail with Terence Sinclair before he died. Julian has been vague, perhaps deliberately obstructive. He still needs to account for his movements in October and November 2017. At least we now understand the altercation with Scott back in 1996 as the main cause of disharmony between Julian and Terence. As for the possible meeting between Scott and Terence, we can't verify this. Julian insists he wasn't there, as does Thomas. If a meeting even happened, that is.'

'Was Julian overseas in that November period?' Arthur asked.

'There's no record of him having flown or passed through customs, no.'

'Where was he?'

'He now says he was on the hills. He's a keen walker, but if he was on his own…' Ruth sighed.

'What about the other son? Luke?'

'His wife says he was working from home on his own business. That's plausible. What we do know from Thomas is that Terence and Scott had fallen out over the debt. Promises to pay some on account were not honoured.'

'What about the rest of the family?'

'We really are clutching at straws, guv. Nothing concrete to go on from this line of inquiry that I can see, however annoying and frustrating they all are. I spoke with both siblings, Luke and Emily. Luke was much more civilised than his brother but couldn't shed any light. Both Emily and Luke were preoccupied with their dad's demise and with family boardroom battles. Emily was outspoken about their troubles and emotional, all over the place.'

'What is it with this family?' bemoaned Arthur.

'Bottom line: the business is going down the pan, the family are at loggerheads, Julian wants to sell up—'

'And the rest don't?' interrupted Arthur.

'Terence didn't, and that's all that matters to Luke and Emily.'

'I've heard whispers that Julian's sold the pub behind their backs, though,' said Arthur.

'Does that matter to us, guv?'

'I don't know, but let's investigate The Yorkshire Belle link and meet with Julian again. Apply some pressure. Bring him in if necessary.'

'Oh – when I met Thomas, the finance director, about the debt, I asked him about a meeting with Scott at the pub. He insists he wasn't there, as I said earlier, but he does have a vague recollection of there being mention of a meeting between Terence and Scott in November 2017. He wondered if Julian or Luke might have been there, but simply didn't know and heard nothing about the meeting afterwards. It was only mentioned in passing when Thomas reviewed debts with Terence.'

'Do you believe him?' asked Arthur.

'Vague recollections, denials, incorrect recollections… who the hell knows?' said Ruth.

'Yes, Tim? Something to add?' Arthur.

'You asked me to look into Scott's mode of transport and I've checked with—'

'Cut to the chase.'

'He had a car, and I've unearthed a traffic report of Scott's car having run a red light.'

'Date?' Arthur.

'Sorry, didn't I say? 10th November 2017.'

'Time? Location?' asked Ruth.

'A64 on the outskirts of York at 11.10,' Tim confirmed.

'Which means he could have been headed to The Yorkshire Belle,' said Ruth.

'Good work, Poirot,' added Arthur.

'There's something else, guv: on that same day at around 10.30 there was a nasty crash on the A64 between a lorry and a car on a notorious accident black spot. The car burst into flames, trapping an old lady and her granddaughter. Traffic screeched to a halt, a guy ran to their aid, risked his life, got them out. Quite the local hero.'

'And this is important to us because…?' Ruth.

'It was our man. Scott Banks, no less.'

'Are you sure?' asked Arthur.

'He was reported as a mystery man who heroically rescued them and then left the scene. There were grainy photos in the press and an appeal for him to come forward. He never did. I tracked down footage on CCTV at the junction. The images aren't that clear but I'm eighty per cent sure it was Scott Banks. Look, I've got the footage here…'

'So, our lowlife's not only a loving, caring husband but now we find he's also a hero. Why did he not come forward to enjoy his moment in the spotlight?' said Ruth.

'Perhaps he needed to stay away from the public gaze?' Arthur.

'Or was dead?' Ruth.

'It puts a different complexion on our Scott Banks, doesn't it?' said Arthur. 'And his son's claim that our lot brought him in for alleged drugs offences is also true. Never charged.'

'So, maybe our heroic lowlife met with Terence at The Yorkshire Belle, a violent row ensued, and he was never seen again? Who was with Terence? He would not have faced him alone,' said Ruth.

'Set up the meeting with Julian at the pub, Ruth. But first I'd like us to search Scott's place,' Arthur said. 'I know we did so previously, but this time let's do it properly and get the sniffer dogs in too. Maybe he was a drug pusher. Might that have produced the cash that allowed him to pay for Penny's care? Perhaps along with whatever he stole from his employers? Another hypothesis for us to go on.'

NINETEEN

DECEMBER 2020

Cassandra was in a sombre, tearful mood. Her family had ostracised her at the funeral and she was surprised to find herself stricken by the loss of her dad. Only a cousin would talk to her. But for him she would not even have known of his death.

'What's their beef, Cass? You've mentioned things are difficult. Why?' Julian said to her over a quiet dinner in a corner of the hotel's small dining room.

'Not yet.' She sat back, her eyes clouded over, the pain acute. 'Soon, I promise. I've taken annual leave owed to me so I'm going to look up one or two friends – I don't have many, mind. And see more of you, I hope.'

'Music to my ears. But will you stay here?' Julian asked, looking around at the drab, run-down surroundings.

'I hoped you might be able to recommend somewhere. Perhaps somewhere close to you? It's a nightmare, navigating these Covid regulations… can you help?'

'Yes, of course I can. Why don't you stay in a cottage? Hotels and restaurants operate under such stringent conditions what with social distancing, table service, and all the rest of it.'

'I thought self-catering was just as problematic?'

'I know someone who owes me a favour. There's a cottage I think I can arrange near York, and I could stay there with you as well if you have no objection?'

'Simply perfect, Julian,' Cassandra said, and her veil of sadness lifted briefly to allow the semblance of a smile.

'It's close enough for me to dovetail between home and the cottage so I get to see Josh daily. Lotte won't like it, but I'm past caring. We're arranging the divorce. Mind you, Christmas may be a bit tricky as we've already agreed to have a truce for Josh's sake.'

'No problem. I won't come between you and…' Cassandra's voice tailed off.

Covid cases escalated even as the government insisted a family Christmas would still apply despite calls to lock down again. Joyous family reunions trumped the virus. Julian smiled wryly at the news. A jolly family Christmas seemed an impossibility. But they had to manufacture glad tidings, comfort, and joy for the sake of Josh, although at fifteen months old he would hardly appreciate the festive tree and all the other trimmings. Nonetheless, Annie, Nanny Barlow and even Lotte had made their minds up. And the marital ceasefire held. The unplanned meeting at The Broken Man had been key. Lotte had dropped all pretence of the absurd claim of Jonathan being her sibling. But she had insisted there was nothing serious in the relationship, just the bit of fun Julian denied her. *Fun*. But it hardly mattered how she rationalised it. What mattered was an end to all the rancour and disharmony.

On the business front, Thomas was working wonders despite limited room for manoeuvre, and he now estimated a stay of execution into February. It gave them ample time to prepare the pre-pack administration arrangements. As to the farm, Henry had once again worked his little black book of contacts and come up trumps when Elgin Corporation expressed firm interest.

'We need to treat them with respect, my friend. No clever argy-bargy. These are in the Premier League,' Henry said. He chortled as he uttered the words, but his eyes implored Julian.

'When will they take a look?'

'I've briefed them, and they've already looked at the business. They've also pulled the map and data together and know all about The Yorkshire Belle, and the land our friends at Optimum own. I'm sure the chance to pull one over on them has its appeal. But we must assume they know of the problems you face at Belle Hospitality. They'll weigh up the pros and cons and timings. They could yet decide to wait until the firm goes up the swanny. I've given them your number and you should expect a call. In the meantime, just sit tight.'

'If they do want to go for a quick deal, how soon could they do it? I need it done and dusted by the end of January at the latest.'

'Who knows? My guess is they could if they wanted to badly enough, but they won't be bullied.'

'Understood, Henry.'

'And a quick deal would come at a price.'

'All understood. Listen, I must dash – another call's coming in.'

Glancing at his mobile, Julian was surprised: Faye Dunbarton. How interesting. He took a deep breath and answered in a flat voice. Emotions firmly in check, hope and optimism kept at bay, even as his heart beat a little faster.

'Julian.'

'Faye.'

'I wondered if we might meet?'

'Always happy to talk.'

'I might be able to resurrect your deal if you want me to…'

'I see.'

'But it would be on Optimum's terms rather than yours… I did try to warn you.'

'Let's meet.'

Henry joined him as they sat opposite an immaculately groomed Faye. Julian had to admire her style, her strength of character, her negotiating skills; a tough woman to deal with. Sat around the coffee table in his lounge, Henry and Faye chatted amiably while Annie brought a tray of tea.

'I'm sorry the deal collapsed, Julian. I did warn you—'

'You said.' Julian played with his wedding-ring finger, almost surprised by the ring's absence. Henry's words came to mind (*Don't scare the horses*), so he sat impassively.

'We've done most of the paperwork, so could complete quickly.'

Julian raised an eyebrow, waited for her to say more.

'Optimum will agree to your two-stage arrangement – gracious of them, I suggest,' she said, looking first at Julian, then at Henry.

'And the price?' prompted Henry.

'We don't mean to be insensitive, but we understand the business context and, shall we say, the likely next steps in respect of Belle Hospitality and The Yorkshire Belle. These are hard times, and we feel for you. But…' Faye paused to sip her tea.

'Your sentiments are, I'm sure, generously intended. What's the deal you propose?' said Henry.

'Neither the pub nor the farm has planning permission for residential development. So, we can only offer the value of the properties given their currently defined use. £2 million tops.'

'I see very clearly what you mean,' said Julian, 'and any such offer would be met with a swift rebuttal, with respect.' He spoke in hushed tones.

'Let me speak candidly, Faye,' said Henry. 'We screwed up the previous negotiations, underestimated your client, overplayed our hand.'

'Your words, not mine,' she said with a half-smile.

'Don't make the same mistake. Optimum's land has planning permission subject to more adequate access. Please don't deny it. This dramatically limits the value of your land, but if you were to acquire the farm and the pub, then, hey presto! Formal planning permission for our land will be forthcoming. The local authority has designated this whole area as residential property development subject to availability – a very recent adjustment to the strategic plan, and one you will be fully aware of. There are also primary and secondary schools within thirty minutes and GP services close by. And I've met with the chair of the planning committee and know he's keen to see this land developed to meet urgent local housing needs. I would be surprised if any of these facts had escaped your client's attention. Now please, let's not mess about. Do you want a deal or not?'

Faye listened patiently and smiled at Henry. 'There's no planning permission granted as we speak. Fact. Will it be forthcoming? We can't be certain. There can be no doubting this impacts the market price. But let me speak with my client. Is there somewhere I can do this in private?'

Julian showed her into the dining room and left her for a while. Within ten minutes she rejoined them in the study.

'I am authorised to offer you £7 million.'

'Your previous offer was twelve; unacceptable then, unacceptable now,' said Julian.

'Okay – I'll report back your response if you're quite sure?'

'Two more things you might like to reflect on: Belle Hospitality will not hit the buffers; it will never be snapped up for next to nothing. Other arrangements are in hand. Additionally, we are in touch with another party who has indicated firm interest,' Julian said.

'Really?'

'Yes, really. You reminded me not to overplay my hand; sound advice,' Julian said, looking at her pointedly. He was raising the temperature, but it was now or never.

'Actually, it was Henry, not me. It's not my style to be aggressive, to criticise or to demean those I negotiate with, Julian. You might like to take a leaf out of my book as you acquire a little more experience.' She stared stonily at him, gathered her things, and said he would hear from her one way or another later today.

'Just one final fact for you, Faye,' Julian said as she reached the door.

Faye turned and raised a pencilled eyebrow.

'My bottom line is £10 million.'

'We'll speak later,' Faye said in a whisper through thin lips, then left.

'What do you think, Henry? You were pushy. I thought the game plan was to be understated.'

'I wanted to play the bad cop. They've given us the runaround, but I sense the tables have turned, my friend. You played it well. Mind you, the price ultimatum was ballsy. You do realise you have nowhere else to go if they still play hard to get?' Henry said. 'But there's been another development. I've just received a text to indicate the price Elgin are prepared to offer: £6 million. I'm sure we can get them up towards your bottom line. But can we get them to do the deal in time?'

Cassandra telephoned Julian frequently. She was bored and felt isolated, neglected. But today she was in her element as Julian introduced her to the Yorkshire Dales, their day starting early as they donned extra layers, pulled on waterproofs, beanies, and hiking boots in the car park in Horton in Ribblesdale. It was still dark, the blustery wind howling, and stinging rain slanted into them as they began their gentle ascent towards the snow-dusted peak. Pen-Y-Ghent would certainly live up to its billing: the hill of the winds. It was the smallest of the Three Peaks at less than seven hundred metres, but Julian thought it the prettiest: the starting point for the Yorkshire Three Peaks Challenge also taking in Whernside and Ingleborough. The plan today was to do the first two and then find a pub fire to settle by. After about an hour and a half they reached the summit in flurries of snow and a biting, penetrative wind. They did not linger, not even against the walled shelter. The obligatory selfie at the trig point was taken, then they stepped through a gate stile to begin their descent. Their progress was much quicker on this fast section as they tracked on good paths over the boggy moors, eventually sighting the Ribblehead Viaduct in the distance. Picking their spot carefully, they found shelter to one side of the viaduct to fuel up on coffee, chocolate snacks, and pork pie. As they did so the clouds parted, and weak sunshine strobed through the arches to illuminate the path ahead.

'I thought you planned to move in with me in the cottage, Julian?'

'Yes.'

'Well?'

'I've been a bit preoccupied with Belle Hospitality, to be honest. We're at a crisis point. Things have been difficult.'

Cassandra looked askance at him, and he felt guilty. He promised her he would make the move next week. She shrugged and he changed the subject.

'Happy to press on, Cass, or head back to Horton?' They had left Cassandra's hire car at the viaduct so they could be warm and snug beside a log fire within fifteen minutes.

'Abort now? And race back to my desolate cottage?'

'Okay, message received.'

They pulled the packs back on and made the summit of Whernside about seven hours after they had set out. It was a good pace given the conditions, and on track to meet the Three Peaks Challenge. A challenge for another day. Standing at the cloud-shrouded summit, they peered through the gloom and saw nothing. Looking at each other, they shrugged, did a high five, took their selfie, and retraced their steps to eventually reach their car an hour or so later. The pub and the log fire beckoned.

'How are things with Lotte?'

'Not easy, but then… let's just say we're agreed on the destination but we've yet to negotiate the route. No change, really, as we prepare for the Christmas festivities. It all seems a bit false but it's what we agreed to do, and Nanny Barlow and Annie are happy to do most of the work. I can't bear the thought of what's to come: forced bonhomie with Bing Crosby, mince pies and sherries as we sit around the Christmas tree. It all seems a bit twee. And in the meantime, whenever Emily and Luke join us, you could cut the tension-filled atmosphere with a knife. Of course, Josh just seems to accept it all, but I worry he's mired in the undercurrent of unhappiness and bile. What about you? Miss your dad? Will you try and patch things up with your family?'

'No. My family ties were severed a long time ago, but my dad's death came as a shock to the system. It awakened old demons. At least the rest of the family were true to form – as cold as ice.'

'How sad.'

'I deserve it, really. As I said to you once before, family can be difficult or easy. I choose to make it easy, reconciled to the irreparable breakdown. The funeral was a blip. I'd forgotten my status with them – a mistake I won't repeat.'

She rubbed her brow and her eyes moistened; she excused herself and headed to the toilets. He resolved to change the subject, lighten the tone when she returned. But she spoke urgently as she plopped back down beside him.

'I've given you a hard time over your past situation. Now I need to share my disgrace with you… you need to know.' She paused and turned to him, grasped his hand tightly.

'Only if you want to,' Julian said, his eyebrows meeting in consternation. He had not seen her so intense, so emotional.

'I was an unruly teenager, easily led. I fell in with the wrong crowd, attracted the wrong sort of boys. I was intrigued with all the usual teenage preoccupations: drink, boys, sex, soft drugs. It was just an awful day, a day I'll never forget. Scarred me forever. You can't see emotional scars, but they hurt more – so much more.'

'Cass, you really don't have to do this.'

'I was a naive fifteen-year-old when I met Toby in the woods close to where we lived. He was the catch all my friends dreamt of. God knows why. He was just another pimply youth really, but we thought he was cool in his designer jeans, strumming a guitar and warbling dreamily like some wannabe Bob Dylan. He was a couple of years older than us and strutted around the youth club; gained a bit of a reputation with the girls. Now I come to think of it, he was more like a predator who circled his prey, bided his time. Like killer whales driving their targets onto a small ice floe from where they were to be mesmerised and eventually taken. But he was hot – or so we thought. Then he made a play for me, and my friends got all giggly, dared me to hang out with him. All the girlish speculation, the imagination and hormones running riot as we envisaged my virginity surrendered to this contemporary Adonis. And the local woods seemed the perfect venue with its dense undergrowth, mossy glades, filtered sunlight. The afternoon sun shone, and we walked hand in hand, happily pulling on cigarettes, and chatted inanely, nervously. His guitar was slung over his shoulder, and I carried a rucksack with the beers and fags, and other stuff. I'd taken a few swigs of my mum's vodka before I ventured out – Dutch courage. Today was to be the day, my friends had suggested. I was up for it too. After all, I was fifteen and virtually an adult. So I thought. Why wait longer? There was just one problem. A big problem. Faith, my younger sister, tagged along. She was twelve and a sweet thing – but a pain in the neck to a teenage girl on an assignation. I couldn't believe my luck. I didn't want her along and she didn't want to be there either. But my mum was insistent: someone had to look after Faith while she worked. She whinged and moaned endlessly until Toby told her to get lost. "Stay close," I shouted after her as we settled into the mossy glade with sunshine streaming through the silver birch trees. Toby popped a few pills and pulled on his beer. I turned down the pills but accepted the can of lager. We swigged and chatted and giggled. He made me laugh, and then it became more serious: he was suddenly pawing me, hands all over. Just two teenagers exploring each other's bodies under the influence of alcohol. At first, anyway. Nothing out of the ordinary, nothing I hadn't anticipated. Eagerly anticipated. What a story I would have to tell as I felt him press against me and experienced his probing fingers. But then he began to force the issue: he was flushed, beads of sweat appeared on his brow, and the situation got out of control. He yanked at my clothes, prepared himself for… I had been up for it, then suddenly I wasn't. "Please stop." He laughed and continued and held me down roughly. I struggled and shouted angrily: "Stop, please stop." I was overcome by a wave of panic. He was too strong for me, ignored my ever more frantic cries. Then he slapped me. Hard. I screamed. He pushed his handkerchief in my mouth. Tears streamed. I gave up the struggle, accepted my fate. This wasn't how it was supposed to be. Where was the romance, the joy of two young bodies in harmony? He knew I was upset; surely he'd take pity on me, wouldn't want to hurt me. He would back off. Surely. But no – the struggle hadn't doused his desire, far from it. I watched in horror as he unzipped and released his boyhood. He ripped my pants off me. Wide-eyed, I fought to control my terror. I went rigid with fear and steeled myself for the inevitable, wondering if it would hurt, until the scene changed abruptly. He howled in pain and tumbled off me, involuntarily rolled away. I looked up and was astounded to see Faith wielding some sort of club. A fallen branch, I guess. She had struck him as hard as she could, but she was just a frail twelve-year-old, and as we both gawped at the scene Toby was gathering himself, roared his anger. He ran at Faith, but she was off – hared away with Toby in pursuit. I screamed after him to leave her alone…' Cassandra wept at the memory but insisted she continue. 'I must. I must tell you now…'

'Did your sister get away?'

'By the time I'd sorted myself out they'd both disappeared. Those woods go on for miles. I just wanted to go home, hit the shower, and curl up in bed. Pretend this nightmare hadn't happened. But I couldn't leave her, so I ploughed on. I eventually heard faint cries and obscenities flung at my little sister. Toby had trapped her in a dark corner with huge, brooding beech trees all around – nettles and brambles blocked her escape route. I heard him scream at her: "I know what you need, you little bitch…" What could I do? He was stronger than me, I was an emotional mess, and he was full of rage, totally out of control. But I had to do something. He didn't know I was there, so I used surprise as a weapon. And a mossy rock. He didn't hear me as he was so entranced, so fixated on Faith, and his legs collapsed under him as the rock struck home. We both ran for it. But… but…'

Cassandra broke down again, the recollections too heavy a burden. Julian pulled her into an embrace and stroked her hair, shushed her like a baby until she broke away. Her words tumbled out of her mouth as tears streamed.

'We lost each other. I wasn't thinking straight. It was a complete nightmare. I searched and searched but there was no sign of her. I came across a dog walker at one stage, and he looked agog at me. He couldn't make much sense of what I was saying, and he stared at my torn clothes, my cuts and scrapes. But he eventually got out of me where I lived, and as dusk beckoned, he escorted me home.'

'And Faith?'

'No sign of her.' She blew heavily into a paper handkerchief.

Julian drew her towards him in an embrace, but again she pulled away. 'Oh my God. Your parents would have been beside themselves.'

'Yeah. They shouted, they cried, they called the police. Search parties went out, and I stayed at home with my mum and a kindly policewoman. It was awful. The longest night of my life.'

'What did your mum have to say about Toby? You did tell her?'

'Of course not. How could I? I felt ashamed, stupid, guilty.'

'But he abused you, tried to rape you, Cass.'

'How could I tell my parents? And Toby would have told a different story. You can just picture it. Anyway, my head was all over the place. I couldn't think, could hardly breathe. I just wanted the nightmare to end, the day to be erased from memory. Ha! Fat chance. It'll live with me forever.'

'Did they find Faith?' Julian gripped her hand tight. She was totally oblivious to a pair of hikers who cast anxious glances in their direction.

Cassandra broke away as tears flowed freely. After a few minutes she composed herself. 'Faith was found at the bottom of the quarry.'

'No, surely not…'

'She'd broken her neck.'

'She wasn't…'

'I'm sorry, Julian. Whatever will you think of me, of my behaviour, the root cause of my sister's horribly untimely, awful demise? I should have told you earlier. I've never told anyone else. I can't forgive myself. I don't want forgiveness. I don't deserve forgiveness.'

'What an appalling experience for you and your poor sister. And your mum and dad. It's just too tragic for words. I don't know what to say.'

'No.' Cassandra pulled out her silver locket and held it reverentially, slowly opening it to reveal a lock of fine fair hair.

'Is—'

'Yeah. I'm never separated from it. The only intimate reminder of my lost sister.'

Julian stepped through a sparsely populated, festively dressed York city centre. All lights and Christmas trees; shop windows displayed their wares: tinsel-clad mannequins wore party dresses, and Christmas jumpers were displayed amongst the reindeer and Santas. Christmas messages of joy sat alongside reminders of social distancing: two only allowed in small shops at any one time; masks mandatory; antibacterial gel to rub on chapped hands. But many shops had closed, and the Christmas market had been cancelled. Piped carols provided a poor substitute for the normal hustle and bustle, brass bands and carollers. And news on the Covid front seemed to be worsening as infections rose. Christmas was under threat despite denials by government as the scientists, the opposition and the media went into overdrive.

He reached his destination and pushed through the swing doors into an anodyne office: all glass, oak veneer, prints of local landmarks, grey carpets, grey walls – a familiar, ubiquitous style found in city office blocks the world over. He awaited Giles, who had a small unit, neighbour to lawyers and accountants, marketeers, PR consultants. He was shown into Giles's office. He was a young man of similar age to Julian with a distinctive style of dress of a previous era: shiny brown brogues, a loud brown check suit with a navy-blue waistcoat harbouring a gold fob watch with a gold chain attached. To top off the ensemble he wore a cravat at the neck. They made to shake hands and then withdrew. They settled for an elbow bump and exchanged a grimace. It still seemed a poor substitute for the traditional business greeting. They sat at opposite ends of the table. Giles told him the room was well ventilated, and took a splash of hand sanitiser.

'Very corporate,' said Julian.

'I suppose you expected a shambolic private eye of dubious character: downtrodden and unkempt, cobwebs and dusty files, empty whisky bottles?'

'I suppose so.'

'Most of my clients are from the professional classes to be found in offices like these. People who have run into domestic turbulence, or need to find someone, or are being blackmailed, or have been caught with their pants down, or—'

'I get it.'

'Happy to get down to it?'

'Always.'

'Okay, well, we have a few suspects, and you need to decide

whether to press on or not. You may find this uncomfortable. A sad business, Julian.'

'So, the rogues' gallery?'

'How sure are you?'

'Very. I have a letter from the lab, which proves that I'm not the biological dad.' Julian handed him a copy of the official letter.

'I see. And from my investigations, we can write off some of the names you gave me. Let's start with those we can rule out: Jonathan and Jeremy for sure.'

'Explain.'

'Both have been lovers. Jonathan had a recent fling but that's run its course. He wasn't on the scene at the critical time. Impossible for him to be the dad.'

'How do you know even this?'

'Let's just say we've used certain house technical skills…'

'You've hacked my wife's digital accounts?'

'You asked me to use whatever means I had at my disposal, and as we are onto this late in the day, we can't dispatch photographers to catch them indisposed – in flagrante, as it were. So, we accessed historical records. None of this would be admissible in a court of law, I should add. But you said—'

'The legal authorities won't be involved. I just want irrefutable proof.'

'Okay. They could subsequently sue you, of course, but it seems an unlikely turn of events. Nonetheless, you need to consider this possibility.'

'We press on.'

'I thought so. Jonathan and Lotte fell out after you recently found them together. Jeremy's still on the scene, but from their exchanges it's a relationship on the wane. You can rule both out.'

'Do we have *any* suspects? They were my best guesses. Don't tell me you've got nothing.'

'I've got two names for you. This may be something of a shock. Let me start with Neville.'

'Not Neville Jackson?'

'One of your pub managers, I believe. They met at a Christmas party, and it developed from there. And Lotte was not his only conquest during this period. I'm pretty sure some of the photos we unearthed weren't of your wife. Quite explicit, too. A Lothario, it would seem, our Neville, with a penchant for erotica.'

'The dates work?'

'Yes, and their affair lasted about six months when Lotte realised that she was pregnant – he soon lost interest.'

'Did he think it might be his?'

'Lotte assured him it wasn't. How she could be so sure, who knows? Maybe he believed her, maybe he didn't, but either way her message evidently suited him.'

'What a bastard! He still works for me as well.'

'Now for the other suspect. Brace yourself, Julian.'

Giles showed him the chain of emails. There remained little doubt. Julian was ashen with shock. Then he was shown the email exchanges incriminating both men. Clearly Lotte had had sex with both at about the time she conceived. Neville was the more likely of the two as their relationship had endured, spanned the time of conception, whereas the other suspect's affair was brief.

'You need to decide where we go from here,' Giles pointed out.

'Let's get incontrovertible, copper-bottomed evidence.'

'I need to remind you it's illegal to obtain human material without consent, and it's obviously inadmissible in a court of law. I can't advise you to petition the court for the right to compel a paternity test be taken by either party, either. Such a petition would stand no chance of success, and of course you would have alerted Lotte. If you choose to obtain DNA samples of either or both suspects I can't have anything to do with the paperwork. I can't be implicated. In fact, I'm duty-bound to advise you not to pursue this course of action,' said Giles.

'Consider your duty done. All understood. Point me in the right direction and I'll get on with it. I'd obviously be grateful for any help in collecting the actual sample. Unofficially, of course,' Julian said.

'I can't, I won't, but I know a man who will. For the right price.' Giles handed him a slip of paper with a telephone number on it.

Cassandra was stony-faced, brusque in her welcome, and he almost tripped over a suitcase by the front door. He followed her into the lounge, spotted her coat and hat on the back of the sofa.

'Going somewhere?' Julian asked.

'Home.' Her manner was curt, her body language tense. 'I thought I could do this, but I can't. And God knows how many Covid regulations I've contravened. These past few days I've not had much to do other than read the papers and watch the news. Your Boris is going to snatch Christmas away, ban travel and the whole hullaballoo any day now. Then where would I be? Trapped on my own while you play happy families.'

'He's certainly not my Boris, by the way. But I thought you were okay with the arrangements? I'll spend as much time with you as I can. Look, I'm sorry about the last week but I've had a few crises to cope with, as I told you.'

'I'm not sure you did. Last time we spent any quality time together was in the pub in the Dales when I bared my soul. I'd never told anyone that before. And what response have I had from you? Nothing. I didn't need sympathy, but I hoped for understanding. I expected you to spend some of your precious time with me. You could have just… just been there for me. But none of this is the point.'

'So, what is?'

'I want to be home in my chalet. I know where I am there. I've seen my dad buried, endured my family's spiteful vitriol, and hung around waiting for you to show up. You said you wanted to spend more time with me, but you ignore me. I feel neglected. A trophy you've won, one you can leave on the shelf to gather dust.'

'Are you sure you're being entirely fair?'

'It's accurate. And yes, I do think it's fair. More than fair. I just feel as if I'm in the way. I'm not happy. I want to go home. You have a dual life: two jobs, two homes, two women.'

'Ouch!'

'Sounds like my taxi.' She threw on her coat and stuffed her beanie in a pocket.

'I love you, Cass.'

'So you say.'

'When I've got this all sorted, I will ask you to marry me, spend your life with me.'

'Words, Julian, words. When your circumstances change…' She reached up to him and pecked his cheek. 'The keys are on the table. Lock up after me.'

He watched her trudge out to the waiting taxi, the driver relieving her of the suitcase. Cassandra opened the rear door and paused, one foot planted on the pavement, the other reached into the car. She looked back at a shell-shocked Julian.

'I'll be in touch, Cass.'

'Merry Christmas, Julian.'

TWENTY

JANUARY 2021

Christmas was as uncomfortable as Julian had imagined, but despite occasional domestic turbulence the ceasefire with Lotte just about held. When Josh was not around the two retreated to their preferred comfort zones: Julian to the study for business, rock music and malt whisky; refuge in a bottle of wine for Lotte, sometimes in her own morose company, sometimes with Emily. One family gathering ended in bitter recrimination when Emily and Luke demanded to see Julian in his study. The peace apparently did not extend to them, and Julian's office was regarded as neutral territory where they could vent their spleens.

'What news?' Luke demanded.

'It's Christmas.'

'Oh, for crying out loud,' Emily said.

Julian sighed.

'Are you going along with this pre-pack nonsense?' asked Emily.

'I'd rather not, but we will probably have no option.'

'So, you leave your family high and dry, cut a deal with the devil…'

'As I said, I'd rather not.'

'What are you really up to, Julian?' said Luke.

'I'm trying my hardest to have a peaceful Christmas for the sake of Josh; work things out with Lotte. And trying not to fall out with my siblings.'

'Failure on all fronts, then,' exploded Emily. 'Belle Hospitality goes bust because of your leadership; you screw around in France; your marriage is up the swanny; you screw your family and line your own pockets.'

'Feel better, Emily?'

'Oh, you're impossible. Bastard.' She stormed out. The door slammed behind her.

Luke sat impassively. He picked up a pencil from the desk and tapped it against his teeth.

Julian sipped his whisky and watched his brother. 'Care for one?' Julian held his glass aloft.

'Why not?'

'Cheers,' said Julian.

'Yeah, cheers. By the way…'

'Yes?'

'I ran into the farmer the other day. Bernard.'

'Oh, yes?'

'I popped into The Belle. A nostalgic visit. Quite sad. The place is like a ghost town, horribly run-down, so outdated. It's a bit like stepping back into history.'

'Yes. I have—'

'I know, I know. But I bumped into Bernard as I locked up. He's moving out – lock, stock, and barrel. Said you knew all about it.'

'Really?'

'I've worked it out, Julian. Are you going to confess? Let me in on the deal?'

'What deal?'

Luke glared at Julian, snapped the pencil in two, stood, swallowed his whisky in one gulp. As he opened the door he paused and turned around. 'Be careful, brother. Be very careful. Emily's judgement about you is soundly based. Merry Christmas.'

Julian's mobile pinged: Cassandra. The message was brief.

We should talk.

Julian sighed. He probably needed to eat more humble pie. Her bitter reproach and rapid exit back to France were warranted. How he yearned for progress on one front or another. He penned a brief but more upbeat response.

Great to hear from you. Miss you more than I can say. Hope for progress on the various issues soon. New Year, new hope, renewed purpose.
    Will arrange a Zoom.
    Love you.
    J x

He sent the message, then reread it and cringed at the stilted language. It was hardly a love letter to set the pulse racing. Why was he so awful at all this? Why could he not express his feelings?

He was shaken out of his reverie by a loud, intrusive knock at the door. Thomas.

'I need to speak with you,' he said with no preamble.

Julian stepped aside as his animated FD crossed the threshold. 'Happy New Year, Thomas.' Julian threw him a look of bemusement. His FD and friend crackled with tension.

'We need to talk.'

'Should you be here? New rules, aren't there?'

'God knows. Who can fathom them or make sense of the logic? Besides, some things are too important.'

'As determined by you, presumably.'

'I've spoken with your siblings and Lotte. A few things we need to straighten out. The thing is—'

'Yes, do enlighten me.'

'Have you lost the plot, my friend? Do you not realise just how—'

'I'm perfectly clear on the stakes, on the dire nature of our circumstances, as you well know. I very much doubt there's anything new you can tell me on those topics. Look, I don't want to prolong this, so let me summarise for you – bear with me… *No*, Thomas, you've invaded my house, my privacy, and you'll do me the courtesy of hearing me out. On the business front, Belle Hospitality alighted on a strategy SI invested in. Then the company under my dad's leadership reneges on the deal. He asks me to become CEO and yet ties one hand behind my back.'

'That's a bit strong.'

'Really? I don't recall you ever saying. Then our underinvested, poorly led company hits the buffers you so presciently anticipated. Next my dad and siblings refuse to take a good offer for The Yorkshire Belle seriously. Now we've reached the destination we repeatedly warned of despite our best efforts. And I'm castigated by the directors – siblings and wife – who refused all wise counsel. How am I doing? Anything you care to disagree with?'

'I worry most about what you're doing now.'

'Really?'

'By your own admission, relationships on the board are in tatters, your wife is at her wits' end, and even your mistress is—'

'My wife and, as you put it, mistress, are off limits, Thomas.'

'We're mates, and sometimes mates must… you know. You've already offended the entire family by your devastating commentary on your own dad's regime. Your siblings have lost it with you. I can't just stand aside as your marriage tears apart and even Cassandra skulks back to France, having lost patience with you. What are you playing at?'

'Cassandra has never skulked in her life, and it's got nothing to do with you. What gives you the right to get on your moral high horse, dear *friend*? You should take stock of your own standards before you lecture others. Proud of your own behaviour? Have you never strayed in thought or deed? Look to yourself before you cast aspersions on others.'

'Julian, what're you talking about? I didn't come here to lecture you. I come as a friend who's concerned for your mental well-being. I'm also worried about an important technical aspect of these deals.'

'Then calm down, leave me to worry about my own mental health, quit the hectoring, stop moralising, and explain.'

Julian stared intently at Thomas, who seemed to wither under the spotlight; he fidgeted uncomfortably and ruffled his hair. His eyes shifted, showed uncertainty. Would he continue to pursue the personal line of argument or head down a business track? He chose wisely.

'Luke's worked out what you're up to. Close to it, anyway. He's not daft, you know. He quizzed me about your farmer. I reckon he suspects you've bought him up. Then it's a short leap to tie in The Belle, and I'm sure he's spoken to one or two of his own contacts in the local authority. He'll rumble you soon, Julian.'

'There's nothing to rumble, is there? There's no deal for the pub.'

'Not yet, but you are duty-bound to take the board into your confidence. At least tell them what you propose. Why don't we call a meeting, come clean, give them hope?'

'No. There's no reason for hope currently. If there's any change, I'll reconsider.'

'Which brings me to the nub of my concern. Should your deal come off and you sell both the farm and the pub you will be acting *illegally*. You don't have the authority to sell without the board's authority and it's questionable you have the right to even enter talks. Come clean, let me call a board meeting. What do you say?'

Thomas's words stung. Julian sat back and looked blankly at him, then stared out of the window at his gardener, who chugged by on the tractor mower. What did he find to do in the grounds at this time of year? Julian was especially needled by Thomas's comments about Cassandra, whose words leapt back at him: *I feel neglected. A trophy you've won… left on the shelf to gather dust.* Why had he neglected her? As for his siblings, he had never wanted relationships to sour, but they had deserted him in his hour of need, had acted against the best interests of the company in pursuit of blind loyalty to their dead dad. He hoped relationships might repair one day, but should he make the steps Thomas demanded? There would be short-lived relief at the prospect of a deal. A sale would be quite a coup, but the odds were stacked against it. Mm. He shook his head sadly, wistfully. He tapped his fingers on his desk, decluttered his mind, and made his decision. His eyes locked back on Thomas's.

'No.'

'Then you will be in contravention of the Companies Act 2006, sections 175 and 177.'

As the end of January loomed, Julian was dispirited. Faye's offer on behalf of Optimum of £7 million had lapsed and the promised call back had not materialised. Elgin had offered £6 million but had still not responded to Julian's demand for £10 million. They had gone quiet on him. Henry counselled patience. He had played his shot and awaited the return. It seemed likely they would wait until Belle Hospitality hit the buffers. And as each day dragged on, the interminable gloom of enforced lockdown, Covid deaths, pessimistic Covid modelling, property deal inactivity, and his business woes took their toll.

Matters weren't much better in France either, with similar Covid restrictions in force. Hotel L'Angleterre was closed, Cassandra seemed further away than ever. Relations between them were cool, although they managed the occasional Zoom call when she could make it through the snow to the hotel. Julian was troubled. He yearned for her, but when she had been close, he had not put in much of an effort. Why? Yes, he was busy. Yes, he was under pressure on numerous fronts. But while her words of censure seemed harsh, they rang true. He could have done the simple things they so enjoyed when together in France: share dinner, enjoy a drink together, savour each other's company. Make love. The consummation of their love had reached an intensity of emotion and pleasure and warmth he had never experienced with anyone else. His love was the real article, the real deal. He did not want to deny it. Why did he not opt to see her most evenings? Sometimes he just did not understand himself.

Being locked up with Lotte was also a strain. The two of them chose to steer clear of each other as much as possible, eating, drinking, sleeping apart. When their paths did cross Lotte could not resist the temptation to lob the odd hand grenade into the battlefield of their marriage – more than the odd barb or sarcastic comment of old. Her comments were laced with bitterness and settled over him like a cloud of mustard gas enveloping the front-line troops: suffocating, sickness-inducing. Their divorce proceedings made little progress. They failed to grip the key issues: custody of Josh, access for Julian, terms of the divorce, sale of the house, timescales. Whenever Julian tried to move this forward, it provoked a barrage of flak so he would back off: a tactical withdrawal. However, he knew he had to navigate this perilous path at some stage, tiptoe through the minefield. So, he donned his emotional body armour, braved a bombardment of incendiaries, dodged Lotte's heavy guns. After an evening of bloody skirmishes, they eventually agreed to arrange a meeting with their solicitors. They opted for separate lawyers despite wishing to do this as a straightforward divorce settlement. All they needed to do was file an uncontested joint petition, but this seemed beyond them as they searched for a landing zone.

Julian logged into his email one evening and his torpor soon lifted. His adrenaline began to surge at the sight of an email from Elgin: a firm offer of £6 million for the farm plus £2 million for the pub. And they agreed the deal construct demanded, with completion by the end of February. Julian reached for the whisky as the tension in his body eased. Then he read the email again. Just to make sure. His mobile suddenly rang to interrupt his thought processes. Henry.

'Have you seen it?' Henry sounded excited.

'Encouraging,' said Julian. A smile spread across his face.

'You don't effervesce, do you? It's bloody marvellous. You know, Julian, I was beginning to despair on your behalf. But this changes everything. Game on.'

'It's still below the threshold, still work to do, Henry. Have you heard from Optimum?'

'You're a hard man to please. Let's cut to the chase, accept the offer, race to the finishing line, and be done with it? In the circumstances…'

'We initially had the farm valued at just shy of £10 million and the pub at around two. So, £12 million was the bottom-line price; our target was north of fifteen. Given our circumstances we dropped the threshold to £10 million, so Elgin's offer is still short.'

'You want to play hardball again, do you, my friend? After last time?'

'Let's just play it canny. I suggest you thank Elgin for their offer, and if they revise it up to £10 million, they have a deal. Meantime, we tell Faye we expect to reach agreement with another bidder by the end of this week.'

'You think Optimum will still come good?'

'Let's give them the opportunity. They could do it quicker than Elgin and they should want it more, given their situation. I can't believe they'll risk it going elsewhere.'

'They could sell their land to Elgin, couldn't they?'

'Unlikely. They'd get fleeced by the bigger player.'

Julian found the Zoom icon and within a few minutes was speaking with Cassandra. They discussed her sudden departure from the cottage in the UK, and Julian apologised for being inattentive. Cassandra acknowledged she had been on edge and spoken harshly. They agreed to put the incident behind them – a huge relief to Julian and, he sensed, to Cassandra too.

'What news from your end, Cass? How do you spend your time given the restrictions, the hotel closure? Are you not a bit lonely?'

'I've always been okay in my own company. When I'm here, anyway.'

Julian winced.

'I volunteered to join the skeleton crew at the hotel two or three days a week to keep the place clean and catch up on backlog admin work. It's a bit mundane but it provides a focus.

Plus, all the usual stuff, really: crafting, reading, and walking when the weather permits. And you?'

'At last, I can report progress. Belle Hospitality can limp on to the end of February, Lotte and I have agreed a process for the divorce, we've got a meeting with lawyers scheduled for next week, and the property deal is back on. I'm hopeful on all fronts.'

'Good to hear. Perhaps one day you'll tell me about the property deals.'

'I thought I had.'

'Not in any detail.'

'I'm dying to see you, but Boris has us all locked down. Travel for business purposes is still possible but it's hard to convince anyone while Hotel L'Angleterre is closed. I can't see a trip being possible for a couple of months.'

'No.'

'Sorry,' Julian added.

'We both have some thinking to do. How are you going to balance the two businesses and a life with me? Where do we live? Access to Josh will be key, but I don't fancy life in the UK. Not yet.'

'Lots to think about,' Julian agreed.

'Listen, I need to go but… I need to say this… especially given our pre-Christmas experience. I'm simply not prepared to contemplate being a part-time partner. Nor am I prepared to continue as we are with a long-distance relationship. You opt in or out. Once your agendas have…'

'Okay. I understand. Let's both think on, Cass.'

'In or out, Julian. No hokey-cokey dance routine.'

TWENTY-ONE

JANUARY 2021

Julian arrived at The Yorkshire Belle early, opened up, and meandered through the neglected pub. As he picked his way through the detritus of abandoned lounges and bars and kitchen areas, he wondered why the police were so insistent on meeting with him yet again. They were a recurring irritant. And why meet at The Belle? Although in a way it was an almost welcome distraction from sale negotiations, business crises. At least the New Year had brought a glimmer of hope, and there was always the fallback position of a pre-pack.

A hammering on the door signalled their arrival – both DI Hemming and DS Dodds.

'Thanks for agreeing to meet us here,' said Arthur.

'I'm intrigued. Why at The Yorkshire Belle? And why yet another meeting?'

Ruth glanced at her DI and received a barely perceptible nod of assent. 'We've checked your whereabouts and travel arrangements – customs, airports, ferry ports – and we're satisfied with your answers. The latest version, at any rate. But we need to ask you about your meeting with Scott Morrison in September 2017.'

'What meeting?'

'You deny there was one?' said Ruth.

'Or do you imply several?' said Arthur, who stood to one side, studied Julian carefully.

'I saw him,' Julian confirmed.

'You're testing even my patience, sir. We have asked repeatedly about your whereabouts, about your association with Scott, about anything you know of our misper. You've lied to us and failed to tell us of your meeting with this man on around 10th September. Now we can continue this conversation back at the station if you wish…' Arthur's quiet voice had a hard edge.

'Look, if you'd let me explain.'

They brushed dust off the seats, Arthur meticulously, and sat around a small table.

'There's not a lot to tell. I shouldn't have sought him out. As I've told you, he's a scumbag, a crook, a nasty piece of work. You know of my teenage experience with him, so you'll understand that I'm not well disposed towards the man.' Julian paused and reached for a glass of water.

'So why meet with him?' asked Ruth.

'I knew there was bad blood between him and my dad. At first that amused me, to be honest. Dad had brought it on himself. Had he listened… anyway, I became aware of a dispute over debt.'

'Scott's debt to your dad?'

'To the business, but yes, it had become personal. Then one day I overheard a telephone conversation, a blazing row, and saw the impact on Dad. It was pitiful, really. I'd never seen him like that. He suddenly looked old, fragile, vulnerable even. I might not have got on with the old man, but…'

'So, you went to see Scott? Where? When?' said Ruth.

'He frequented an old pub, The Blue Moon. I knew the manager, so found out when he usually drank there. It wasn't hard. Most days just before closing. Downed a few pints, abused a few people, had the odd scrap, and hoped for a lock-in.'

'Manager's name?'

'Jane Swan.'

'It wasn't an arranged meeting, then?' said Ruth.

'It was more of a shouting match. Utterly pointless. Lasted all of five minutes.'

'So why? What did you hope to achieve? It seems out of character.'

'Bad judgement. Maybe for once I let my emotions get the better of me.'

'Lose your temper, did you, sir?' suggested Arthur.

'Yes,' said Julian: contrite, regretful.

'We all have the capacity to lose it occasionally, don't we? And with such a lowlife who provoked you, intimidated your dad. Threaten him, did you? Strike out?'

'Steady on. No. Speak to Jane—'

'Oh, we will,' said Ruth.

Julian insisted it was a one-off occasion, and it was the last time he had seen Scott. 'You didn't say why you wanted to meet here.'

'Can we take a look around?' asked Ruth.

'Do you have a search warrant?'

'Do we need one, sir?' asked Arthur.

'No. Be my guest. I'll show you if you like.'

Julian then started his tour in the upstairs rooms and gradually worked his way down to the kitchen and bar areas and into the lounges. The police poked into toilet areas, cupboards, fridges, outside storage areas where a bemused Julian watched them move aside old kegs and crates and rubbish bins; smiled at Ruth's reaction as a rat scuttled out.

'If you tell me what you're looking for then maybe I can help,' Julian offered.

'Can you show us the cellars?' Ruth said.

'Sure.' He took them through to the rear lounge. 'It's years since I went down there.'

Julian led them through the underground rabbit warren of interlinking corridors, through the various beer and wine and bottle cellars, and the passageway became narrower with lower ceilings. Julian and Arthur were forced to duck their heads. Ruth shook her head and ran her hand through her hair to release dust and bits of flaking plaster. Arthur constantly dusted down his once-pristine jacket and trousers, looked disconsolately at his cobweb-coated leather brogues. Turning the corner, they reached the end of the labyrinth. Arthur said he had seen enough, and they ascended the steps to emerge into a bar, then made their way to the front door and out into welcome fresh air.

'We'll speak with Jane Swan at The Blue Moon,' said Ruth.

'And return with a search warrant to examine the pub and cellars,' said Arthur.

Julian watched them off the premises, then turned back to switch off the lights and lock up. But first he wandered through to a room that had captured his attention earlier. A big area, once a busy lounge with a large fireplace, which now housed a wood-burner stove. He could almost hear the hubbub of old. He looked around him. What had struck his subconscious as different? Then he alighted on the concrete slab, remembered the old wooden flooring and trapdoor, which had given access to a small cellar down rickety steps to a storeroom. He had not noticed this patch of flooring before, probably because there used to be old rugs and furniture in that area. In preparing the pub for sale they had removed much of the furniture and disposed of threadbare carpets, and other detritus. He thought about it and was sure that the cellar he recalled was beyond the brick wall that had signalled the end of the cellars where the detectives had turned around. Julian's mind replayed snatches of his youth when he and his siblings would run amok underground – in the early days their imaginations had conjured ghosts and smugglers and witches. That had given way to hide-and-seek, and in their teens the cellar complex became a favourite haunt to smoke or swig from a forbidden bottle. They had known those cellars like the backs of their hands.

He retraced his earlier steps to find the brick-wall dead end. Yes, he was certain that beyond was the cellar with dodgy steps up to the lounge through a trapdoor. Julian inspected it closely but there was no way through without demolishing the wall. He thought about doing exactly that. Then a thought struck him. He turned around, and as the corridor turned left there was a small nook on the right. He pushed himself into the narrow space, shone the torch on his iPhone, and saw the low-level gap. And it came back to him. Getting down on his hands and knees, he crawled further, ignored the accumulated filth. He tried not to think about the damp patches and sludgy bits he pushed through, and crawled for perhaps fifty feet to reach an open arch, partially blocked by a cupboard of some sort. After a lot of effort in a tightly constrained space he managed to shove it aside sufficiently to enter the hidden cellar, where he could now stand and stretch. Yes, this was it. A cursory inspection revealed a rack with maybe twenty dust-encrusted bottles of wine along one wall. Brooms and mops and buckets were clustered in a corner, a crate of bottled beers, packing cases, and a corner with rolls of old carpets and rugs. He took a closer look and worked his phone torch round the room methodically, peered behind the debris and gallimaufry of abandoned cleaning materials. He reached the corner with the carpets and pulled them aside. There in the corner was a mound of rugs and sheets and debris. They seemed to be piled high upon a large object. He cast aside cardboard boxes and dust sheets, curtains and rugs, until the object was revealed: a substantial-sized trunk. It was not locked, and the lid groaned as it yielded to his curses and tugs.

Well, I'll be damned.

An unseeing skeleton stared up at him.

TWENTY-TWO

JANUARY 2021

Julian was shown into the interview room.

Ruth asked what they could do for him. 'It's somewhat unusual, you asking to meet with us, sir.'

'Indeed.'

'And?' said Arthur.

'I think I've found your Scott Banks,' Julian said with a smile. He was calm and perfectly in control: no signs of anxiety, no nervous tension. He told them what he had found, offered to show them.

As the first month of the New Year drew towards a close, the police sealed off The Yorkshire Belle site, much to the disgruntlement of Bernard Archer, who made a beeline for them as the police tape fluttered. He accosted Ruth who directed operations, made protestations, waved his arms around. Ruth smiled, flashed the search warrant, assured him the owners had been informed, pointed to Julian who was also in attendance, and left Bernard to stew. A systematic search of the pub unfolded as a small team of officers wearing forensic suits, overshoes, masks, and gloves set about their painstaking task.

'Bloody hell,' grumbled the unhappy farmer as he strode away, calling his dog to heel.

Julian wore unfamiliar protective gear as he led Ruth back through the cellars, showed her the nook and the opening through which he had crawled. Ruth concluded that the best way of accessing the cellar was through the brick wall. A team were directed to the bricked-up cellar, although narrow access and the confined space meant that only two people could work there. Having press-ganged a surveyor to assess the situation, his advice was taken on board. A few hours later the ceiling had been shored up at each end. Ruth spoke to Arthur: demolition works could now begin. He soon appeared on site. Julian was told to leave the police to it.

'Let's get on with it,' Arthur said in uncharacteristically brusque terms.

Arthur squeezed himself into the space and signalled for them to begin. He pulled back as the two workmen wielded their masonry saws and sledgehammers. It was hard work made more difficult by cramped conditions. The air was soon full of dust despite the damping-down process, and after a while the workmen stopped what they were doing and confirmed the completion of that phase. They allowed Arthur room to ease forwards, step over piles of rubble, and peer into the void beyond, but it was impossible to make anything out. They would have to wait for the dust to settle.

'How's the pub search going?' Arthur asked Ruth.

'It's slow, but nothing yet. What about down there?'

'The wall's down but you can't see jack. We'll give it an hour or so and then I'll go have a peek. Then the guys need to clear a path, which will no doubt necessitate further downtime before we can see what bounty the room might reveal.'

'Other than a skeleton, you mean… I'll join you…'

'No room for us all. You stay here and oversee the search. I'll give you a shout when we can see what's what.'

At last, he could gain access, and instructed the workmen to remove themselves. He thanked them for a job well done and asked them to stand prepared to assist further. Arthur flicked on the powerful torch and shone it around the small cellar, clouds of dust motes dancing in the light. The room was as described by Julian and the trunk had been exposed from beneath the carpets and rugs and old curtains. It stood proudly centre stage. Arthur creaked open the lid and grimaced at the contents.

Scott Banks, I presume.

Peering behind the trunk, he could see an object, but could not reach it without further disturbing the scene. He left it where it was. He was careful not to disturb anything more than was necessary; he should have already admitted someone to take photos.

He turned his attention back to the trunk's contents and spotted a jacket, screwed up, stained, almost certainly blood encrusted. He grabbed it, reached into the right inside pocket.

Nothing.

He examined the left inside pocket.

Nothing.

Frowning, he rummaged in the side pockets but found only a few coins. And then he spotted it. Lying at the bottom of the trunk beneath the jacket was an envelope. Arthur reached in, extricated it, partly unzipped his forensic suit, popped the envelope inside, and re-zipped.

'How's it going, guv?' a voice shouted at him from the corridor. Ruth.

'Be right with you,' he said as he restored the scene.

Arthur left the cellar to join Ruth and the two of them made their way outside and to the relief of fresh air. He confirmed to

Ruth the trunk's skeletal contents and instructed her to get the CSI team to do their stuff. They all knew the routine.

By the end of the afternoon, they could reflect upon a successful search: body found, a likely weapon also. If forensics confirmed the dried stains on the iron poker were blood, then all they need do was match that to the body to confirm murder. Almost certainly Scott Banks, their elusive misper, had been found. And perhaps government property too. Over to forensics and science for confirmation. Patience was once more needed until a definitive outcome was determined.

'Oh, Ruth. Please reiterate to Julian that he must not divulge the find. To anyone. I include his own family members in that. To do so will expose him to charges of impeding a police murder investigation.'

'He's already confirmed the news will be treated as confidential. Funnily enough, I believe him. He's got enough on his plate without more family histrionics and speculation. He also knows we will need to interview him further as a potential suspect.'

Arthur sped away and his thoughts were not of Julian, nor of Scott Banks, nor of murder or the various suspects, but of the extricated envelope. He would look at the contents in private later. He shared this news with no one. But Arthur's weary smile morphed into a frown. His guv could easily deny any such instruction, which would leave Arthur holding potentially incriminating material.

TWENTY-THREE

MONDAY 1ST FEBRUARY

Josh jabbered amiably, and Julian's anxieties lightened as he played with his son. Josh was unusually responsive, and time slipped away as Julian delighted in his son's sunny mood. It was inevitably spoiled when Lotte launched into one of her tirades.

'Please, Lotte, I'm just playing with Josh. Let's not—'

'Makes a change…'

'A good daddy,' said Nanny Barlow. 'Daddy always plays with Josh when he can, always reads a bedtime story…' She stared at Lotte and stood her ground despite turning the colour of beetroot.

'Have you arranged the joint meeting with the lawyers, Daddy dear?' said Lotte, her facial expression and tone lacerating, excoriating, toxic.

'Not in front of Josh. We agreed.'

'Just tell me, for God's sake.'

'Your solicitor should have confirmed. Tomorrow at midday.'

Lotte tossed her blonde hair back, threw Nanny Barlow a scornful look, and stormed out.

'Sorry, Nanny. Not fair to sound off in front of Josh.'

'You get on, Julian. I'll calm him.'

Julian called the contact his solicitor had given him.

'Hi, Esther, it's me, Julian.'

'Good morning.'

'Any progress?'

'Samples obtained and submitted. As you paid their extortionate bill, we should have the results later today.'

'Thanks.'

Just then his office door swung open, and Annie bustled in with a tray of coffee and a plate of mince pies. 'By the looks of you a caffeine fix is overdue, and Christmas might be over, thank the Lord, but I know you like your mince pies.' She plopped the tray down, took one look at him, and sat down opposite. 'You worry me, Master Julian. You work too hard, take too much on yourself, and she's… she's poison. You can't half pick them. Now, I never have a bad word to say about anyone, as you well know, but I might have to make an exception with her. When's it all going to be over? If you ask me, you're better rid. And that poor little mite. Love him to bits. Good job he's got you and Nanny Barlow is all I can say. Now, what do you say to that? Eh?'

'Coffee and mince pies are great, Annie. You're a diamond.'

'Well, I can't chat all day. Things to do. Her Ladyship to mop up after… have you seen how much booze she tucks away? Well, I never.' She scowled, struggled to her feet, and headed to the door. Storm Annie had blown in and fizzled out.

Julian's mobile announced the new caller. Interesting.

'Hello, Faye. Happy New Year.'

'To you too, Julian. I trust you're well. Have you got five?'

'Always, Faye.'

'We got Henry's message about your supposed alternative offer…'

'Our only offer. Yours expired.'

'We're prepared to give it one last shot. Remind me of your timescales?'

'Friday.'

'We should be able to do it this week. All the legal documents have been done, the due diligence was completed previously, although we may need to do a brief top-up assessment. And the documents may need minor amendments.'

'I'm all ears, Faye. You know what our bottom line is.'

'Yes, you've been clear.'

'So?'

'I'm authorised to increase our final offer to £8.75 million.'

'I see.'

'Nothing more to say?'

'I'm grateful for your ongoing interest and the offer. What can I say? Frankly, the other offer is the one I'm working on. I'm confident we'll get to my bottom-line price. The deal is theirs when they confirm they will meet my price – or yours if you pip them to the post.'

'Still flexing your muscles, Julian? Even after last time?'

'No. Not what I'd want you to think. Prior to Christmas your client offered £12 million. Your tactics will have saved them a cool £2 million. You've done your job, Faye. Most impressive. I'd love to work with you in the future – with the proviso that we're on the same side.'

He sensed Faye allowed herself a brief internal smile. She would enjoy the professional compliment.

'I'll get back to you.'

Henry agreed to follow up with Elgin to establish progress, to inform them of another interested party with a higher offer. It was transpiring into a contract race. Neither of the runners and riders inspired total confidence. But surely history would not, could not, repeat itself?

Julian took various business calls. Thomas informed him of further draconian cuts, of customer debts they had not managed to collect, many hiding behind the excuse of Covid lockdown. He was not sure he could hold the bank off. He feared they would take precipitate action. Julian shuddered. He needed a few more days.

'Speak to Zoe at SI. They carry some influence. In fact, I'll drop her a brief note. A few more days, Thomas. It's all I need.'

'I thought you said the property deals were dead in the water?'

'They were.'

'But something's changed?'

'Not yet.'

'But it may?'

Julian said nothing.

'You're not going to enlighten me, are you?'

'When I have something to say you'll be one of the first to know. Must go.'

He rubbed his brow and heaved a huge sigh. He needed air so grabbed his coat and boots and strode through the hallway, ignoring Lotte's plaintive cries. Very soon he hoped her moods, her drinking, her histrionics would be a thing of the past, something he could forget. Ha! Fat chance. After all, they were parents to Josh and ongoing contact was inevitable. Desirable even. He would have to find a way to deal with it. Whatever agreement they reached, she could always use one pretext or another to defer and disrupt his time with Josh. He crunched down their gravel drive, ignored the grey skies and the incessant drizzle. He could still see in his mind's eye Lotte in the clutches of Jonathan. Julian stopped and turned back to picture her tottering up the drive – a happy drunk prior to denial, deflection, obfuscation. His mobile pinged every few moments as he pushed through the gate. He glanced at the rain-splashed screen. An email from Faye caught his eye but it was just a holding position. Henry had yet to hear from Elgin. Something from Esther was of more immediate interest: the results were in. All he had to do was settle her bill and then she would ping him a scanned version and put the original in the post. Julian downloaded the invoice. He raised an eyebrow at the sight of the charges and smiled a wry smile. Everything had its value; everyone had their price. Time to head back. How far had he managed to walk? What he could really do with was a brisk ten-miler on the moors. Another day. Duty called.

He made the bank transfer, and within the hour the results shouted at him from his screen. So, it wasn't Neville Jackson after all. He had sort of hoped it might be. He spoke with Giles, relayed the results to his private investigator, who said he was surprised Neville was not the man.

'He's still culpable. He's screwed around with my wife and destroyed trust. I'll deal with him. Please send me the audit trail: emails, phone records, photographs. Especially photographs.'

'You can't use—'

'I've no intention of doing anything other than using it in discussion with him.'

'I'm not comfortable with this, Julian.'

'It was part of our agreement. I'll keep you out of it. You have my word. *Again.*'

'And you presumably want the same in respect of the others as well as the biological dad?'

'Yup.'

'How can you be sure the DNA test has been correctly processed and is valid? How can you know she's not mixed the samples up? And all this is illegal. It can't—'

'Be used in a court of law. I know. You said. I'll know when I speak with the biological dad. I'll see it in his eyes.'

'This is all ethically questionable.'

'Don't get squeamish on me now, for God's sake, Giles.'

Giles went quiet, and the crackle on the line could have been the whirring of his mental cogs, the synapses going into overdrive as he wrestled his dilemma. But it was perfectly simple. If he wanted his account settled… 'Very well. I'll wing it over. And my account. Then I don't want anything further to do with you. You're like a man possessed. I don't like being press-ganged into overstepping the line.'

A private detective with a heightened sensitivity seemed an oxymoron. Oh, well.

'Thank you. I'll transfer the funds as soon as I'm in receipt of the material.'

Julian ended the call and moved on. He would soon have what he needed to enter the endgame on this agenda at least. Now for Neville Jackson. But Luke beat him to it.

'Hi, Luke.'

'What the hell's going on at The Belle? Police swarming all over the place.'

'Yeah. I understand a statement will be made shortly. Spoke to that nuisance detective… what's her name?'

'Have they found him?'

'Who?'

'Don't play games – you know damned well who. Have they spoken with you recently?'

'Well, I guess it's all about that Banks character, but I've been a bit busy, Luke.'

'Only Emily reckons they've found him… heard his son on

some radio station talk about police incompetence, government cover-ups. She reckons they've unearthed a body.'

'Luke, I just don't have time for this. The business hovers on a precipice. Remember?'

'Of course… is this it, Julian?'

'Not quite.'

'What's the plan?'

'We meet next Monday.'

'Let's meet sooner.'

'You need to give me a few days.'

'To do what?'

'Please be patient. I don't have time to tell you and there may still be nothing to say anyway. Bear with me.'

'Emily's shouting and screaming, Thomas is exasperated, and Lotte is—'

'I know, but hysteria won't help.'

'Give me a clue as to what you might be doing, at least.'

'We've asked Zoe to reach out to the bank to defer the meeting with them until next Monday. Meanwhile, Thomas is doing all he can to keep a lid on events. I have a few irons in the fire. I'll probably fail, but I'm trying to complete a deal to save our bacon.'

'How stupid do you think I am? This is about the farm and The Belle, isn't it?'

'I've never in my life considered you stupid… a bit dull, perhaps.'

'I'll fight you every inch of the way if you try to sell The Belle from under our feet.'

'As you have from the very beginning. Why, Luke? Why so stubbornly resist the only solution available to us… hang on, I've got incoming. Got to take this call.'

Julian ended his conversation with Luke and sat back heavily in his chair. He had said more than he'd intended, had let his guard down, and now he'd insulted Luke. Then he recalled the times when Luke could have used his skills and brainpower to support Julian and the business. Countless examples.

TWENTY-FOUR

TUESDAY 2ND FEBRUARY

Julian's morning routine was interrupted by a sharp ringtone: an incoming message from Elgin. They had increased their offer to £9.15 million. Good progress. Furthermore, they underlined their readiness to complete on the requisite two-pronged deal structure by the end of the week.

'What do you think?' asked Henry on the landline.

'Encouraging. I've not heard from Optimum yet, though.'

'Look at the evidence, Julian. It's compelling. Optimum have played silly buggers throughout, run circles round us. We can't trust them—'

'I don't trust either of them.'

'Take it, my friend. They've increased their offer from an initial £6 million to £8 million, and now this. They have the funds. Their team will get there on the legal documents. Take it.'

'Let's see where Faye is, let's play it out. *You* counselled patience, Henry.'

'Touché. You've balls of steel, Julian, balls of steel.'

His office door swung open, and a red-faced Annie bustled into his midst. 'Door, Master Julian. I seem to be doorman now, too. A Neville Somebody-or-Other. He's in the hall.'

'Thanks, Annie. You're a…'

But she had gone.

Julian smiled, sorted through his papers, and left it for a few minutes. The meeting had been arranged at a time when Lotte would be around. As Julian strolled down the hall, Lotte was in whispered conversation with Neville Jackson. Julian paused in the shadows for a moment and had to admit they made a good-looking couple. Lotte had grown her hair, and tight baby-blonde curls bounced as she tossed her head back in high dudgeon; then flicked her hair while narrowing her eyes. Flirtatious tools of her trade. Her body language exhibited collusion, consternation, confusion. Her hand gripped Neville's arm as she looked earnestly into his dark eyes. He was a handsome, swarthy man for sure. But their body language undermined their natural self-confidence. Their whispered entreaties were no doubt speculative. Time to break cover. Julian filed away his smile.

'Neville. You're late. Let's get to it. My office.' No handshake offered, no elbow-bumping.

'What are you up to now, Julian?' asked Lotte. 'What's the game?'

'I thought introductions unnecessary. You know each other well, don't you?' He directed the shadow of a smile at his wife. 'Excuse us, Lotte. Business.'

Lotte turned on her heels and headed for the lounge, slammed the door behind her.

'What's this about?' demanded Neville.

His attempt at bravado was lost in his facial twitches, his flickering eyes. He crossed and uncrossed his legs, fiddled with his watch. Julian scrutinised him, allowed the ensuing silence to thicken. He reached for the coffee pot, poured, splashed in milk, plopped in a cube of sugar, and stirred. He sipped without his eyes straying from Neville, who was not offered a drink. The tension settled – like dust slowly descending, coating every surface. Julian took satisfaction from Neville's discomfort. A small consolation. Now it was time to mete out retribution.

'Thanks for coming over.'

'Against all the rules…' Neville sat forward, then pressed himself back in his chair under Julian's gaze.

'How long have you worked for us?'

'Five years or so. Why?'

'And you're a social animal?'

'What?'

'Earned a certain reputation for yourself.'

'Where's this going? I don't know what—'

'Perhaps you'd like to tell me how well you know my wife?'

'What sort of question—'

'One a cheated husband might ask.'

Neville ran his finger along the inside of his collar, pulled at his tie.

Julian placed half a dozen photographs face down on his desk. 'Nothing to say? No puffed-up denial, no protestations of innocence?'

'I'm shocked. Sure, Lotte and I saw each other a few times—'

'Saw rather a lot of each other, didn't you?' Julian turned over the photographs one by one. 'My darling wife, I believe… now unclothed. And this one is you, is it not? And as for this photo – it's rather explicit, don't you think? My goodness, your passions were roused, weren't they?' Julian said, feigning close examination. 'And here's one with my wife showing all her charms. Quite erotic, I suppose. And—'

'Enough. What do you want from me?'

'I have emails, more images. I'm sure some of these would trend on social media.'

'What do you want?'

'Your resignation, a written admission of your affair, and your forfeiture of all employment rights and notice period payments.'

'You're joking.'

'Try me.'

'You wouldn't release anything to implicate your wife. You're bluffing.'

'Did she not tell you? We're divorcing. Bluffing? Try me.'

'Okay, you can have your poxy job. It's all going down the pan anyway.'

'And one more thing. I retain all this... what shall we call it? What euphemism might dull the pain? Audit trail. I shall retain the *detailed, colourful, explicit* audit trail for future reference, should you choose to pop up in my life or contact any of my family at any point in the future.'

'*Bastard.*'

'Better believe it. Now get out.'

The afternoon's call promised to be more challenging: the first virtual meeting with both solicitors. Julian hoped Lotte's solicitor had counselled her, advised her to control her emotions, focus on the required result. Perhaps Neville's appearance might have unsettled rather than angered her. But Julian was unsure. Maybe he had got the timing wrong. But it was too late to harbour doubts. Anyway, he knew there had been no chance for discussion between the two of them after his meeting as he had walked Neville to the door. He had watched him storm down the drive, kick a wheelbarrow over. Julian had chuckled as his gardener shouted after Neville, receiving a proffered finger of insult in response.

Julian's solicitor kicked the virtual meeting off, Julian Zooming from his office, Lotte from the sitting room. The two solicitors set out the ground rules as Julian and Lotte confirmed their intention to seek an uncontested divorce. They would need to file a joint petition, they were reminded. So far, so good.

The matter of the prenuptial agreement was raised, but Lotte's solicitor knew nothing of this until Lotte reluctantly acknowledged its existence. A copy of the document was immediately sent via email as they discussed it in principle. It went to the heart of the matter in determining a financial settlement. The prenuptial contract ring-fenced Julian's business interests, his cars, and the main property, all predating their marriage. Lotte and her solicitor reserved their position on this matter pending a review. Fair enough. The meeting seemed to inch forwards positively.

Then Lotte threw in accusations about Julian's conduct, his affair with the 'harlot'.

'We grew apart very quickly, Lotte. You said you didn't like the real me, you were lonely, you were unhappy. We aren't suited. It's not your fault and nor is it mine. It didn't work. We made a mistake. Inevitable we would both meet others. Why do we need to drag this up?'

Lotte's solicitor tried to intervene, but she would not let him.

'Don't you bloody well implicate me. The issue is your infidelity. It drove a wedge in our marriage and now you plan to throw me out on the streets without a roof over my head.'

'Don't be so melodramatic. You've already admitted an affair with Jonathan. I've just sacked Neville Jackson, with whom you also had an affair, and I know there've been others… just having fun, you called it.'

'All lies.'

'I have explicit photographic evidence.'

'You're bluffing.'

'I'll save your blushes, but we can pore over the images later if you insist. Stop messing about. My main concern is open and free access to Josh rather than financial matters. We need to get over our personal feelings and create some sort of tolerant relationship in the best interests of our son. We agreed this process was not to allocate blame. If we are to file a petition to the courts, we just need to agree the division of the spoils, and access to Josh. They're the main things. Can't we just focus on our priority – Josh – get this business over, and get on with our lives?'

'Quite a speech from Mr Monosyllabic.'

Both solicitors quickly took their opportunity from the silence following Lotte's sarcasm to urge them to begin to tease out the financial details. Julian was invited to make an offer, given his stated intentions of generosity.

'I'll vacate the house and give you up to twelve months to find somewhere else. The house will be put up for sale after six months for completion following your tenancy.'

'So, I've suddenly become a *tenant*? And you call this *generous*?'

'You've no call on the proceeds given the nuptial agreement—' Julian ignored her protest.

'If it holds water.'

'It will. Nonetheless, I'll give you twenty per cent of net proceeds. I can also agree to a maintenance allowance until such time as you marry or cohabit with a partner. And an allowance for Josh's upbringing, of course. I'm determined to be involved in his life, and I want to help fund it. The lawyers can help us nail down the figures.'

'I can't believe you're being so miserly.'

'This is generous, Lotte. Do you realise what this would mean financially to you?'

'You will, no doubt, have the numbers off pat. Just tell me.'

'The valuation I put at a little over £3 million, less a £750K mortgage and costs – so I estimate your proceeds would be something approaching £500K, give or take.'

Lotte said she wanted fifty per cent. 'And the prenuptial agreement is null and void.' She gave no justification for her assertion. 'And the jewellery you gave me remains mine,' she blurted out.

'Of course.'

'And all my personal possessions, and an equal split of the furniture and our joint possessions.'

'I furnished the house prior to our wedding, but we should split all the things we bought as a couple. Just list what you want, Lotte.'

'And my shares.'

'I gifted those to you, so of course they're yours.'

'Bloody worthless, mind, given your incompetence.'

'You can't resist taking a potshot, can you?'

Julian's solicitor interjected and suggested they had covered enough ground for this initial meeting. The two solicitors would review the prenuptial.

Julian sighed with relief, albeit tinged with sadness. They had both screwed up. It was a disaster. He reached for a ten-year-old malt with ice and put some music on: Free's signature track, 'All Right Now', seemed to hold some sort of irony – a classic track. In truth he was far from all right on any front. They inched forward, but a great deal could still go awry. While he worried about Cassandra's present state of mind there was progress on most fronts, so he raised his glass in a silent toast.

His satisfaction was short-lived as Lotte burst in. She had worked herself into a lather, was almost incoherent with rage.

'Calm down, Lotte.'

'Don't you "Calm down, Lotte" me. What's all this about Neville? Why do you rake up the nonsense about Jonathan? How dare you downplay what she – Cassandra – has done to our marriage? And how dare you have her shacked up just down the road over Christmas?'

Julian remained calm, sipped his whisky, and watched.

'Well? You couldn't stop speaking in the meeting when you had an audience. What now? Back to the tight-lipped automaton?'

Julian looked intently at her contorted features and, without taking his eyes off her, revealed two of the incriminating images. He watched her eyes cast downwards, noted her facial changes as the anger gave way to shock. And then dismay registered. Or was it shame?

He said nothing.

Her colour drained, and the tears came without warning.

She shook her head slowly and her eyes could no longer hold Julian's.

TWENTY-FIVE

WEDNESDAY 3ʳᴰ FEBRUARY

Julian allowed himself an hour tuned into BBC Radio 4's *Today* programme before his two-minute commute. The pandemic news was gloomy: infections high, deaths mounted, and scientists' strictures were dutifully repeated by ministers. When would all this end? And why was it such a threat after the hailed vaccination programme, he pondered before his attention was diverted by an incoming call. Faye.

'Good morning, Faye.'
'Hi, Julian. I'm pleased to tell you the legal documents are nearly complete. We just need to enter the agreed purchase price and away we go.'
'I'm all ears.'
'I've worked hard on this for you—'
'For all parties, I imagine.'
'And my client has pushed the boat out to get as close to your ask as we can.'
'And?'

'£9.245 million for both: £7.5 million and £1.745 million respectively for the farm and the pub.'

'I see.'

'Can I tell my client we have a deal?'

Julian paused, allowed the silence to settle like dust. Faye said nothing.

'I'm grateful to you for your interest and your efforts, but you haven't reached my bottom line. I have a board to answer to and my mandate is £10 million.'

'Oh, come off it, Julian. The farm's nothing to do with your company. Do your board even know about this deal? Well, do they?'

'You and your client have your own internal processes to navigate, we have ours. I have no greater insight into yours than you into mine.'

'I wonder. I took a call from your brother.'

'How interesting.'

'A fishing expedition.'

'I'm sure Optimum has its own internal politics as well, Faye.'

'So, you reject our offer? Out of hand?'

'I respectfully ask you to reach the £10 million price to finalise a deal. I continue to talk to the other party, and they are similarly reconsidering their bid. We will finalise this by 5pm tomorrow, Thursday 4th February, and complete the transaction by midday on Friday 5th.'

'Best and final offers, then? *And* a contract race?'

'The finishing line is defined for both parties. I'd like the winner to be you, Faye.'

Julian was surprised when Lotte asked him to join her in the dining room for a light lunch. They had not shared a meal since Christmas. He expected rancour, but he resolved to be the model of restraint whatever the provocation. He was met with a forced smile and Lotte at her most stunning. She had dressed as if for a lunchtime date: a figure-hugging black dress and scarlet shoes. Her blonde hair flowed, and her green eyes sparkled. And the smile beat the anticipated scowl. It reminded him of their early dates when she had been flirtatious, charming, wonderful company. A joy to be with. A bottle of white wine remained unopened in the ice bucket, and platters of cured meats, smoked salmon, prawns, and salad with crusty bread were set out on the table between the two places laid either end. Julian raised an eyebrow in appreciation and complimented her on her appearance. They helped themselves to food and he opened and poured the wine while they made polite talk.

Lotte topped her glass up. 'We should talk about the arrangements,' she said. Her voice was quiet; she looked intently at the contents of her glass, then swallowed deeply.

'Yes.'

'What will you do afterwards, Julian? Move to France?'

'I don't know.'

'No? You can hardly see much of Josh if you're on the continent.'

'I hear what you say, and Josh comes first.'

'Ahead of—'

'Let's not go there, Lotte. It was such a good idea of yours to do this. Let's not spoil it. Let's focus on the areas where we might reach agreement and then agree a list of things we need to work on.'

'Okay. But you need to be flexible. None of your brinkmanship bravado, none of your games.'

'Agreed. What are your plans, Lotte?' He did not expect her to be forthcoming, but he had a keen interest given his quest for access to their son. And anyway, he wanted her to be happy. She needed a positive agenda to move into a new phase of her life, and if she could do so it would inevitably help Josh. However toxic their relationship had become, they had known good periods, and Julian had once loved her, she him too.

'I'm not certain but I think I'll head to London. I know more people there. Yorkshire just doesn't suit me.'

'Whereabouts?'

'A girlfriend of mine has a large apartment. I can stay there for a while.'

'I see. Not great for Josh, though, is it?'

'I know. Like you, I'm not sure.' Lotte lapsed into silence and took another slurp of wine. Her eyes locked back onto Julian's, seemed about to say more. Her inner turmoil was evident in her body language and searching eyes. What did she want to say?

'Yes? Have you thought this through, Lotte?' He spoke kindly, softly.

'No. I need to think more.'

He watched her eyes narrow, harden, and she became distant. Quite a mood swing. She seemed to be stiffening herself to deliver a practised line, perhaps the real reason for the meeting. Then she leant forward and spoke briskly.

'So, to the list… I want fifty per cent of the net proceeds of the house, and I'm not sure about Josh.'

'Meaning what?' Julian tensed and instinctively reached for his naked wedding-ring finger. What could she mean? He shifted in his seat, crossed his legs, and swirled his glass. Lotte's eyes, hard now, lasered on him. Julian tried to force himself to relax.

'I'm uncertain as to what's in Josh's best interests so I'll take advice from the lawyers, from doctors… you, too.'

'Meaning what?' he said weakly.

'Let's discuss the house and all the other stuff first.'

He sighed inwardly but said, 'So long as we can get back to this.'

She nodded.

'Anything we agree only applies if we agree to access to Josh.'

'So, the house?'

'The prenuptial puts the house out of the equation. I've said I'll do more than already offered, but only when you admit its existence.'

'I do.'

'You do?'

'My solicitor says I have no choice.' She shrugged and flashed a wry smile. 'But you claimed you'd be generous – so fifty per cent, please.'

'I'll stretch to twenty-five per cent.'

'Okay.'

'What?'

'I agree. Here's the list of possessions I wish to take with me.'

Julian crossed out three items and added two to the list. 'I bought those prior to our marriage, and this one I inherited from my grandparents. The two I've added we bought, and I've no need of them.'

'Fair enough.'

'Good progress, Lotte.'

'And this is a list of my jewellery.'

'All agreed.'

'I need to speak further with my solicitor on child maintenance and your proposal for me too.'

'The standard calculations for child maintenance provide a baseline, and I can top up as required. And you should soon become self-sufficient, shouldn't you?'

'So, you're going to row back on your previous offer?' Her tone was abruptly strident.

'We just need to be guided by the lawyers and by your own earnings.'

'How can I possibly earn a living if I'm looking after Josh full-time? You made no mention of Annie or Nanny Barlow, so I assume I'm to be denied their support? How do you expect me to manage, let alone earn a living?'

'Millions do. There are such things as nurseries and schools. It can be topped up with childcare arrangements. If Josh has special needs, he should qualify for financial support too. But I'll share any burden with you.' She was on the brink of an emotional outpouring, and Julian quickly added, 'Are you okay?'

'Of course I'm not bloody okay. How can I be? Don't be so bloody insensitive. Can't you see how worried I am about all this? From a big house with all the hired hands to being cast adrift. I'll have to find a home in a new city, find work, and all you can do is go on about money.' Her voice wavered, her hands went up in despair, and she reached for a tissue to dab watery eyes.

'I get it. And the impact on Josh worries me terribly. This doesn't have to happen all at once, though, Lotte. I'll help all I can.'

'Ha!' she said with derision. 'And all because you couldn't keep your dick in your pants.' The emotional floodgates opened, and she fled the room, banged the door behind her.

Julian reached for the wine and poured himself a glass. He wandered over to the window and looked out. What should he make of this conversation? She'd sounded genuinely scared about the future. Beneath the outgoing, confident young woman... the more he thought about it, the more muddled her thinking seemed to be. Why would she want to take Josh to the big city? And as for living in an apartment... and what did she mean about being unsure of Josh's best interests? Why the vagueness? One minute she was straightforward, and agreeable, and the next vague and emotional. Where was she going with all this, and did she even know?

TWENTY-SIX

THURSDAY 4TH FEBRUARY, 10.00

Julian's head was full of the loose strands of his life, but it was the business deal that held centre stage. Could he pull it off? It was close, so close. Wrenching himself away from anguished thought processes, he accepted an incoming call.

'Yes, Thomas, what is it?' Julian was sharp, irritable almost.

'Good morning to you, too. Did you see the emails I sent over?'

'Yes.'

'We need to meet with the board and shareholders tomorrow at the latest.'

'We've been round this loop before. Monday.'

'I can't hold them or the bank off.'

'Just do it.'

Julian ended the call despite Thomas's anger. But it was time to make some personal representations. His first port of call was Zoe at SI, and then the account manager at their bank. The former was philosophical and broadly supportive, the latter sceptical and distant. As promised, he followed up with an email to both, copied to Thomas. His FD would be surprised and frustrated to see Julian act without consultation. Too bad. He reread the key paragraph.

Thomas has kept me fully briefed of our financial plight and of the imminent decision point. Our options are limited. We've almost run out of time. I'm under no illusion as to the seriousness of our position. Our board and shareholders have an emergency meeting on Monday, and I'll revert to you immediately following. In the meantime, I'm hopeful of a significant breakthrough in negotiations on a parallel matter. I'm not at liberty to divulge confidential matters at this juncture given legal obligations, but I expect to be able to impart good news on Monday and consign these difficulties to the past. All I ask is the time to reach a conclusion in this regard.

He could only hope it would do the trick. He had shared with Zoe the bare bones of the deal; she promised to do what she could to persuade the bank. Julian then tapped out a note to his siblings and Lotte, with copies to Zoe and Thomas: he was in touch with both SI and the bank; a meeting prior to Monday would be premature. He expected to be able to engage openly with shareholders then, and he hoped to be able to end the uncertainty that hung over them like Damocles' sword.

Thursday 4th February, 14.00

He checked his email again.
    Nothing from Henry.
    Nothing from Optimum.
    Nothing from Elgin.
    This was going to the wire. Again. The process was defined, and they would either cooperate to enable Belle Hospitality to rise, phoenix-like, from the ashes – or not.

Just then Annie blustered in, handed him his post, and mumbled her complaints about the pandemic, Covid rules, the inequity of it all. Getting no response, she sighed and retreated. Julian extricated a letter in handwriting he immediately recognised. She had not written for a while. He grabbed it and found a comfy chair in the small library area outside the main bedroom for peace and quiet, the mobile abandoned. He opened the letter with a frown, a sense of foreboding. His furrowed brow deepened as he read and reread the contents, hardly able to believe them:

I'm about as good as you at expressing my feelings, sharing emotions. What you read is a mishmash of jumbled thoughts, I fear. Better sharing than keeping locked inside. Maybe better. Not what I normally do. Nor you. I once castigated you for deceiving me. I've not been completely open with you, though. I've told you more about my past than anyone else. But not everything. It was just too painful. It still is. But you deserve an explanation, and I don't trust myself to tell you to your face. So, I hope you'll forgive me penning this note.

You know so much about me, Julian. My sister's demise, my excommunication from the bosom of my dysfunctional family, my disastrous relationship with my fiancé. But there was more. I'm just going to blurt it out. I can't see how I can soften the blow for either of us. What I hadn't told you is I was four months pregnant when my 'wonderful' husband-to-be set upon me. Fuelled by drugs and drink, he convinced himself that another guy had made me pregnant. There was no reasoning with him. He's an animal. Before he threw me out, we had a blazing row and, well... oh, God. He became violent. He slapped me, he punched me, he... raped me. His final act of terror. Ruined my life. I was in a sorry state. I haemorrhaged. Blue-lighted to hospital. It was too late. They had to operate. I lost the baby. A baby boy: Lucas. The awful upshot is, I can't have children now.

Julian stared at the words, utterly shocked. He felt pinpricks of emotion, tasted salty tears. He had not been able to cry for his dad, but he ached for Cassandra, felt her pangs of grief, wanted to hold her, tell her it would be all right. Somehow it would be all right.

So now you have the bones of the whole story, the reason I opted for a life of contented solitude in the beauty of my simple mountain retreat. Then you came along. At first I revelled in the seclusion, peace, and contentment we slipped into, and I found elusive, enveloping, enticing love. But slowly my peaceful existence was disrupted until it all became, well, you know.

It's impossible, Julian. We've tried to contend with all the complications of my past, of your past, of the complexities of your circumstances, of your hectic life. I can't live a life of turmoil and uncertainty. Worst of all, I can't bear you children or give you the family life you crave. Anyway, I doubt Lotte will give you unfettered access to Josh while I'm around, and I can't say I blame her. And your business life is so complicated. Sometimes you're like a man possessed. Scary. It won't work, Julian. I've come to understand it's impossible. Let's just be honest with ourselves and park our love, our hurt. I need to return to my life as a mountain hermit. It at least provides contentment. Please release me. Please understand.

I will always love you.
All my love, forever and always,
Cass x

Thursday 4th February, 16.00

Henry called in search of news.

'What? Oh, the deal. No.'

'Are you okay? You sound distracted.'

'I'm fine. Nothing your end?' asked Julian.

'No. I put in a call to Elgin and was given short shrift. They understand the process and the timescales. They were totally uncommunicative. I've no idea if they'll party, Julian.'

'I got a similar response from Faye earlier.'

'With an hour to go. How are your nerves, my friend?'

'Speak later. Must go. Another call coming in… no, it's neither of our party poopers.'

Julian spoke with his solicitor, a short conversation. Lotte had put a pause on proceedings. Why? He updated his lawyer on their meeting yesterday, on the progress made, and on her cryptic comments about Josh. No, he did not know what was driving her, nor what she was likely to do next.

Thursday 4th February, 16.40

Henry arranged for them to Zoom with Elgin's investment director, Samuel Thistle, and his in-house solicitor. Julian could hear the energy and excitement in Henry's voice. He wished he felt the same.

'Good to speak with you again, Samuel,' said Henry.

'And you both,' Samuel replied in a calm, cool, corporate voice.

'How can we help?' Henry.

'I'm about to send our best and final.'

'Okay.' Henry again.

Elgin intended to bid, and Julian was pleased, but could hear the 'but' in Samuel's tone and knew the offer would fall short. He remained silent.

'£9.35 million: £7.6 million for the farm, the remainder for the pub,' Samuel said without preamble.

'Really?' Julian said. His tone was flat.

'We're enormously grateful for your interest and for the offer. Aren't we, Julian? We recognise you've moved your position substantially, done all you can to work with the defined process. May I ask if you're ready to complete the legals?'

'Yes. So, you accept our offer?'

'No. It falls short, with respect.' Julian.

'Err… look…' said Henry. 'Can we revert to you shortly? We need to reflect, sort a few things out our end. Is that okay?'

'Very well.' Samuel ended the call.

Julian answered his mobile and listened to Henry's urgent tones, could feel his frustration.

'I'm not angry – just dismayed, Julian. It's the best offer we've had, and the deadline looms. We've still got nothing from Optimum. This is *madness*.'

'I hear what you say, but let's wait to hear from Optimum.'

'For how long? Do you expect Elgin to hang around and dance to your tune?'

'They have so far. This isn't about emotion and relationships, it's about business. Money. Returns on investment. Elgin know it's a good deal. So do Optimum. And they've yet to get to £10 million. We hang in there.'

Julian decided to take time out with Josh. His son had been fed and Nanny Barlow had bathed him. He smelt fresh and was relaxed. Story time.

'You pick, Josh. Look, how about *Room on the Broom*?'

They curled up on the toddler's bedroom beanbags, gathered the various cuddly toys around him: giraffes, seals, whales, bears, elephants. Quite a menagerie. Josh gripped Green Dog tightly. For once he was calm and happy to be cuddled and entertained, frequently pointing with his expressive index finger. Just then the door creaked open. Lotte. She held her finger to her lips. Leaning over, she kissed her son lightly on the forehead and he glanced up briefly. Lotte settled into the semi-gloom in the far corner and watched as Julian completed the story, then put Josh to bed. Lotte bent over, kissed Josh goodnight, and followed Julian out. As they walked quietly down the corridor Nanny Barlow was headed towards the nursery with raised eyebrows. Julian followed Lotte into the lounge, accepted the offered gin and tonic. He glanced at his mobile. No call, no message. Raising his eyes back to Lotte, he caught her scowl of disapproval.

'Good to see you with Josh,' she eventually said. 'You're good with him. I wish…' Her voice tailed off; the wistfulness struck a poignant note.

'Yes?'

'Nothing.'

'You had something to say, Lotte?'

'Why do you keep on looking at your mobile?'

'Sorry. I'm expecting an important call.'

'All I ask is for a few minutes. Will you turn it off? Just for a while.'

He nodded.

'I've been thinking. A lot. I hate being where we are. We used to love each other, and we have a son. A future if we want to reach for it…' She looked enquiringly at Julian, but he held a steady gaze, hid his astonishment. 'It's been a difficult period for both of us. The thing is, you've brought me to the brink. I've stared into the abyss, and I don't want to jump. It's too scary. The most important thing is Josh. We should do everything we can. Children need to grow up with a mum and a dad. Role models. Us.' Lotte lapsed into silence, sipped her G&T, and stared into space.

'What are you saying?'

'Maybe we should make a go of this, step back from the brink, make our marriage work. I'm prepared to forgive you, Julian. It won't be easy… but I'll try. So long as you—'

'And are you asking for forgiveness too?'

'Let's not fight.'

'I don't have time for this. I must get back to it.'

'But what do you say?'

'We can't turn back now. You can't be serious. We've agreed how to proceed.'

'No. No, I won't give you a divorce. I've offered to forgive and forget. What more can you ask?'

'An apology? Contrition? How many partners have you had during this time?'

'I told you, it was just a bit of fun while you were away – and you always were. Shacked up with your harlot. And it's you who's got himself into a serious relationship, by all accounts. For God's sake, I'm giving you a way out. Take it. For once in your life, opt for the easy route. Do the right thing. I'm serious. Let's make a go of this – wipe the slate clean.'

'You've slipped into a familiar mode, I note. No, Lotte, no. It's too late.'

'I won't divorce you, so you're stuck, aren't you?'

'Very well. Wait there and I'll be back in a moment. Just remember you drove me to this. I've tried to play nice but have it your own way.'

Julian walked calmly back to his study and grabbed his papers. He invited her to read the emails. She refused.

'This is an audit trail of messages between you and Neville Jackson, together with explicit photographs of both of you.' He spread them out on the table. 'This is the audit trail of messages and emails between you and Jonathan over a briefer period. But equally explicit in their messaging, don't you think? And what do you think of these photos? What do you think the courts would have to say? Do you not think there's enough evidence to ensure I get the divorce I want? The divorce you said *you* wanted?'

'I have pictures of you too, remember.'

'They're a bit lame in comparison, aren't they?'

'No, I don't think so, actually.'

'And there's more. Do we have to go there? Can't we just cast all this to one side and reach an amicable end to hostilities?'

'Yes, we can. Forget it ever happened. We're married. All couples have their problems.'

Julian looked scornfully at her, ran his hand through his hair, and then said, 'Lotte, this is the *end*. You choose whether we do it the hard way or the easy way. I've got to get back to my study.'

'You said there was something else. Let's have it all on the table.'

Julian looked at her. His eyes narrowed. Pause.

'Well?' she demanded.

'I'm not Josh's biological dad.'

Lotte opened and closed her mouth. No noise came out. She was wide-eyed, then her hand clasped her mouth, imprisoned the unspoken words.

TWENTY-SEVEN

THURSDAY 4TH FEBRUARY, 19.20

He had a string of missed calls: Henry, Thomas, and one from Faye could all wait, as could the emotional messages from Emily and the veiled threats from Luke.

'Samuel.'

'Julian.'

'I saw your message. Sorry I've been indisposed this last—'

'No matter. I can ease the price up a bit. But only a bit.'

'To what?'

'£9.45 million.'

'Thank you. I'll get back to you in the hour.'

Julian sat back briefly, eyed his malt whiskies, and mentally selected the one he hoped to drink once this process concluded. He smelt victory. But there was more work to do. He ignored Henry's incoming call and dialled Faye.

'Good evening, Julian. You received my message, then?'

'No, I don't think so.'

'Do you want to hear our BAFO?'

'I'm all ears.'

'£9.55 million, made up of £7.8 million for the farm,

£1.75 million for the pub. It's a good offer. The best I can get from my client. Take it, Julian. I've pushed them as far as I can.'

'Split the difference with me and it's yours. £9.775 million and you have a deal.'

'No. And I can't go back to them. If I do, they say they'll pull the plug. I believe them.'

'You would, though, wouldn't you?'

'Maybe, but it happens to be true. Take it, Julian.'

'When could you complete?'

'Noon tomorrow.'

'Do it by nine tomorrow morning and the deal's yours.'

Silence.

'Agreed,' she said after a pause.

'It's been an experience, Faye. Let's get over the line and then share a glass of champagne.'

'Definitely. Must dash – a few lawyers to round up and papers to get signed.'

Julian reached for his glass and poured a generous measure. Now for Henry.

'Where the hell have—?'

'We have a deal, my friend.'

Julian smiled as Henry spluttered, quizzed him for details.

'Come round and share a whisky with me. I'm deeply grateful to you, Henry. Mind you, you won't do so bad out of this, given our arrangement, will you?'

'Bloody right. The hardest-earned fee of my life. Don't drink all that whisky, I'm on my way.'

'Great. Just one other thing. Round up our solicitors and have one alerted to the need to draft some papers for me outside this deal.'

'What are you up to now?'

'See you soon.'

TWENTY-EIGHT

THURSDAY 4TH FEBRUARY

The expected summons arrived, and Arthur pushed open the door into Ted Beech's office.

'Arthur.'

'Sir.'

'A result, then. Well done. You got there in the end.'

'You're too kind.' Arthur's words were laced with sarcasm.

Ted raised an eyebrow, allowed a half-smile of acknowledgement, then adopted an officious tone. 'What leads are you following? Can we expect an imminent arrest?'

Arthur had given Ted a written report with all the details, but wearily gave the requested overview anyway. He confirmed that the victim was Scott Banks, and that the murder weapon had been located. There was DNA proof that the poker had been wielded to terminal effect. Then the body had obviously been manhandled into the cellar. It may have simply been rolled down from the cellar trapdoor that then existed. But getting a dead body into the trunk was almost certainly the work of two people.

'Who?' asked Ted.

'We are checking DNA samples of Julian and his two siblings, Luke and Emily, plus Thomas the finance director. Multiple prints were also found on that poker, unsurprisingly. We are tracking down staff who would have been employed at around that time and who might have had legitimate reason to use it. It seems highly unlikely that the chairman, CEO, FD, or siblings would have stoked and prodded the pub's wood burner.'

'And the government's property?' Ted's eyebrows lifted enquiringly.

'Property?' Arthur feigned ignorance.

'You well recall our discussion about said property. Don't bugger around.'

'I don't recall any discussion about government property in any *official* meeting we had, sir.'

Ted sighed. 'And in any *unofficial* conversations we may have had? Off the record.'

Arthur paused, looked down at his hands nestled in his lap, before he locked eyes back on Ted. 'No sign, sir.'

'Even off the record?'

'On or off.'

'Quite sure, Arthur? I promise you the document's too hot to handle. The consequences don't bear thinking about.'

'What document would that be? *Sir.*'

TWENTY-NINE

FRIDAY 5TH FEBRUARY, 9.30

'What's this about Josh not being your son?' demanded Lotte.

'Not what I said. He will always—'

'You did, you did. Exactly what you said. Why do you do this? Why do you lie, make falsehoods, and then deny everything? What's the game now?'

'I said I wasn't Josh's *biological* dad.'

'Same bloody thing. What do you mean? Of course you are.'

'Look at this, Lotte.'

They argued their way to the study. Now he placed the paper on the desk in front of her. She looked at it, but was so heated, so emotional she did not understand, the words a blur on the page. Julian told her about the DNA test, explained there was no doubt. The science was clear. Lotte fell back into the chair, picked the papers up and scanned them. He doubted the words on the page registered. He gave her a few minutes as she began to speak and then stopped herself. She returned the document to his desk. She shook, struggled to compose herself, to find the right words.

'So... so... so you're distancing yourself from Josh as well? Rejected me, now him. You are—'

'Before you say something you may regret, of course I don't reject Josh. Where did you find me? What was I doing? What did Nanny Barlow say the other day? What do your own eyes tell you?'

'I just don't understand...' She paused, and then it was as if a light flicked on. She found the right question. The question she needed to ask. And the question demanded an answer. 'Then who?' Lotte's words were whispered.

'You might like to think about the dates, who you were with.'

'So, you don't know?'

'Do *you* is the question?'

'What do you mean by... oh... but do you know?'

'I suggest you think about this and where it leaves us, Lotte. You know my position. I've briefed my solicitor about your apparent change of heart. I suggest we revert to plan A.'

They were all assembled: Emily, Luke, Lotte, and Zoe. Julian's siblings' conversation halted abruptly as he entered the tension-filled room.

'Have you heard?' said Luke.

'Heard what?' asked Julian.

'An arrest is imminent... the Scott Banks thing.'

'Told you,' Emily said.

'They found him, then?' said Julian.

'And his son's going ape,' said Emily. 'He's issuing threats, talking about murder, conspiracies, cover-ups.'

'An arrest?' said Julian.

'Don't tell me you haven't followed every morsel of news on this. A body was found at The Belle,' said Emily.

'Now that's pure conjecture,' said Julian.

'Well, they didn't say as much, but The Belle is still out of bounds, and they were there all day and then the following day too... and a body's been found.'

'Speculation and rumours won't help us. Please can we focus on our business meeting? We all know what's at stake here,' Julian said.

'Thanks for bringing the meeting forward,' said Luke. He had gathered himself, spoke in an ameliorative tone, and looked at Emily and Lotte. His eyes pleaded for calmness. Luke nodded and his expression seemed to say, *Let's hear him out.*

Emily grunted; Lotte glared.

'Good morning, Julian,' said Zoe. She directed a thin half-smile in his direction.

'Where's Thomas?' enquired Luke.

'The police haven't—' began Emily with bright eyes, ever theatrical.

'I can't imagine why the police would be interested in Thomas. He's not here because he's not invited. This is an informal shareholder gathering prior to our Monday board meeting.'

'When we fall on our swords, penniless and cast aside, while you do your bloody pre-pack, I suppose? I just don't know how you can live with yourself, dear brother,' said Emily. She drew thick-lined geometric shapes on the page in front of her, then screwed it up, threw it over her shoulder.

'It depends on what we conclude this morning.'

'Why's Thomas not here? He provides the financial clout to our meetings,' persisted Luke.

'One of your few allies,' said Emily.

'I don't need his input, given the agenda.'

'Do we have one?' asked Zoe. In contrast to Emily's, her voice was soft and measured. She had insider knowledge as to the game plan. Gave him his cue.

'I won't summarise our predicament or go into the reasons why.'

'As we all know it's your fault,' shouted Lotte.

'Quite right. Hapless and hopeless,' agreed Emily.

Julian heard the opprobrium without comment. 'We're all well versed in our recent history—'

'Under your malign regime.'

Julian sighed and continued, 'Unless we secure a last-minute injection of capital, the company will go into administration.'

'So SI to the rescue after all?' enquired Luke, raising his eyebrows.

'Our position is unchanged,' Zoe said.

'I wish I had a pound for every time you've said that.' Luke grimaced, perhaps regretful of his lapse of self-discipline.

'I've alluded to a deal I've been trying to pull off in my private life. Contrary to expectations, we managed to get it over the line. I'm able to offer an injection of capital. Belle Hospitality will survive to pursue an exciting, expansionary strategy.'

Julian sat back and looked at their expressions of amazement. They looked at him in disbelief, then assailed him with multiple questions.

'The farm?' Luke said.

'It doesn't matter.'

'Yes, it does. And what about The Belle – are you selling the pub too? You can't without the board and shareholders' authority. Is this the game?'

Julian remained passive. Luke was not to be underestimated, as Thomas had warned. It did not matter, though. The die was cast.

'We promised never to sell,' said Emily, incredulous at the turn of the conversation.

'For the record, Emily, not so long ago you called for exactly that,' said Zoe.

Emily glared at her.

'And now you revert to your original position? It's hard to keep up,' Zoe said.

'I don't propose the sale of The Belle,' said Julian. 'The sole reason for this meeting is to inform you of my offer to buy out your shareholdings.'

'What?' asked Emily.

'Buy you out.'

'Go to hell,' said Lotte.

'No way,' said Emily.

Luke held his counsel and then leant forward and asked Julian for the details.

'The business is worthless without an injection of capital.'

'Because you ran it into the ground,' said Emily. 'Why even listen to this? He's about to offer us a penny for our shares when they were worth millions when Daddy was alive.'

'I'm not sure they were,' said Luke. He spoke quietly and with authority. 'Let's hear him out. And Julian's right about one thing, at least. When we entered this room, we all expected the end. I for one want to hear more.'

Julian nodded and handed out envelopes to each of them. 'These contain the offer details. There's a contract for you to sign and return to me by first thing Monday morning. But the offer only stands if you agree in principle before we conclude this meeting. In other words, if you agree subject to the legal review you will need to undertake. It's all been drawn up by my lawyers and the terms are generous, given the circumstances.'

'And if we don't agree?' asked Luke.

'Back to square one,' Julian answered.

'A pre-pack?'

'Yes.'

'If we decline your deal you could put in your capital and avoid a pre-pack.'

'Why would I want to repeat the experience of the last couple of years and pay for the privilege?'

'So, you have us between a rock and a hard place,' Luke said.

Emily and Lotte watched the exchange, open-mouthed.

'I offer you a way out and the company a way forward.'

'And I suppose SI are supportive?'

'We are. SI will also inject capital into the company, and I expect the bank to restructure the debts in support. The business plan is compelling and always has been,' said Zoe.

'We need an hour on our own,' Luke said.

'Of course.'

'But show some respect. Tell us something of your deal. Don't you think you owe us some sort of explanation? You bought the farm and have just sold it. Yes?'

'About the size of it.'

'To a property developer?'

'Yes.'

'As I thought. And they wouldn't be interested in The Belle as well, I don't suppose? I warned you, Julian,' Luke said, shaking his head.

Julian was about to respond when the door opened. DI Hemming and DS Dodds appeared. Board discussion ended mid-sentence. Julian watched the various reactions.

Emily licked her lips and leant forward.

Luke cast his eyes down and sighed.

Lotte sat back in surprise.

Zoe raised an eyebrow.

'I don't know how we can possibly help you now, but it will have to wait until after our shareholders' meeting. We have important matters to conclude here,' said Julian, irritation to the fore.

Arthur nodded sagely, half-smiled, smoothed his hair, and

addressed Julian. 'However important your meeting might be, I'm afraid our business trumps yours.'

'I doubt it,' Julian countered.

'What do you think, DS Dodds? Does murder trump insolvency?'

Julian sat back in his chair, cast his eyes around the table, watched the shock register on their faces. Emily and Lotte gawped. Zoe muttered to no one in particular, 'Well, *this* is a new experience.' Luke and Julian swapped anxious glances.

'You see, we've found our misper. In The Yorkshire Belle's cellars. A murder weapon too. So, I suggest that murder most definitely trumps shady property deals and business shenanigans, if you will allow me to observe. I wonder if you'd be so kind as to accompany us to the station, sir?' Arthur had turned to address Luke.

'My guv'nor means, "You're nicked, sir",' said Ruth.

Emily wailed.

Lotte gasped.

Zoe's eyes widened.

And Julian's hand clasped firmly over his mouth as Luke sagged in his chair.

'Good of you to provide the interpretation, DS Dodds. Now, if you'd read him his rights…'

Julian left the other shareholders to their meeting, as did Zoe, as emotions were unleashed. No one could quite believe what had just happened. Nor could Julian. No matter how hard he tried to imagine circumstances which might lead to Luke killing another human being, it was beyond his comprehension. But he could not let go of the business before them, and hoped that sooner rather than later his siblings and Lotte would focus back on the deal. Money would eventually talk as they all adjusted to the turn of events. He assumed they would reach out to

Luke via the family solicitor, who had been swiftly contacted to support their sibling.

In the interim period he rang Hotel L'Angleterre, but Cassandra had rung in sick. Mm. Perhaps she was just keeping below the radar. She would not relish a call, and he was still not sure what he would say. Perhaps he should convey such a message in a letter. He seemed to be stuck in something of an impasse. Even if he could overcome Lotte's obduracy, he struggled to reconcile Cassandra's hermit instincts to remain in the Alps with his own determination to see Josh. How could he possibly choose between them? He told himself he had to take this step by step. As in business, it was best to break down insurmountable problems into bite-sized chunks: his love for and refusal to release Cassandra; the property deals; the turnaround of Belle Hospitality; his divorce; Josh. And now Luke's situation. He resolved to pen a letter and an email to Cassandra to express his love for her, however inadequate his words might be. She would forgive his clumsiness. And he could also say the divorce was progressing, albeit not without challenges. Quite an understatement, but he needed to project positivity and optimism. The other things were all within his grasp. *Almost there.*

THIRTY

SATURDAY 6TH FEBRUARY

Thomas was stony-faced. 'I can't believe what I'm hearing about Luke. You don't think he had anything to do with it, do you? He couldn't have. Not Luke.'

'Not the reason we are here, Thomas.'

'I guess not. I hear congratulations are in order, my friend,' began Thomas, who wore a sour expression, his nose put out of joint by his exclusion.

'Thanks.'

'You've bought your siblings out, then?'

'I hope to.'

'And you're putting in capital along with SI? You didn't think to involve your FD in this new strategy? Why cut me out of the loop?' Thomas was on edge, agitated.

'I didn't ask you here for that, Thomas. It's a private matter we need to discuss. You'll recall the chat we had in this very room a few weeks ago. You tried to lecture me on my conduct, my relationships with siblings, spouse, and mistress; lectured me on my morals.'

'And you challenged mine, I seem to recall. Where's this going, Julian?'

'It's time to come clean.'

'What?'

'Time for you to own up to your behaviour, your betrayal of my trust. Molly's too.'

'Leave my wife out of this.' Thomas stood, placed his hands on the desk, and glared down at Julian, his face flushed with anger.

'Would you like to tell me about your relationship with Lotte? The wife of your *good friend*?' The emphasis was delivered in a withering tone.

Thomas stared at him, nonplussed, and then slumped back down as realisation dawned. He sighed, shook his head, and then sat with crossed arms; a scowl darkened his features. He said nothing. Julian could see his eyes calculating. He chose to keep his own counsel.

'I know everything, Thomas.' Julian spoke in barely a whisper. 'I have the email audit trails, images... everything.'

'I don't know what you're talking about.'

'Shagging your good friend's wife. I wonder what Molly will say?'

Julian reached into his drawer and took out copies of some of the emails, and showed pictures of Thomas and Lotte posing for each other in various stages of undress. Thomas spluttered, his face glowed, and he looked desperately at Julian.

'Lotte seems to have exhibitionist tendencies you obviously reciprocate... well? I'm all ears... *my friend*.'

'I'm sorry... a mistake... something and nothing. All over no sooner than it started. I'm sorry. I just don't know what came over me. Just a bit of—'

'*Fun?*' Julian grimaced.

'It was a long time ago. A terrible error. Please accept my sincere apology.'

'No. No, I don't think I will. Your infidelity had a long-lasting impact. Your congress with my wife has significant ramifications. And does Molly know? You didn't say.'

'I've not… what can I say? Please don't…' Thomas's voice was suddenly weak – it wavered, it beseeched. 'Please. Things are difficult between us. This would kill our marriage.'

'Like mine, you mean?'

'What did you mean, "long-lasting"?'

'Remember I commented on how little resemblance Josh has to me?' Julian let his words hang in the air and watched as Thomas began to grasp his meaning.

'You're not serious? Please tell me. No… surely not? Dear God. We only ever… you know… twice…'

'Even now you lie. At least four times. Compelling evidence too, would you not say?'

'Please just spell it out for me.'

'I'm not Josh's biological dad. You are… my *friend*.'

Monday 8th February

The board meeting was held mid-morning and attended by Julian, Zoe, and Lotte. The family solicitor had been allowed access to see Luke, who had granted power of attorney to Emily to enable the completion of the sale of their shares to Julian. Their resignations from the board were noted at the outset, as were the details of the reinvestment into Belle Hospitality by both Julian and SI. Julian also informed the board of the resignation of Thomas with immediate effect. He would be on paid garden leave for the six-month duration of his contract, required only to support the handover to an interim finance director who would commence her duties tomorrow.

'Why has he resigned?' asked Lotte.

'Betrayal of trust.'

'Meaning what?'

'I'm not at liberty to say. We have a non-disclosure agreement.'

'This is a board meeting, and you've a duty to disclose.'

Julian glanced at his wife. While she opposed him, the tone was soft. There was a degree of restraint too, and he had to admit her point was valid. 'I'll take an action to outline the essential details at the next meeting. I'll also consult with board members during the week on the separation of board and shareholder meetings.'

'Good practice,' said Zoe.

'You're both saying I'll be excluded. Why not be honest?'

Julian breathed deeply. *Here we go. Any time now.* 'I envisage a board of top executives with key shareholder representation—'

'SI, you mean?' said Lotte.

'Yes.'

'And the shareholder forum?'

'As I said, I will consult, but I expect it to become an annual general meeting.'

'Sensible,' said Zoe.

'I agree,' said Lotte.

Julian and Zoe both looked sharply at Lotte.

'Thank you,' Julian said. 'There's just one other item for today: to agree the sale of The Yorkshire Belle to Optimum. The details are all enclosed in this paper. My proposal is to draw the funds down this week. It just requires the board to agree, and I'll execute the arrangements.'

'Agreed,' said Zoe.

'I can't agree. In consultation with the previous shareholders, here's a solicitor's letter. It's self-explanatory.' Lotte spoke in a businesslike manner as if the words were rehearsed. She handed the letter to him. A cursory glance indicated that

Julian's authority to discuss, let alone set up, such a deal was challenged. He was in breach of sections 175 and 177 of the Companies Act 2006, the letter claimed.

'We'll consider this with urgency, but it doesn't change the proposal today. Zoe agrees on behalf of SI, as do I, so the proposal is carried. Your objection will be noted, Lotte.'

'Fair enough. On a separate matter, I also resign from the board,' Lotte indicated, and pushed another letter across the table to Julian. 'I will no longer reside in the UK.'

Lotte watched as her bombshell registered. She flashed a brief smile at Julian, stood, and left the room.

Lotte's departure allowed them to conclude the formal board meeting. Then Julian and Zoe considered the matter Lotte had presented them with. The essence was a claim by his wife and siblings of a conflict of interest in pursuing both a private sale of the farm and an unauthorised sale of the pub: a 'situational conflict'. He had also failed to notify his board colleagues of his intention to enter discussions on the sale of the pub, referred to as a 'transactional conflict'.

Julian was in breach of his statutory duties as a director of the company. Thomas had warned him, he recalled, and he said as much to Zoe. 'But given previous exchanges, their position seemed intransigent. We were headed for the—'

'I know, but why did you not simply rely upon the pre-pack we'd agreed?'

'I obviously thought about it as the least risky of all options. But I just felt a deep family duty to do what I could to save the company, our heritage, our reputation. Grandad's reputation, mainly. And to prove I could do so.'

'Despite all you said about your dad?'

'He told me so often how useless I was and then he asked for my help… it doesn't matter. This way we save the company, pay our debts, keep the bank onside, and take the strategic route previously agreed. And my siblings have pocketed good value for their shares when they'd lost all hope of such a prospect. Who's lost out?'

'You, possibly. I suggest you call Stubbings and Garner.'

He did so, with Zoe listening in. The corporate lawyer said the allegations seemed valid. But Julian was insistent they proceed as planned and expedite the deal's conclusion tomorrow.

'Are you sure you want to run such a risk, Julian?' the lawyer said.

'The board decided this morning. The deal's done, my siblings have resigned, and the company has moved on. What can they do?'

'Have you removed as a company director under the Company Directors Disqualification Act 1986. They might take out an injunction or bring a private suit. Or they might even enforce the rolling back of the transaction. Think about the implications. I imagine you'd then be in dispute with Optimum as well.'

'I know Luke and Emily. They just want their pound of flesh, retribution. It'll cost a bit more in compensation and may be messy, but they'll drop the case. I have in mind another sweetener.'

'Luke will presumably have other things on his mind too,' said Zoe.

'Possibly, but he didn't do it. The police will let him go soon enough. My brother just hasn't got it in his make-up to harm another human being. He will have briefed Emily. But his absence isn't ideal as at least Luke can be sensible, whereas…'

Julian ended the call and the two of them discussed their options further as Zoe asked him to explain the so-called 'sweetener'.

'Let me work it through first.'

'And you'll no doubt tell me when agreed? You need to

learn to trust others, Julian. Right now, you need my support.' Zoe gathered her papers, slotted them in her bag, and departed. Her warning shot was delivered quietly but it hit home.

The four participants logged in and Lotte's mic was muted. Julian was intrigued.

'My client would like to conclude this matter and has empowered me to reach agreement on her behalf within certain parameters. She doesn't anticipate speaking but will consider any written questions should there be points of clarification,' said Lotte's solicitor.

'I welcome the objective,' said Julian.

'Subject to the details, my client agrees we should file a divorce petition this week.'

'We've already agreed most of the details, haven't we?' Julian's solicitor commented. 'Prenuptial, possessions, jewellery, proceeds from the sale of the house, tenancy period...'

'Let me outline the concluding arrangements proposed. We don't seek any maintenance arrangements; we don't seek to remove any items of furniture or possessions beyond personal items and jewellery. My client wishes to secure a one-off settlement independent of the sale of the house: a finite sum of £1 million.'

'I will need to speak separately to my client on this,' said Julian's solicitor.

'I agree to the principle proposed, albeit with staged payments,' said Julian quickly.

'Agreed.'

'And subject to open access to Josh.'

'Ah, this is most delicate... my client has given this matter a great deal of thought and... Lotte, are you still content for me to respond as discussed earlier?'

Lotte unmuted her mic for long enough to say, 'Yes.'

'This has been a difficult matter for her to contemplate. Lotte is solely driven by Josh's best interests. She hopes you understand. Our proposal is for Josh to remain in *your* custody, Julian. Motherhood is not for her – an agonising conclusion to have reached. She's decided to relocate to another country after a period of travelling. Lotte…'

Julian heard no more.

He could not believe it.

He had thought about all the possible reactions he might meet, all the options. But never this.

Suddenly, after all this time, the future seemed clearer.

A way forward.

This was beyond his wildest dreams.

Had she really proposed this?

THIRTY-ONE

8TH FEBRUARY

Arthur and Ruth took their seats in interview room two. She opened her file, notebook at the ready, pen poised. Arthur nodded. Ruth turned on the tape, announced attendees, undertook the formalities, sought and received Luke's and his solicitor's acquiescence to commence.

'Where were you on 10th November 2017?' said Arthur.

'No comment,' said Luke, maintaining his stance since arrest.

'This really won't play well for you, Luke. The evidence is compelling. One more chance. Where were you on 10th November 2017?'

Luke looked from Ruth to Arthur, and beads of perspiration broke out on his forehead, while damp patches spread under his arms. He glanced at his solicitor who nodded his encouragement. Luke bowed his head and mumbled, 'Okay, okay.'

After a moment he confirmed that he was at The Yorkshire Belle to join his dad for a meeting with Scott Banks. It soon became adversarial. 'Scott was hostile. It shocked me. He threatened all manner of violence in colourful language. But Dad had discovered an ongoing direct debit that was paid directly into an account set up by Scott.'

'To his Barclays account?' asked Ruth.

'No. It was in one of those new internet accounts.'

'Name?'

'I don't recall.'

'We'll come back to that. Please tell us what happened.' Her voice was calm, measured, respectful as she encouraged him to take them through the events of that day.

'Oh, it was terrible, a dreadful day I wish I could erase.' He took out a handkerchief, wiped his brow, blew his nose, and his hand shook as he reached for a glass of water. 'Dad and I got there a bit before him, opened up, and sat around waiting, really.'

'Was anyone else there?'

'No. Business wasn't good, and we closed in the afternoon most days…'

'Please continue.'

'Dad was in a foul mood, furious. I did my best to calm him down. The thing was, not only had he realised that Scott had previously pinched booze, fags, cash, but he'd set up this direct debit. So not only did he owe him… Dad and he had previously agreed that he'd pay something back in compensation – to the pub, the business, you understand. Not Dad. But it transpired he'd set up this direct debit. So, the business paid into *Scott's* bank account every month.'

'How much was it for? And when was it set up?' asked Ruth.

'I honestly don't know. Dad was so het up it was hard to fathom exactly what had gone on. I don't think he knew really, and he couldn't believe that it had gone under the radar. I think it was probably a small amount. I don't know – I assumed £50 or so.'

'Do continue. What happened when Scott arrived?'

'His breath stank of booze; he was belligerent from the get-go. The meeting was arranged to draw a line under the whole sorry story. But discovery of the direct debit scuppered that. I think the recent business difficulties had prompted a detailed review of every single payment, and this one was apparently under some obscure name and, as I said, it was for a small amount… Scott swore at Dad, told him what he thought of him. Me as well for good measure, and he had a few choice words to offer about Julian too. They had history. I guess you know all about that…'

Ruth swirled her hand, encouraged him to continue.

'Scott threw a bag at Dad, which had a few quid in it, and said that was it. End of the matter. He was effing and blinding, said that if any of us attempted to contact him again we'd regret it. He was explicit, didn't wrap it up, and I honestly believed him. I tried to calm him down, and my dad also, who'd become incensed and swore back at Scott. It was bloody ridiculous, really. Two grown men shouting at each other, and the temperature just kept rising and rising, and suddenly Dad was on his feet, his chair clattered to the floor, and he stood toe to toe with Scott. I tried to intervene, but they wouldn't listen. I pulled at him, tried to drag him away, and he slung an arm, caught me in the face, drew blood.'

'Your dad or Scott?'

'Dad. He didn't mean it. He was out of control; Scott was rarely in control even when sober. Then Scott prodded Dad in the chest. Well, you can imagine. It just escalated. Dad pushed back, Scott swore and raised his hand. I grabbed it just in time, but he easily pushed me away, and I fell and banged my head on a table. Meanwhile Dad pushed him again, and this time Scott swung and connected, once, twice, and Dad fell. He was hurt, his nose bled profusely; Dad was badly shaken. He was getting on, didn't enjoy great health even then… then Scott kicked him as he lay on the floor, and set about me. Dad let out a feral scream, and I just picked up whatever was at hand and… and… I didn't mean to. If only I could turn the clock back. I'm so sorry. I can't tell you what a relief it is to unburden myself at last.'

'Go on, Luke,' said Arthur.

'I grabbed it—'

'What?' asked Ruth.

'I think it was a poker. And I swung. It was just… just horrendous. He went down but came back at me snarling and spitting and said he'd kill me. I knew he would, so I… I…' Luke broke down and needed a few minutes to compose himself.

'Go on,' said Arthur.

Luke's solicitor whispered in his ear, suggested he say nothing further, but Luke shook his head. 'No. It's been too long. I should have… he was unconscious, so I turned to Dad. He shook like a leaf, held a handkerchief to his nose to stem the blood. I got a bowl of water and some tissues and cleaned him up as best I could. His injuries weren't serious, but he was distressed, dazed. We'd been a bit concerned about his health. Me and Emily. Julian wouldn't even have noticed.' Luke paused, leant back in his chair, and let out a sigh.

'You need to tell us everything, Luke,' said Arthur.

'And you'll feel better,' added Ruth.

Luke nodded, took a deep breath. 'I got Dad to a chair in the corner and then turned back to Scott. I honestly thought he was just unconscious…' Luke looked with despair at both detectives.

'But he wasn't?' Ruth.

'He didn't move, didn't respond to a prod. It was then that it began to dawn on me. I felt for a pulse. Nothing. He was… he was…'

'You have to say it,' said Ruth.

'He was dead, stone dead. I'd killed a man. Me... I... I...' Luke's words came out in a whisper; he put his head in his hands and sobbed.

'What did you do with the body?' Arthur.

Gradually Luke recovered some poise after a short break. And then he continued his account. Luke had pushed the body through the trapdoor, and once his dad had gathered his strength, they'd both descended the rickety steps and manhandled him into a long-ago discarded trunk. He told them that he and his dad had arranged for the bricking up of the subterranean corridor access, and then for a contractor to concrete over what had been the trapdoor entrance at ground-floor level.

'So, you admit that you murdered Scott Banks on or around 10th November 2017, Luke?' asked Arthur.

'No, no, I don't. It was self-defence.'

Arthur turned to Ruth and smiled. 'Oscar-worthy performance, would you say?'

'Worthy of a nomination, certainly,' confirmed Ruth.

Luke looked at the two of them, raised his hands, palms up, as if to say, *What the hell?*

Arthur rocked on his chair and then stood and clapped. 'What a performance... now try the truth.'

'My client has cooperated fully, given a full account—'

'Tell us about the drugs, Luke,' said Ruth.

'Explain why you owed thousands of pounds to Scott Banks—' Arthur.

'£47,573, to be precise,' interjected Ruth.

'Your drug habit. Tell us about it.' Arthur again.

'I don't know what you're talking about,' Luke said.

'Okay. One last opportunity. It won't play well if you persist in your lies. Show him, Ruth.'

Ruth produced a holdall, swung it onto the table in front of them, and invited them to look at the cache of drugs inside – amphetamines, cocaine, ecstasy, heroin. Luke was wide-eyed but said nothing. She then produced a black book and turned to one section that was headed up 'Luke Sinclair', with columns of dates, drugs supplied, and monetary values. 'All of this was found by our lovable, friendly sniffer dogs at Scott's place.'

'And right now, their boundless energy is being directed to your abode, Mr Sinclair. You wouldn't like to tell us what their search will reveal, would you?' Arthur.

'I assume a search warrant has been obtained?' asked the solicitor.

'Of course.' Ruth.

'I've never taken heroin... whatever he might have listed,' Luke managed to say.

'But you did take drugs supplied by Scott Banks?' asked Ruth.

'Yeah... just a bit of dope at first and a few pills... slang. That sort of stuff.'

'And later?'

'It escalated: coke, speed...'

'We are searching as we speak,' said Arthur. 'Tell us what we will find.'

'Okay, okay. Pills and stuff in the loft at home. Probably a bit of everything I've mentioned. No heroin, though. I'm not that daft...'

'Most would think that cocaine and ecstasy was more than daft,' suggested Arthur.

'I know. Crazy. And there's more at work. I'll show you. No need to get a warrant.'

'Too late.'

'Okay. Look, all I said was true except...' Luke paused, sighed.

'Yes, Luke?' Ruth.

'The argument with Dad was exactly as I said. But angrier, more violent. I do have a recreational drug habit. It's long-standing and it got out of hand back then. Still a problem, to be honest. He'd supplied my habit from when I was a teenager. Back then it was something and nothing, but it sowed the seeds… seeds of destruction, I suppose you might say. My family knew nothing about it, still don't. When my business got into trouble, I took my hits more often and he let me have some on credit… that racked up the money I owed as he doubled the cost every month my debt wasn't paid. Then I'd borrow from the business to pay him off until the business hit cash-flow problems, then the debt to Scott would pile up, I got stressed so I needed more gear, ran up more debt, and so the spiral continued. Sold my car, spent my savings. On that… that day Scott was in no mood to compromise, refused to leave until he'd been paid. Mumbled something about needing to pay his wife's debts. He wasn't coherent, he was so angry, so aggressive. He did hit and kick Dad. All that happened. But then he set about me, and he grabbed the poker. In the struggle he dropped it, I broke free, picked it up and swung with all my might. I've never hit anyone before but we'd both lost the plot. It was him or me. Dad was badly shaken, shocked. The rest is what I said earlier. I'm so, so sorry.'

Arthur buttonholed Ruth as they wrapped up matters for the day, insisted on taking her for a drink at the local pub. They discussed how to proceed with the case against Luke. It was all straightforward, routine, but Arthur was keen to lay the plans out clearly. Ruth looked at him askance; he was not inclined to labour such procedural steps. And they had worked together for a few years, knew each other's approach, were a good team. Arthur paused, took a sip of his largely untouched beer. He seemed troubled. To distract him Ruth spoke about family matters, station gossip, discussed other cases in the in-tray. But he was singularly focused on wrapping up the Scott Banks case.

Ruth looked at him, said gently, 'Are you okay, guv?'

'Me? Sure. You know me…'

'You seem preoccupied.'

'Do I? Goodness, is that the time? I must dash.' Arthur felt in his inside jacket pocket, made to extricate something, changed his mind. He stood up, pushed his beer aside, and took a stride away from the table. A perplexed Ruth watched his every move. He stopped in his tracks and turned back to her. 'It really has been a great professional pleasure to have worked with you, Ruth.'

'Guv?'

'The thing is… I'm going away for a while: a long-overdue break.' He looked her directly in the eye, shook her hand, then pulled her into a light embrace. 'Take care.'

THIRTY-TWO

FEBRUARY 2021

She waited for him with arms crossed across her chest. She stood in front of the fire and scowled. Lotte was seated, in attendance to support her friend, wine glass at the ready. Emily unfolded her arms, strode across to her own glass, gulped her fill, and resumed her hostile pose as Julian entered his own lounge.

'Did you see Luke?' asked Lotte. Her tone was soft, measured.

'Yes,' Julian answered as he collapsed into his seat. 'Please sit down, Emily. I'm as shocked as you are. A turn of events none of us could have anticipated.'

'It didn't happen.'

'Did you know about it all, Em?' His eyes pleaded; he did not want to provoke an emotional response.

'You *bastard*. How could you ask such a question?'

'I'm sorry. It's just that you were as opposed to the sale of The Belle as Luke... well, until your recent wobble on the matter. It would provide the explanation I've searched for all this time. There had to be a reason other than—'

'*Bastard.* I told you of my reasoning. I made a promise to Daddy, we all did. Only you broke it – *only* you. And anyway, Luke couldn't have done it, wouldn't do it, *didn't* do it. It's not in his nature. He's a gentle, loving, peaceful man. How can you believe such things?' She now paced the room, waved her arms around.

'I didn't. Until he admitted it to me a short while ago. Aided and abetted by Dad. He was severely provoked, denies murder. Hopes for manslaughter, I guess. I don't know much about these things.'

'I *hate* you, Julian. He didn't do it. End of.'

'We must face facts, Em. He's admitted everything, explained what happened, and apparently it all fits. His prints are all over the weapon, which was alongside the body. I don't want to believe it either, but it happened and it's going to be all over the papers. Better you hear it from me than…'

Emily dissolved into tears as Lotte attempted to soothe her, provided tissues, gently removed the wine glass from Emily's reach. She called for Annie to make some tea. Julian looked on, astounded. His wife administered love, kindness, sense, and reason.

'What was their plan, Julian? Let's hear the full story.'

'Luke wanted to go to the police straight away, but Dad wouldn't let him. Said something about Luke needing to grow some balls. He made Luke promise to go along with the plan.'

'Which was?' Lotte enquired.

'They bundled the body into a trunk in the cellar, cleaned up, shut the trunk's lid, boarded up the cellar access, and later concreted over the trapdoor. It wasn't an elaborate plan. The hardest thing was to stay quiet, pretend nothing had happened. The intention was to simply forget about the incident, the body, the cellar. Brick up access from the other cellars. We never really used it for anything anyway. Then get on with life.

The Yorkshire Belle would pass on down the generations and Scott Banks would never be found. After all, his was not exactly a celebrated life.'

'And Luke told you all this?' said Emily.

'He said it was a relief to get it off his chest. He's full of remorse, regret, guilt. But there's more, Em.' Julian proceeded to tell her of Luke's drug habit, the cache of drugs found at his home and at work, and that Luke had confessed that debts he owed to Scott Banks had been the main cause of the escalation of violence, of Scott's death.

THIRTY-THREE

MARCH 2021

Julian packed his suitcase. He had to see Cassandra after several dispiriting conversations. She had become withdrawn, reticent, reluctant to engage: *I've said everything there is to say.* He was not prepared to give up on her. The lifting of Covid travel restrictions was a relief, although there were still bureaucratic obstacles to navigate.

As he zipped his case shut, he was assailed by Emily on the mobile, who insisted on a meeting. A flurry of exchanges between the legal representatives had failed to make headway on the claim against Julian. Despite the trauma over Luke's crimes, Emily was still determined to bring it to a head; Julian would need to play his trump card, his sweetener.

As he headed to the meeting he smiled. He relished the prospect: he was confident this would put the matter to rest. In Luke's absence, Emily awaited him. Lotte was also there. The mood was sombre. Emily reminded Julian of their objections – no doubt scripted by Luke in absentia. Julian had illegally exceeded his authority and would be held to account. He reminded them that they had all benefited. Emily sighed deeply and tossed her hair back, but otherwise stayed quiet. As did Lotte.

'Despite Luke's news, the family shame, you still want to pursue this?' said Julian.

'Luke is adamant I do so. It's his wish.'

'I see.'

'Well? You acted without the board's authority. You need to account for that.'

'Fair enough. I get it. I understand what you're saying. And technically, off the record, I guess you're right. But it worked. We're all better off as a result.'

'Not the point,' said Emily.

'So, what do you want?'

'To take you to court unless you persuade us otherwise.'

'What's your price?'

'We're open to offers.'

Well, at least there was no pretence.

'Look, I want to say something. We've had our differences—' Julian began.

'Understatement of the year. What are you on? You cheat us, you lie and deceive, you renege on a deathbed promise to Daddy…'

'I know you see it like that. But I never promised Dad what *you* promised him. It was you who said you'd never sell, not me. My words were chosen carefully. I know, I know – you see it as being disingenuous. But The Belle was the only way out of a mess of his making. In your heart of hearts, you know the truth of it. I took on the challenge and promised Dad that I'd make it work. It became my mission. I wouldn't let go no matter how hard you made it for me. I vowed to see it through to the end, and pulled off every trick in the book to save the business. I knew you wouldn't be natural business soulmates, but I never envisaged you'd make it so impossibly hard.'

'We don't share your damning verdict on our dad's stewardship. There was just something so toxic, so intense, so personal between you two…'

'Yes. *Very* personal.'

'It clouded your judgement, Julian.'

'Oh, come on.'

'You've just no idea, have you?' said Emily. 'It's about time you heard the truth. Did you never question your first deal? Why you got the investment in the first place? You're so bloody arrogant you never even stopped to question why or how. You'd no track record. So, why did they invest in you?'

'They liked the compelling business case, Emily.'

'They liked Dad's cash and his security even more.'

Julian pulled up short, frowned, paused. 'You mean…'

'Yes.'

Julian looked at her. So, his dad had oiled the wheels as banker of last resort. His mind raced. He had pondered Emily's questions, but he had not seen his dad's input. And why? The room was quiet as attention fixed on Julian. He gazed outside as the wind howled, the skies darkened, and hail hammered against the windowpane, the drive turning white. Then images assailed him like lightning flashes: steel-capped boots, vomit-spattered blue suede shoes. He instinctively fingered his facial scar, felt his perpetually sore leg, recalled the pain of his dad's mistrust, his scathing words. It was his dad's way of making good the harm he had caused. All those years ago, yet so vividly, painfully recalled, never far below the surface. It could be the only explanation. His dad had always found it difficult to acknowledge fault, let alone apologise: *Julian… I'm so, so sorr…* uttered on his deathbed, his last words. Julian was rocked by the news. His hand gripped the desk as if hanging on to a lifeline as the ship sank. Emily and Lotte looked at him and let the news sink in. He slowly recovered his poise, sipped water, and then drew himself up straight, ready to re-engage.

'"There will always be a Yorkshire Belle," is what I said to him. I need you to see something.' He leapt to his feet, reached for his car keys. 'It's a few miles away. Follow me.'

'No!' shouted Emily.

'Just do it,' Julian shouted back.

Emily's surprise registered her brother's anger; the mask had slipped.

'What are you up to now?' said Lotte.

'Come with me, Lotte. We can chat about a few things too.'

'Okay.'

Julian was surprised she agreed, but pleased. They had not talked about the agreed divorce proceedings, the deal they had come to. The papers had been filed and the process would now meander its way to a conclusion, but he still wanted to smooth things over with Lotte if possible.

He drew to a halt in the car park of The Friesian, a run-down pub not a mile from The Yorkshire Belle on a lane just off the main road into York. It was even more neglected and mournful than their dad's beloved Yorkshire Belle: flaking plaster, rotten window frames, missing roof tiles. Julian carried a file of papers and brandished the keys to allow entry. It had the feel of abandonment. It was dark, depressing, dismal. There were cobwebs everywhere, dust and ingrained filth, and signs of rodent activity made Emily shudder. They wandered around the two bars: one large, the other more of a snug. Nicotine-stained wallpaper from a previous era peeled off two of the walls, the windows leaked, and the carpets were mildewed. There was no stock bar a few packets of peanuts and a half-box of salt and vinegar crisps. A jar of pickled eggs sat uninvitingly on the bar. Julian pulled on one of the pumps. It coughed into life and spewed forth a noxious-smelling beer well past its sell-by date. He wrinkled his nose and grimaced. They viewed the large, cavernous kitchen, glanced in the fridges (devoid of produce except for a mouldy round of some indeterminate cheese and a box of rotten vegetables). They climbed rickety stairs and peered into the upstairs rooms, perhaps once used for functions. Three antiquated bedrooms with grimy sinks. Two upstairs bathrooms – one male, one female, from an era devoid of modern fads like nonbinary loos – lurked at either end of a narrow, gloomy corridor. Looking through the grubby rear windows, they stared at what had once been a beer garden. It was hard to imagine happy family groups on a warm, sunny day, children playing on the slide and squealing their delight on swings, now broken and rusty. The garden was so overgrown and tangled it was hard to work out its topography. Back downstairs they poked their heads into the toilets, then swiftly retreated.

Julian lay a local street map on a table and overlaid it with a new layout on translucent paper.

'Why are we here?' asked Emily.

Julian pointed to where The Friesian was situated on the map. The depicted roadwork scheme had been approved by planners and was due to commence next year, he told them.

'So what?' Emily said.

'It'll be on the direct route into York,' said Julian.

'What's it got to do with us, though? Why have you got the keys?'

'Take a look at these papers.' He handed out copies. He watched them struggle with the contents, tried to gauge where their puzzled expressions took them.

Emily sighed and looked at Julian helplessly.

Lotte stopped reading the papers, her eyes glazed over, she shrugged her shoulders. She had told Julian that her plans gathered pace for the next stage of her life. Perhaps she was already on the road in her mind's eye. Lotte had been thoughtful and balanced in conversation on the journey here. She was clearly remorseful at having reached her conclusion, but insisted it was right for Josh. She shed a few tears as she said, 'I want Josh to know how much I love him. This decision is for him. I'm not cut out…'

'You will always have free access, Lotte.'

'I won't dip in and out of his life. Better to have a clean break. Sorry, I know I look bad… so bad. It's been hard, Julian. I'm convinced it's for the best.'

'If you change your mind…'

'I won't.'

But they had not spoken about who the biological dad was. He assumed she knew. Had the two of them discussed it? There was no way to tell. He imagined Thomas would be keen to avoid the topic as he fought to save his marriage. Julian felt betrayed by Thomas's actions. But Molly was a wonderful mother and Thomas a great dad. He was hardly the first person in the world to stray. No – Julian silently wished him the luck he would never articulate.

'This pub is the primary asset of a company called TYB Limited, whose shareholders and directors are the four of us… including Luke,' explained Julian. As an afterthought he said, 'If he's allowed to be a director given… anyway, Emily and Luke will have thirty per cent each; Lotte and I will both have twenty per cent. I'll be a silent partner and accept only dividends when your board chooses to make them. I won't be a board member. Nor will Lotte. The assets of the company are the freehold of this property and £250,000 in cash.'

'Why would we want this dump?' asked Emily. She threw her hands up theatrically.

'Because it'll be on the main thoroughfare to York with huge commercial potential. But it'll cost an awful lot more than this to make it work,' Julian said. 'I envisage you calling it The Yorkshire Belle. All the memorabilia from Grandad's day have been put aside. Furthermore, we can dismantle and reassemble the sixteenth-century front doorway of the original Belle, and the ruins left by the Luftwaffe bomb. You know, the shrine our grandad erected, complete with information boards, as part of the heritage. He was a natural marketeer before the word had been invented, a true entrepreneur. You could do similar if you wanted to – you have the grounds to accommodate it. On the investment front, you won't have any trouble in raising cash with the right business plan. It will need a clear branding strategy and conceptual overhaul, and I've got a few ideas if you're interested. Up to you.'

'What's the catch? Oh, wait a minute… I get it. You want us to spend our proceeds from Belle Hospitality? Well, go to hell. You really think we're so stupid?' said Emily, who now paced around the gloomy pub lounge.

'You'll need to spend a little of the proceeds,' said Julian.

'How much?'

'1p each.'

'I see. Our pay-off. All this if we drop the claims against you.'

Julian looked at his sister and slowly nodded his head, and added, 'If you say no then I'll undertake the venture on my own: the restoration of The Yorkshire Belle. I promised there would always be a Yorkshire Belle. The only question is whether you want to make this happen. It's your chance to make your own mark, oversee the reincarnation of the Sinclair family heritage. I had envisaged Luke running it, so you will have to discuss alternatives with him.'

'Don't you think he has other things on his mind?' said Emily. But she said it quietly, thoughtfully.

As Julian walked down the rain-sodden path a doleful funeral party filed past and turned their backs on the freshly dug grave, a near neighbour to his dad's. He suddenly felt an overwhelming sadness. It both surprised and reassured him. Not as effusive as Emily's brand, but emotion, nonetheless. He *could* do emotion after all. Julian stopped just short of his dad's grave and looked around him to take in the surroundings, the bigger picture. A small clutch of teary-eyed mourners on the far side; a little girl placed flowers on a grave close by and chatted gaily as she did so, while her mother wiped away her own silent tears; an old lady sat peacefully, held the lead to a faithful Labrador with dutifully mournful eyes. Life had been lived, had ebbed, had died. The clouds darkened, and the persistent drizzle threatened more. Crows cawed and squabbled, and a distant car horn provided an untimely reminder that life continued. Narrowing his focus, he read the tombstone for the first time:

RIP Terence Gerald Sinclair
1950–2020
Loving dad of Luke, Julian & Emily

And then he cast his eyes over the inscription at the bottom:

Local businessman extraordinaire

His eyes clouded and he frowned. Then a smile breached his features, and he allowed a small chuckle. Extraordinaire indeed. He could not have put it better. But he had not come here to take issue with his dad, with his siblings. All firmly in the past. He just wanted to share a few thoughts, sign off without rancour, say a final goodbye.

'Banker of last resort, then?' He spoke aloud. What a shame his dad could never express his regret, could never say sorry, but instead chose to hide it in a grand gesture meant to lie undiscovered. Perhaps their relationship could have been so different, if only… no point. 'I said I'd do it my way, rescue the business, save the legacy. You made it hard, so hard. I now understand why you didn't want The Belle slipping into others' hands. What a sorry mess. But I've kept my promise: there will always be a Yorkshire Belle.'

Julian sighed, pulled his collar up tighter, and took a step back from the grave.

Time to move on.

Time to put his own life in order.

'*Goodbye*, Dad.'

As Julian waited for his flight to be called, mask removed, he sipped coffee as he caught up with his inbox. A note from Bernard Archer caught his eye. What could the farmer want now? A cursory scan of the letter told him: compensation, more money. Julian shook his head. *What is it with these deals? They won't stay in the outbox.* The farmer claimed overage. Julian forwarded it to his solicitor, who rang ten minutes later.

'I'll deal with it, Julian. Nothing to worry about. We dealt with it in the contract. He's no leg to stand on.'

'Remind me – overage?'

'If a parcel of land's sold and subsequently built on following planning permission there's a possibility of a claim arising for overage. He'd then be able to recoup money from you as you've profited to excess.'

'Got it. After all, he extracted a price twice the market value.'

'Indeed. You've legal protection as we carved out the possibility of any subsequent claim for exactly that reason. He effectively signed away his rights. It's just a try-on. Leave it with me.'

Julian boarded his early flight and turned his mind to Cassandra. Their relationship had seemed so vibrant, so dominant, but had then been relegated to the background by force of circumstances and geographical distance. This wretched pandemic had much to answer for. But he could have done more when she had been in England. He bitterly regretted his neglect of her. He had been relieved that they had put it behind them, but her latest revelations threatened their future. Now he was the bearer of wholly positive news to ensure a future together. He hoped the sun's rays would penetrate the claustrophobic gloom of their recent relationship.

The weather was balmy compared to home. As he meandered through the villages and lanes, he savoured the warm sunshine. The profusion of Alpine Spring flowers in the meadows signalled the welcome transition to spring: snowdrops and snowflakes, crocuses, primroses, and little blue flowers whose name escaped him. It was too early for the orchids, whose beauty Cassandra's enthusing had taught him to appreciate. For too long he had had no headspace for anything other than business trauma, deals, and personal crises. It was such a relief to appreciate the gentler, natural things in life. And this place just seemed to relax him as tension dissolved in the sun's rays. It was magical. As for Cassandra, well, if she refused to live elsewhere then he could fashion a wonderful family life here for the three of them. For the moment he cast aside the challenges of Josh's undiagnosed ADHD. Any learning difficulties would necessitate support wherever they chose to live.

Cassandra was surprised to see him, but any awkwardness dissipated as the evening wore on. The usual prescription of simple food, wine, and the serenity of the mountain retreat worked its magic. Slowly but surely the two of them relaxed and Julian stretched out on cushions on the floor in front of the log fire, his back against Cassandra's chair, his head nestled in her lap. She reached down and ran her long fingers through his hair, and he sighed with contentment.

'What's your agenda this time, Julian?'

'*You*. You and me. Can't you feel it, Cass? Despite all we've been through, what we have is so special. I've never experienced this with anyone, and I think you feel it too. Oh, God – I wish I was a wordsmith rather than a businessman. We just… we just belong together. Don't we?'

'But how?' Whispered, wistful words.

'You told me to talk to you when I had more than just empty words. Well, now I can. Lotte and I have filed for divorce, and we seem to have found some sort of equilibrium after all the hostility and bitterness, the recriminations. We've reached concord. The decree nisi should be through in about six months, although Covid seems to delay everything…'

'I'm pleased for you.'

'Cass, it's amazing. Have you ever thought of being a mother…?'

Her fingers stopped working their magic. She froze, shrank back from Julian, and instinctively reached for her locket, drew it out from beneath her blouse with trembling fingers. Cassandra prised open the two halves and touched the strands of hair within. A chasm opened between them. Suddenly she was miles away, withdrawn into her own world.

Julian reached for her and squeezed her hand. 'Sorry, Cass. I didn't—'

'How can you ask such a question?' Her voice was shaky. She was on the edge of tears. What had he done? Oh, God. Idiot – his choice of words unbelievably crass.

'No… no, you don't understand. I didn't mean… what I meant was, would you like to be Josh's mum, Cass? Would you? You'd be wonderful. We could have a family life.'

He got up onto his knees, turned to her, looked imploringly into her liquid eyes. 'I'm sorry. Your message was… there aren't words to describe it. What you went through. What you've lived with all this time. But not all men are monsters. I love you, Cass. Please marry me. Please be Josh's mum. We can live wherever you like.'

He embraced her, and Cassandra released her emotions, sobbed quietly into his shoulder, held him tightly. After what seemed an age they separated, and Julian topped their glasses up before returning to his armchair so they could look at each other.

'I don't understand…'

He told her of Lotte's decision.

'I can't believe any woman could give up her child.'

'I never saw it coming either. Quite the opposite. I'm told it isn't unheard of – unusual, yes; unique, no.'

'What about your business life, Julian? I've told you I can't cope with…'

'Whether we live in Yorkshire or here, it's time I moved to the next phase of my career, the next phase of my life. I plan to become executive chair of whichever company I'm living geographically closest to, and non-executive chair of the other. My days of pinging between the two are over. Whatever we decide to do. I need to prioritise Josh. And you.'

'Are you sure it would make any difference? The least little thing and—'

'We will employ a CEO in each location. It'll work. My role will be wholly different. But of course, I still need to provide for my family, so I'll still have a busy business agenda. But the reason for my frantic lifestyle was because I was mired in the operational side of the business. Oh, don't get me wrong – I revelled in the excitement, in the buzz it gave me. But I've found a new business vibe to allow me to be more hands-off. I love the strategic dimension and the investment in new brands, catering concepts, and buying and selling businesses.'

They spoke for a long while about what he had in mind. He seemed to have thought it through, he seemed serious, she acknowledged.

'So, will you, Cass? Will you marry me? Be Josh's mum? Where would you like to live?'

'I'll sleep on it, Julian. Now stop talking and take me to bed…'

www.ingramcontent.com/pod-product-compliance
Ingram Content Group UK Ltd.
Pitfield, Milton Keynes, MK11 3LW, UK
UKHW051117300325
456866UK00004B/24